AN ART TO LOVE

by Helena Harte

By the Author

Call to Me

Scripted Love

AN ART TO LOVE

by Helena Harte

2022

This trade paperback original is published by Butterworth Books, Nottingham, England

Cataloging information
ISBN: 978-1-915009-23-4
CREDITS
Editors: Victoria Villaseñor
Cover Design: Nicci Robinson, Global Wordsmiths
Production Design: Global Wordsmiths

Butterworth Books is a different breed of publishing house. It's a home for Indies, for independent authors who take great pride in their work and produce top quality books for readers who deserve the best. Professional editing, professional cover design, professional proof reading, professional book production—you get the idea. As Individual as the Indie authors we're proud to work with, we're Butterworths and we're *different*.

Authors currently publishing with us:

E.V. Bancroft
Valden Bush
Michael Carter
Michelle Grubb
Helena Harte
Lee Haven
Karen Klyne
AJ Mason
Ally McGuire
James Merrick
Robyn Nyx
Simon Smalley
Brey Willows

For more information visit www.butterworthbooks.co.uk

Acknowledgements

My continued gratitude to everyone at Global Wordsmiths for making this publishing stuff so easy and so much fun. Special thanks to my editor, Victoria Villaseñor, for your patience, sentence-titivating, and contstant encouragment. Thank you to Margaret Burris for her excellent attention to detail in the proofing process, and especially for weeding out all my naughty Britishisms! And most of all, thank you to all the lovely readers who continue to read my words and tell other people about them. I'm so grateful for that, I can't even put it into words. I hope you love Jamie and Lauren as much as I do.

"All the art of living lies in a fine mingling of letting go and holding on."

~ Havelock Ellis

CHAPTER ONE

LAUREN GRAY ENTERED THE boardroom and made her way around the large group of people chatting in small clusters. She welcomed each of them with a warm greeting, including their name or preferred moniker and something small about their family, loved one, or an interest. She considered knowing such things vital in building solid and trusting connections with people, regardless of whether their working relationship was to last a few hours or several years. She walked to her usual chair, opened the soft khaki leather portfolio in front of her, and smiled. This huge stack of paper represented eighteen months of meetings, negotiation, and compromise coming to fruition. She ran her fingers across the top of the pile, appreciating the soft touch of the more environmentally friendly paper choice. Shifting to stone from traditional tree-based paper was one of the first things she'd changed here, and it had made them stand out in the crowd.

Her right-hand woman and best friend, Whit, came up beside her. "Big day, boss."

Lauren winked and whispered, "We make a hell of a team."

Whit grinned. "You know it. We're going for drinks after this, aren't we?"

"We're going for *all* the drinks." She nudged Whit. "Especially if you're buying."

"What happened to sharing the load?"

Lauren gave a quiet laugh. "That's only when it works to my benefit."

Whit shook her head and laughed too. "I could destroy your saintly reputation if I told everyone who you really were."

"Are you sure about that? Aren't all CEO's *supposed* to be egotistical, maniacal sociopaths? If you exposed me, I'd probably be headhunted by Amazon and offered a gazillion percent pay raise."

"Huh, like you do this for the money."

Lauren thought briefly of the plans she and her twin sister, Kayla, had for education in their hometown and beyond. Somehow, they had yet to come to anything. Her thoughts soon flipped to the new model of Aston Martin she coveted. "Think what I could do with all that money though. And all the women who'd fall at my feet when I got out of my $200k DB11."

"Women fall over your feet because they're so damn huge, Bigfoot."

"Ouch. Feeling catty much?" Lauren settled into her chair, rotated her ankle, and glanced at her size eleven and a half feet before she pulled herself closer to the table. "They're not *that* big, and with my height, I'd look ridiculous with tiny feet. I'd probably topple over."

"They don't make Louboutins in your size—that's how giant your feet are. Quit dreaming and get this party started so we can get our after-party started."

"That's not true," Lauren muttered and gently kicked Whit's shin before she turned her focus back to the people taking their seats around the enormous circular table at LitLot, the organization of which she was CEO. In eight years, she'd grown it from a small, city charity that was barely sustainable to a multi-million-dollar non-profit covering six East Coast states, and she had no intention of stopping there. She wanted to set up LitLot franchises across the rest of the country, and Whit, who'd been her first hire and wing woman from just three months in, shared that ambition.

But before that expansion continued, there was this: finalizing the contract to see LitLot delivering writing workshops in every state school in all the major cities across New York. And gathered in this room were the people who had the power to make that happen. She and Whit had moved mountains to get the project to this stage, and all they needed now was for everyone present to sign the contract sitting on top of the hefty mountain of paperwork in front of them.

She was about to officially begin the meeting when her phone vibrated. A photo of her mom came up on the screen. She pressed ignore. "Good morning, everyone. Shall we get started? I think we could have this done within the hour and be eating Jackie's gourmet lunch by noon."

Everyone laughed, and some looked more excited at that prospect than they'd ever looked when discussing this project in previous meetings. Jackie's deli wasn't exactly the best in Boston but compared to the school cafeteria food some of these folks were used to, it was heavenly.

Her phone vibrated again. Her mom again. Lauren frowned. Her mom didn't call often. Not anymore. She had when Lauren first left Damarron,

Ohio to attend Harvard and later when she'd moved to a big city to pursue dreams bigger than the tiny town could ever offer, but Lauren was almost always too busy to answer or call back. More than ten years later, and those unanswered calls had become fewer and farther between.

Something was wrong. She'd had a vague sense of dread for the past few hours but had put it down to this meeting since so much was riding on it. Nausea was always strong on the day of a big project closure. She hovered her finger over the green call icon.

Whit placed her hand on Lauren's forearm. "Is everything okay?"

Lauren shook her head slowly. "I don't know."

Whit followed Lauren's gaze back to her phone screen. It stopped vibrating for the merest of moments before a third call from her mom came in.

Whit frowned. "You should answer it. Your mom barely calls, and she certainly doesn't call repeatedly."

Whit knew Lauren's family history. It wasn't complicated. It was just meh. Other than her tight relationship with Kayla, she could take or leave time with everyone else. They were just so different. If it wasn't for her twin, Lauren would seriously believe she'd been adopted.

In the time she'd mused over that, the call had ended and started again. "Please excuse me," she said to the rest of the room after a quick nod to Whit, "I have to take this call." Lauren hurried out into the corridor as she answered her phone. "One second, Mom. I'm just coming out of a meeting." She took a left toward the small seating area near the window and sat on the arm of a large leather Chesterfield couch. She took a deep, cleansing breath and raised the phone to her ear. "Hi, Mom, what's up?" she asked, affecting a breezy tone she'd never used with anyone ever. She barely recognized her own voice.

A sob erupted on the other end of the line. More wailing than sobbing. What the hell was happening? "Is it Dad? Has there been an accident at the factory?"

"It's not your father," her mom said between heaving breaths.

Lauren lost the grip on her cell, and it dropped to the hardwood floor. The dread she'd been feeling had nothing to do with the meeting. No, she was being silly.

She retrieved her phone and rolled her eyes when she saw the glass back was cracked. God dammit, she'd only just gotten this new model.

"Sorry, Mom, I dropped my phone."

"It's your sister, Lauren. She was in a—"

Her mom broke down again, and there was a rustle before the crying went silent.

"Kayla was in a car crash, honey."

Her father sounded stoic. She could almost imagine him standing there, ramrod straight just like his Vietnam vet father had drilled into him. Her mom was overreacting, that was all. That's why her father had taken over. Her parents' words sank in. *Kayla.* "She's okay though, Dad, right? A broken leg, maybe? Mom's just being hysterical." The words felt hollow and empty coming from her mouth. They held no truth.

"I'm sorry, honey. She…she didn't make it."

Her father's stuttered words registered in her ears, but they couldn't be real. He never stumbled over his words. He might not be the most eloquent of people, but he never struggled with something to say.

"She died an hour ago."

"NO!" Lauren released the phone as if it were suddenly white-hot and had seared her hands. She slid from the arm of the sofa and thudded to her knees. "NO!" Lauren heard the banshee-like scream as if it were outside her body. The boardroom door flew open, and Whit darted across the corridor to join Lauren on the floor.

She pulled Lauren into her arms and held her tight. "I've got you," Whit whispered over and over.

Lauren wrapped her arms around Whit's waist and held on, fearful that if she let go, she might fall and never land. Kayla couldn't be gone. Lauren would've felt it. They were twins, connected by more than blood and DNA. The warmth from the underfloor heating did nothing to stop the icy cold grip of grief curling around every cell in Lauren's body.

Now she felt it.

Now she was alone.

CHAPTER TWO

One week later.

JAMIE NELSON PICKED UP the bucket of beers from the bar and headed back to the booth where her friends waited for their first round of the night. She slid into her seat, and the three of them pulled out a bottle each and clinked them together.

"To the unholy trinity," they said in unison and drank half in one long pull.

"God, I love Saturday nights," Terri said after she placed her beer on her coaster. "Don't get me wrong, you know how attached I am to my job, but I look forward to this all week."

Jamie laughed and pointed to the bottle Terri had turned so that the label faced toward her perfectly. "Looks like you're still doing your job."

"When you're as OCD as me, stacking shelves isn't work, it's therapy *I* get paid for." Terri positioned the remaining bottles in the bucket in the same direction and settled back in her seat.

Fran grinned at Jamie, reached over the table, and turned the bucket around to shift the beers. "It's good to challenge your foibles, Tez."

Terri's eyes widened, and Jamie placed her hand on Terri's forearm before she rearranged them again. "Relax, buddy, Fran's just messing with you," Jamie said and jutted her chin toward Fran, who rolled her eyes but set the beers back in a way Terri would be happy with. "Okay, who's going first?"

"Five bucks or ten?" Fran opened her purse and took out her wallet.

"It's the end of the month," Terri said. She slapped a ten-dollar bill in the center of the table. "It's always ten at the end of the month."

Jamie and Fran dropped their money on the pile, and Terri tidied the bills into a neat stack before she drew them closer to her.

"That confident, Tez?" Fran raised her eyebrows. "You're on a five-week losing streak."

Terri smiled widely. "I'm going to break that tonight, I'm sure of it. I've definitely got a winner."

"What about you, Jamie? What do you think your chances are?"

Jamie thumbed the condensation from the neck of her beer. "Slim, as usual. You guys see a lot more people than I do."

"And yours are mostly dead." Terri laughed and clinked her bottle to Fran's.

"We've been playing this game for a while now," Jamie said. "I'm thinking it's time to change it up."

"Ha! You only want to change it because you hardly ever win."

Jamie gave Fran a light shove. "That'd be a good enough reason for anyone, no?"

Her friends shrugged.

Terri tapped her bottle with her ring repeatedly. "I'll go first. Once you've heard mine, you'll realize you've got no chance of winning."

"You have the floor, buddy," Jamie said.

"It was just after midnight on Wednesday, and I was at the door stopping last-minute customers from coming in—"

"I wish I could stop people from coming in after midnight." Fran stuck out her bottom lip.

Jamie chuckled. "Sure. Limit all emergencies from nine in the morning to midnight. Let it be known that you can only chop your finger off or stick a sweet potato up your butt in those hours."

Fran closed her eyes briefly and shook her head. "*That* was a gruesome night."

"And *that's* why you keep winning this game," Jamie said. "I still can't look Old Man Mitty in the eye when he visits his wife at the cemetery."

Terri tapped her beer bottle on the table a few times. "Do you want to hear my story or not?"

Jamie held up her hands. "Of course we do. You were at the door stopping people from coming in—"

"Right," Terri said. "I'm at the door, opening it for people to leave and not letting anyone else in. I'd just pressed the button for the door to close after letting out this pregnant woman and I'd turned around to push a cart into line. Then I hear this clip-clopping thundering of hooves, and a whitetail deer comes running in before the doors slide shut."

Jamie slapped her hand on the table. "No way! You're making that up to win the pot."

"Am not." Terri looked offended.

Fran tilted her head to the side. "The store's close to the Camden Forest. I'm surprised something like that's not happened before."

"Trust the nurse not to be fazed by a giant animal careening into a grocery store," Jamie said.

Fran wrinkled her nose. "A lot of the people I see every day are giant animals, trust me."

"So, what did it want?" Jamie tried not to laugh at the serious expression on Terri's face. "Crunchy peanut butter or some flowers for his doe back in the forest? Which aisle did it head for?"

"The one straight ahead, of course," Terri said and looked at Jamie like she'd asked the most stupid question in the world. "But Anne hadn't quite finished cleaning up a spill in the central aisle. The deer lost its footing and went headfirst into one of the ice cream freezers. Knocked itself clean out. And then three shelves full of Ben & Jerry's tumbled all over it."

Jamie and Fran dissolved into laughter, while Terri looked suitably smug that her story would win the week's pot. She placed a single finger on the money and drew it a little closer, very slowly.

"Oh my god," Jamie said between chest-bursting laughs. "How long did it stay unconscious?"

Terri bounced a little in her seat, clearly psyched to be the cause of so much glee. "Long enough for Anne to spring into action, grab some rainbow duct tape from the crafting aisle, and hog tie it."

The trio laughed some more, clinked their beers together, and drank.

"That could be the best any of us have ever had," Jamie said.

When Fran had recovered sufficiently to speak, she shook her head. "You might be right, Terri. This week's money might be yours. All I've got this week is a kid swallowing a dollar coin for a dare."

"A dollar coin? I don't think I've ever seen one," Terri said.

"Well, I saw one in his chest, and it looked like a full moon on the X-ray. We sent him home and told his parents to keep searching through his scat until the dollar passed." Fran shoved Jamie hard enough to shift her across the seat. "Your turn, Jamie. Have we saved the best till last, or is Terri finally going to end her record losing streak?"

Jamie took another swig of her beer before telling them about the worst thing that had happened at work that week. She hadn't seen much action in the way of vandals or high school kids making out on the gravestones. There'd been no streakers running through anyone's final services, and there'd been four funerals, three of which had died of natural causes. Her worst thing was something she wouldn't—and didn't want to—win their weekly bet with. Her worst thing that week had been something far too personal and close for comfort. It had also been a cold blast from a past she'd pushed way down into the depths of her memory banks. But it wasn't her experience that made her story cruel, it was the injustice of losing a life so young, one full of vitality and promise, one of the town's best, most kind, and generous of people. "We buried Kayla Gray."

A cloak of sadness stifled the oxygen of their previous mirth, and the smile fell from her friends' faces. None of them were close to Kayla, but all of them knew of her and her work with the town's kids. Each of them had donated their time, money, or belongings to one of Kayla's funding drives. Jamie had even given one of her sculptures to Kayla for an auction, and Jamie *never* let the product of her hobbies out of the confines of her garage.

She tried to smile but feared she'd failed miserably. She raised her almost empty bottle, and Terri and Fran met it gently. "To Kayla."

Terri and Fran echoed her words, and they finished their beers. They put the empties down and took a second bottle from the bucket. Ice-cold water dripped from Jamie's onto her hand and along her forearm. The chilled caress reminded her of losing her grandmother a few years ago. She still struggled to talk about her with her mom and hadn't quite reached that place where she was supposed to be able to celebrate and cherish the time they'd had together. Instead, Jamie was mired in lamenting the time she would never *get* to spend with her grandmother, who'd essentially been a second mom to her after her father's death.

Fran nudged her. "Where'd you go?"

Jamie offered a tight smile. "Nowhere good." She took a long pull on her beer before she pushed the thirty dollars to Terri and raised her bottle. "All yours, buddy, just like the next round."

Terri collected her winnings, but she didn't look as happy about it as she had before Jamie told her story.

"I saw Lauren at the wake," Fran said. "Did you talk to her, or did you worship her from afar like you used to do in high school? And junior high. And elementary."

Terri laughed, and Jamie appreciated Fran's change of direction. They came here to have fun and get away from work, and Jamie didn't need to be reminded of death when she was around it all week. Her occupation taught her to live in the moment and enjoy life for all it had to offer. She wished she'd had that same mindset back when she had a massive crush on Lauren, who'd been amazing through every one of her formative years. "Even if I'd wanted to, I don't think that her sister's funeral would've been the right place to approach her, do you?"

"Maybe you'll still get another chance. I hear she's sticking around for a while to clear Kayla's apartment." Fran blew out a deep breath. "I can't imagine what she's going through."

"She's staying at Nancy's B&B, if you want to accidentally bump into her," Terri said.

"Where'd you hear that?" Jamie wondered why Lauren wasn't staying at her parents' place. They still had the old family home, so they'd have plenty of room. Unless they'd repurposed the sisters' rooms after they'd left. Or maybe Lauren couldn't face the ghost of Kayla and her childhood memories. As an only child, Jamie had no concept of the connection she had with her sister, but everyone knew twins were usually closer than regular siblings.

"It's one of the places Ethan cleans," Terri said.

"Your brother's cleaning now?" Fran asked. "I thought he'd started a boat business."

Terri rolled her eyes. "I told you two months ago; that went up in flames—literally. His boat blew up." She shook her head. "Now he's got a cleaning business. If I were Nancy, I wouldn't have hired him. He shouldn't be allowed anywhere near flammable materials and liquids."

Jamie grinned. "Remember the time he blew up your rabbit hutch? It was a good thing that you had Bugs, Rugs, and Sugs hidden in your bedroom at the time."

"People talked about that explosion for months afterward. Everyone thought your brother was crazy." Fran shoved a handful of nuts into her mouth and did a googly eyes impression.

"Mom and Dad got him checked after, but the doctor said he was just inquisitive." Terri looked wistful. "Those bunnies were the cutest though, weren't they?"

Fran wrinkled her nose. "If you ignore the rabbit poo all over your bedroom floor and them constant banging each other even though they were family, sure they were cute."

Terri shook her head. "They only pooped in their area, and I kept it super clean, you know that."

"Anyway," Fran said after washing her nuts down with a drink of beer, "we digress. Nice try, Jamie, but back to Lauren. Are you going to talk to her now that you're all grown up or not?"

Jamie shook her head. "What's the point? I doubt she's even into women, and if she is, she's probably got some hot, model-type waiting for her back in Boston. She couldn't wait to get out of this town, so she'd never be interested in someone like me."

"Meaning you still haven't got the gumption to ask her out. I call BS," Terri said.

"I second that." Fran held up her hand, and Terri high-fived her.

"Gumption? You need to update your vocab, Grandma. What does that even mean?" Jamie laughed, though Terri's jibe wasn't far from the truth. Lauren had broken her heart without ever knowing it. She wasn't about to give her the chance to do it again. And Jamie's stomach had fluttered just like it used to when they were younger. She hadn't expected that. She'd thought she was over Lauren by a long shot. But her breath still caught in that stupidly clichéd way, and other parts of her reacted in a more adult way that was entirely inappropriate for a funeral.

Jamie slid out of the booth. "I need the bathroom. Why don't you order us some wings and another round while I'm gone?"

Terri and Fran chanted the ridiculously childish song about sitting in a tree and made over-the-top kissing noises as Jamie retreated to the back. She headed straight to the sink and splashed cool water on her face, though it did nothing to chill the heat rushing through her body from thinking about Lauren. Sure, she could be gay just as easily as any person alive could be, and that made it worse. But she'd be heading back to Boston soon enough. How hard could it be to avoid running into her in a small town like this?

CHAPTER THREE

"Is the place where you're staying okay?" Whit asked.

Lauren looked around the drab, tired space with its flock wallpaper, garish flower curtains, and multi-colored carpet. "It's not bad." She turned the phone camera around and swept it across the room slowly for Whit to take in its wildly rustic charm.

"Tell me again why you're not staying at home?"

"Because this is easier for everyone." And she wouldn't have to sit having awkward conversations with her mom and dad, whom she had nothing in common with. She also knew she couldn't be in the place where she and Kayla had grown up. She wasn't ready for that kind of pain on top of the constant ache she already carried with her every day. "I left home when I was seventeen. My parents probably thought I was gone for good and turned my room into a mini cinema or a meth lab for all I know."

Whit chuckled. "You're so dramatic. Did they ask you to come home?"

Lauren shrugged. "I told them I'd booked a room at Nancy's, so they didn't have to make any excuses. One second." She put the phone down and pulled on her coat before picking it back up. She left the room, locked the door with an actual key—with a chunk of wood attached so you didn't leave with it—and made her way downstairs. "They don't want me home any more than I want to be there."

Whit grunted. "You don't know that."

"Whose side are you on? One second." Lauren placed the key on the front desk. "I'll be back in a few hours, Nancy."

"Aren't you having breakfast before you go? Patrick's making his special waffles." Nancy wagged her finger at Lauren. "A few waffles would do you a world of good."

"I'm good. Maybe tomorrow." Food couldn't mend her broken heart. Why *did* people think eating was a cure-all? Lauren pushed the meandering thoughts away, headed for the door, and made it out onto Main Street with Nancy calling after her that Patrick would make extra, just in case. She raised her phone again and rolled her eyes.

Whit laughed. "It's nice that she's trying to look after you. It wouldn't hurt for you to take this time to slow down and recharge a little. Everything is under control here."

Lauren trusted Whit implicitly but driving without her hands firmly on the steering wheel had never been her management style. "How's recruitment going for the new contracts?" She'd been out of the office for just over a week, and after COVID, the new proliferation of Zoom users across the country, and the world, meant that she'd been able to orchestrate the new schools project with Whit almost as easily as if she'd been in the office. The ease with which they'd achieved it despite the distance conversely had her feeling a little ill-at-ease. She enjoyed the buzz of the office, the people darting in and out to see her all day, and the travel all over New England and beyond. Remote-working subdued that enjoyment somewhat, and it wasn't something she was prepared to get used to.

"Really good. I'm heading to Manhattan tomorrow to meet the short-listed project managers for New York. Next week is Albany. Did you get the updated schedule I sent?"

Lauren nodded and looked up to cross the street. "You're pulling Charlotte in to help, aren't you? I know she's spent most of her career in operations, but I think she's got management potential. One second." She stopped at the florist to pick up another pre-ordered bouquet for Kayla. Pink carnations, purple hyacinths, and dark crimson roses. He'd been ordering them in specially since Lauren dropped in with her very specific requirement the day after the funeral and today, he had them ready at the counter for her. "Thanks, Simon." She nodded toward his magenta bow tie and baby pink shirt combo. "Looking sharp, as usual."

"I try," he said and handed her the beautiful arrangement.

She tucked it under her arm and tapped her watch to the card machine to pay. "Do you think I'll get to see all the bow ties you own before I leave?" So far, he'd worn a different one each day she'd seen him.

He tilted his head and wiggled his rather bushy eyebrows. "That depends on how long you're staying. It's good to see your face around here even though the circumstances are heart-breaking."

Lauren swallowed hard and gave him a quick smile, suddenly needing to get out of there fast. "Thanks." She swung the front door open entirely too hard, and it smashed into several metal tubs of flowers, knocking them all over the floor. "Oh my god, I'm so sorry."

He waved her off. "Not to worry. Off you go."

She took a big gulp of fresh air when she hit the sidewalk and closed her eyes momentarily.

"Lauren, are you okay?"

Startled, she brought her cell back up when Whit's voice sounded in her earbuds. She'd briefly forgotten she was still on a call with her. "Yeah. I'm fine. That yoga class must be working. I nearly ripped that door from its hinges."

Whit arched her left eyebrow. "That's not what I meant."

Lauren ignored the distinction and walked on toward her destination. "We were talking about Charlotte."

"Are you sure she's ready to take a step up, even a temporary one?"

"I am." Lauren crossed the street and stopped outside the coffee house she'd been patronizing since she'd gotten into town. It wasn't the best, but she knew if she went to the town's best place, owned and managed by her old high school BFF, she wouldn't get out of there for hours. She owed Beth a long visit, but she wasn't quite ready for the trip down memory lane that would inevitably lead to a palace of pain. She hadn't seen her parents since the funeral and wake either. Lauren had never been one to delay facing tough situations, but this wasn't her work life, and losing her sister was like nothing she'd ever experienced. She felt the burn of tears flame at the back of her eyes and blinked hard. *Concentrate.* "One second," she said and realized by the answering expression on Whit's face that she'd said that one too many times in this conversation. "I need both hands. I'm switching to voice." Lauren turned off her camera, slipped her phone into her back pocket, and entered the coffee shop.

The baby-faced barista from the previous morning greeted her and held out a takeout cup. "Double-shot Americano with coconut milk, Ms. Gray."

"You're an angel," she said and paid.

"Same time tomorrow?" he asked.

Lauren picked up the hint of hope in his voice and shook her head. She needed to avoid this kind of thing *and* she should go see Beth. "I don't think so." She retreated to the door and waved back at him.

"You have an admirer already?" Whit asked.

"Please. He looks like he's eighteen."

"That means he's legal."

"Then I'll drop him your Tinder username next time I go in." Lauren stopped at the lights and waited for the walk sign. Not that she really needed to here. It wasn't exactly Boston traffic.

"You know I have no need for dating apps."

Lauren took a small sip of her coffee and sighed at the weak flavor. She definitely needed to get her morning hit at Beth's place tomorrow. "The internet would explode if you went on a dating app." Lauren smiled, and it felt good to do so genuinely. The smiles she'd been giving out the past week barely stretched her cheek muscles. She missed Whit. She hadn't spent this much time away from her since that disastrous vacation a few years ago with a woman who turned out to be a crazy stalker.

"Truth," Whit said.

Lauren crossed the street. Her destination was only a few hundred yards away, so she had to wrap this meeting up. "Give Charlotte a try with the New York meetings and let me know how it goes. It'll work out, I'm sure."

Charlotte had been a volunteer on an early literary project, and Lauren immediately knew she had the makings of a great manager, but she'd had to wait to recruit her until she finished college. She'd been learning the ropes in operations for the past two years, and Lauren was certain she was ready for the next stage.

"If you're sure, I'm sure," Whit said. "Are you nearly there?"

"Yeah." Lauren could just see the black gates with the ornate gold lions standing guard on either side of the entrance. She'd always thought them too flashy when she lived here. Now that she was visiting daily, their ostentatiousness grated on her nerves even more. There was nothing to celebrate within.

"I love you, babe."

"You too." Lauren tapped her right earbud and ended the call. She stopped at the threshold of the gates and pulled the flowers from under her arm. "It's not supposed to be like this," she said quietly before opening the side gate and entering the cemetery for her daily pilgrimage to Kayla's grave.

She looked for something new to focus on as she made her way forward, her shoes suddenly as heavy as concrete. With the florist, the café, and work talk with Whit to focus on, Lauren could almost ignore the gravity of her destination and delay contemplating the feelings of finality and desperation. But once inside the pretentious gates, the reason for her walk could no longer be ignored.

Someone was walking toward her holding a set of ladders under their arm. That was new. The place had been desolate on her previous visits, and thankfully, she hadn't bumped into another living soul. She scoffed internally at the unintended faux pas. There was one too many dead souls in this damn place.

Lauren studied the person, still quite a distance away on the long, gravel path that led her inexorably toward a meeting she wished she didn't have to attend. There was something familiar about them, which wasn't surprising since it seemed she'd been the only one to escape this one-horse town, and everyone she'd known throughout her childhood and teenage years was, depressingly, still here. Such a lack of ambition and waste of natural gifts. She'd attended school with some truly talented and intelligent people, but all of them had been content to follow in the footsteps of their families and keep their roots firmly in this soil.

As the person drew closer, Lauren saw they were carrying a can of paint in their other hand. Probably for the god-awful gates. If only they were carrying a sledgehammer to destroy those gauche lions. The person stopped and looked behind them as if they might've forgotten something. They started toward her again then stopped again. Their shoulders sagged a little, and they headed Lauren's way again.

Now they were closer, Lauren could see the person was a woman. With cropped, dark hair and dressed in work jeans, tan boots speckled with paint and grass stains, and a puffer vest over a white T-shirt, Lauren pegged her as queer. It wasn't her appearance alone that led to that conclusion, it was the way she walked, with that butchy swagger Lauren had always been a big fan of. Except when the woman had stopped-started hesitantly a few moments ago. That wasn't indicative of confidence at all.

The woman was just a few steps away and seemed to be looking everywhere but at Lauren until she finally met Lauren's eyes. The shy smile and kind eyes were familiar, but not enough so that she could put a name to them.

"Hi, Lauren," the woman said and adjusted her direction to continue walking beyond her.

Lauren frowned. She was good with faces and names; she'd made a fine art of it in her work life, so it bothered her that she had no idea who this was. She disliked not remembering anyone she'd met. It made people feel insignificant and not memorable, and she disliked making anyone feel bad even more. Equally, she wasn't one to bluff and pretend she remembered someone, because that could lead to an embarrassing situation. She remembered a time when she'd been with Whit when a guy approached them, and Whit had no idea who he was. She'd played along, thinking it was someone she'd slept with and said they should do it again, but he turned out to be the kindergarten teacher of Whit's young niece. She hadn't picked the poor kid up from school since. "I'm sorry, do we know each other?"

By the time Lauren asked the question, the woman had walked past her, but she stopped and half-turned. Now she looked a little forlorn.

"I guess not," she said, her voice deep but quiet. "We used to go to the same school when we were kids. And teenagers. All schools. While we were growing up."

The woman kicked at the gravel, and a chunk flew up and hit Lauren's shin.

"Ouch."

"Oh my god, I'm so sorry."

"It's okay, don't worry about it." Lauren put her flowers down on one the benches along the walkway and bent over to inspect it. "It hasn't— oh, it has broken the skin." She wiped the small amount of blood away that had begun to seep from the wound and straightened. She didn't have anything on her to wipe the blood on. *Damn it.* She dragged her finger across the top of her coffee cup lid then took the lid off and dumped it in the trash bin beside the bench.

The woman hurriedly placed her ladders and paint can down and pulled a white cloth from one of the many pockets on her workpants. She dropped to one knee in front of Lauren then stopped.

"It's bleeding pretty bad. I'm so sorry. This is clean. Can I just, kind of bandage it for you?"

Lauren extended her leg to see the woman wasn't wrong. The sight of her own blood made her a little light-headed. She pointed to the bench and placed her takeout cup on its arm. "I'm going to sit down a moment."

When she was seated, the woman scrambled over, still holding the white cloth. "Seriously, I need to wrap this around it. It's clean, I promise. You can check."

Despite the dull throbbing pain in her shin, Lauren couldn't help but laugh. "How clean can a rag in your pocket be?"

"Actually, I only just opened the packaging, so it's practically sterile," she said.

Lauren suppressed another laugh. "*Practically* sterile? As in anti-bacterial, COVID-safe sterile?"

The woman's expression fell, and her cheeks flushed red. "Well, no. It's not." She held it up like limp lettuce. "But look, it's clean."

Lauren shook her head. She could see it was clean and new; the folds in the crisp, white material were still evident. "Okay, wrap my war wound."

"Jamie," she said, pulling a buck knife from a leather holster clipped onto her workpants. "I'm Jamie. I used to watch you. Play soccer, I mean. And the swim meets."

Jamie sliced into the material and created a long, thin strip before she put her knife away. Lauren would've thought it slick had it not been accompanied by Jamie's comical ramblings. She took a closer look at Jamie while she was busy tending to the damage she'd created and finally recognized her. "Jamie Nelson," she said so loudly that it startled Jamie, who looked up, wide-eyed. Yep, more memories clicked into place. "You hung out with Francesca Rogers and Teresa Caddy. You guys were like the Three Musketeers." She smiled down at Jamie, who now looked baffled. The rest of the school had invented other names for the group, but none of them were as flattering as the one Lauren had just used, which explained Jamie's expression. Lauren had never been part of the bullying crowd, but she'd known who they'd targeted, and they'd given Jamie and her friends a hellish time from elementary through to high school.

"Yeah." Jamie pulled out a roll of duct tape, ripped a piece off, and used it to secure the material around Lauren's leg. "You've got a great memory for names, if not for faces."

"Ha, it's been a while," Lauren said, surprised at the little jab. "You've grown a few inches and," she gestured toward Jamie's shoulders, which strained against the T-shirt she wore, "gained some muscle. And you've changed your hair." Now *she* was rambling and trying to find excuses for not recognizing someone she'd had such little real interaction with as a kid. But Jamie's lost expression when she hadn't recognized her made her feel awful.

Jamie stood. "I'm really sorry about this." She looked toward the depths of the cemetery grounds. "And your sister. She was a wonderful woman."

And there was Lauren's cue to go. She was barely holding it together when people didn't talk about Kayla, but she wasn't ready for a conversation about her with someone who was basically a stranger. Breaking down in private wasn't something she did regularly, so she definitely wasn't about to start doing it in public. Lauren tossed her coffee into the trash, picked up her flowers and stood. "It was lovely seeing you. Take care." And she hurried away, wincing slightly at the pain in her leg but not letting it stop her escape.

She reached Kayla's resting place a few minutes later, placed the flowers in an empty vase, and sat cross-legged on the grass in front of the marble gravestone. Her gaze fell on the inscription.

Kayla Gray
Loyal and loving daughter and sister.
"Don't cry because it's over,
Smile because it happened."
9/19/1988 – 6/19/2022

Dr. Seuss books had been their favorites as children, but reading the quote now sent a raging fire through her veins. She clenched her fists, pressed them against the soft ground, and looked up to the sky to stop her tears from falling.

She failed and doubled over, the sobs racking her body. She wanted to scream out and ask why? Why Kayla? Why so early?

But there was no one to answer that question. Kayla's death wasn't part of some grand design. There was no sense to it. And there was no one to blame.

Except maybe Lauren could blame herself. When she'd gone back to Boston to pursue her grand ambitions after they'd attended college together, she should've brought Kayla with her. They would've done such great things, made such a huge difference to thousands of lives, moved mountains together. But Kayla had said that she wanted to go home, that she needed to stay close to their parents.

She shuffled closer to the headstone and leaned against the marble, cold even in the warmth of the spring morning. "I'm sorry, sis. I should never have let this happen."

CHAPTER FOUR

Damn, damn, damn. What had she been thinking? Of course the most popular girl in every school year didn't remember who she was. They hadn't seen each other for over fifteen years. Lauren must've thought Jamie was crazy. Or a stalker. She should've kept her mouth shut and walked on by. She was visiting her sister, for God's sake. She didn't want to be bothered by someone who hadn't even been her friend. And then she'd made matters worse by—

Jamie pulled the silver wire down with too much force. It slipped through her hand and sliced her palm. "Shit."

"Are you okay, honey?" her mom asked as she peered around the edge of the barn door.

Jamie held up her hand. The blood was already running down her wrist and along her forearm toward the rolled-up sleeve of her shirt. *Great. Today's theme is blood.* She dropped her arm down, pulled the bandana from around her head, pressed in onto her palm and closed her fist around it.

"Jamie, no." Her mom hurried toward her. "Let me see." She opened Jamie's hand and looked beneath the makeshift bandage. "Oh, it's not that bad. You're a tough cookie. You'll live."

As her mom held her hand, Jamie noticed she was wearing her best watch and her favorite bracelets. She looked at the rest of her and saw her mom was also rocking a plunging neckline blouse, hip-hugging skirt, and her fancy heels. "Are you off on another date?" Jamie asked, trying to keep the amusement in her voice to a minimum and pulled her hand back.

"What do you mean, *another* date?" Her mom pressed her palm to her bare chest and seemed to be going for a demure look. "Do you have me on a quota? Are you at war with love and need to ration my innocent meetings with suitors?"

Jamie laughed. She might not have a traditional mom but what she lacked in cooking skills, she made up for with wit. "Is it with Jeff again?"

She took a step back. "No."

"What happened to Jeff?"

Another step back. "Too tall."

"So it must be Henry?"

Her mom was almost out the door. "No. He turned out to be a taxidermist, and I'm not dating someone who sticks fluff up the butts of dead animals all day."

Jamie grinned. "I don't think that's what they actually do, Mom."

"I don't care. No dead animals fixed into weird human poses. I'll put up with a lot of things, but that's just not right." Her mom stopped and came back into the barn. "I saw Sharon at the nail salon today. She said that Lauren Gray hadn't left town yet. Have you seen her since the funeral?"

Jamie studied her injured hand as if it were a sculpture by Paige Bradley. "Maybe. A couple of times." She'd seen Lauren every day since the funeral and watched her from afar like a creepy weirdo. She'd been trying to work up the courage to approach her but hadn't wanted to disturb what looked like deep and intense discussions with her sister's headstone.

Her mom gave a small laugh. "I should be more specific. Have you talked to her yet?"

"A little bit. It didn't go well." Understatement. First contact had been disastrous.

"Did you ask her out?"

Jamie scoffed. "Of course not. Her sister just died, Mom. I doubt she's in the mood to be hit on."

"It doesn't have to be a date, does it?" Her mom picked up a rag and dusted off Jamie's work stool before she hitched herself up onto it.

Jamie sighed. Her mom was staying a while, apparently. "I thought you were just heading out?"

Her mom ignored her and rolled on with her unsolicited interference. "You could just ask her if she wants to get coffee. Catch up with what she's been doing all these years. Find out why she barely comes back home. See if you've got anything in common." She gestured to Jamie's sculptures scattered around the barn. "You could tell her about your art. Think of it as a reconnaissance mission to see if she's even worth your time."

Jamie didn't need an elaborate plot to discover Lauren was "worth her time." Lauren was a sophisticated, successful, and sweet woman with a heart of gold who worked for a kids' charity. She was worth the Dalai

Lama's time. Google had been a mine of information, but it hadn't yielded Lauren's love interest or marital status. The internet seemed to have been scrubbed of that useful information. "This isn't art. It's a hobby to keep my mind occupied. And I'm really not desperate enough to take dating advice from the woman who's had more bad men than Taylor Swift."

"So you *do* still like her, and you *do* want to date her. Interesting that your flame for her hasn't died out in nearly two decades."

Jamie frowned. "Jeez, it's not two decades. That makes me sound old."

"Still, it's a long time to have a crush on someone."

Jamie rolled her eyes. She wasn't winning this one. "Crushes are for teenagers, Mom. Yes, she's still attractive." Another understatement. Age had only increased Lauren's level of hotness. Like a fine wine, she was simply improving as she matured. "But she barely knows I exist, just like in school. And she might not even be into women. Whatever she's into, she's about as likely to be single as…something very unlikely. Have you even seen her since she got back?"

Her mom shook her head. "I don't need to. *I'm* not the one who's in love with her."

"Whoa, I am not in love with her. You can't be in love with someone you haven't seen for over ten years." Jamie opened her palm and peeled her bandana off. Her mom was right; it wasn't that bad. She tossed the stained cloth onto a nearby work bench. "And I probably wasn't in love with her when we were at school either. I didn't know what love was back then."

"Oh, and you do now after *all* the relationships you've had."

"What are you saying?"

"I'm saying it's hard to know what love is when you don't stick around long enough to find out, honey."

Her mom's expression softened, and she gave Jamie that look that could always make her cry when she was trying to hold back her tears. *Like mother, like daughter.* But Jamie held back that surprisingly bitter response, not sure where it had come from. Her mom was looking for love, and pretty damn earnestly. But she had standards and a checklist, and after Jamie's dad, no one had what she was looking for. And maybe her mom was right. Jamie didn't have the greatest track record when it came to love, but there were slim pickings in this town and most of the time, it just seemed like too much hassle. Where was it written that she *had* to find someone to settle down with? She had Fran and Terri, both single, and they had a pact that, if they were still single at fifty, they'd get a place and grow old together. They'd made it when they were seventeen and fifty seemed like a lifetime away. Fifty was ancient. Her mom was just about to hit the half-century mark herself. She said it was the new thirty, and she was *still* looking for love and companionship.

Jamie sighed and fiddled with the wire she'd been working with. She used her discarded bandana to clean her blood off the metal. "Someone told me that if I stopped looking, love would find me."

Her mother huffed. "Whoever that was didn't live in a little town like this."

Jamie laughed and nodded. "Seriously though, I'd like to get to know thirty-three-year-old Lauren, I would. But she's grieving, and spending time with a stranger probably isn't high on her agenda."

Her mother tilted her head. "Talking to someone outside the family might be exactly what she needs, honey. She's been distant from her parents for a long time, and I doubt she's maintained any friendships with old school friends. And you're a wonderful listener."

Jamie flicked at her wire creation then stuffed her hands in her pockets to concentrate on the conversation fully. Lauren was spending a lot of time by herself at Kayla's grave, talking up a storm, and Jamie's mom was, annoyingly, almost always right about everything. "Maybe. I did try to talk to her today." She recounted the sorry tale. Her mom clasped her hand over her mouth partway through and alternated her expression between mortified and thoroughly amused.

"Sounds like it was going quite well until you mentioned her sister."

Jamie nodded. "It felt right to give my condolences, but she practically ran away as soon as I did."

"It's only been a week, Jamie. Maybe next time you see her, talk about anything *but* Kayla. And if she wants to talk about her sister, she'll bring her up when she's ready." Her mom straightened the wedding ring she wore on her right hand. "If something's meant to come of you two, it'll happen. I always thought she was such a lovely girl, and by all accounts, she's turned into quite the woman. Find out who she is." Her mom held out her hand, and Jamie took it. "And let her find out who you are. You never gave her that chance in high school. Don't make the same mistake now."

They stood in silence for a few moments, and Jamie twisted her mom's wedding ring around and around her finger, its presence still a strong reminder of her dad for both of them.

"If it's not Jeff or Henry, who is it?" Jamie asked, lightening the unexpectedly somber mood switch. "Aren't you running out of eligible men within a twenty-mile radius of the town? You'll be heading off to Rock Lake soon."

Her mom gave her a wicked grin. "I ran through Rock Lake a year ago. I'm going to have to join one of those dating apps Sharon keeps talking about. She says she doesn't have enough days in the week for the action she's getting."

"Ew, Mom!"

Her mom slid off the stool and hugged Jamie hard. "Don't get carried away in here and forget to walk Olly." She released her and headed for the door.

"I love you, Mom," Jamie called after her. She might not know what it was to really love a woman, but the love she had for her mom was stronger than her platinum wedding band.

"I love you too, honey." Her mom turned and winked. "Don't wait up."

Jamie rolled her eyes. "At least text me to tell me you're safe."

Her mom nodded and left, and Jamie heard her chuckling all the way back up the driveway. She turned back to the piece she was working on and blew out a long breath. She wasn't feeling it anymore, and like her mom had said, Olly needed his last walk of the day. She flicked the lights off, locked the barn door, and headed back to the house. She thought of Lauren and her sweet smile and resolved to heed her mom's advice. Jamie didn't want any regrets, or any what ifs in her life. If she crashed and burned, if Lauren wasn't interested in even being a friend, that'd be okay. But what wouldn't be okay was not knowing what might've happened if she didn't try.

CHAPTER FIVE

AFTER HER MORNING VISIT to Kayla's grave, Lauren headed back to Nancy's to change. She chose a silk blouse, suit skirt, and block heels for her meeting with Whit and Katie from the LitLot board. First, it was time to visit Beth.

She'd grabbed coffee at her regular place against her better judgment, but the horny teenager who'd been serving her had been thankfully absent. The coffee was still sub-par, and it'd put off her visit to Beth, so it was worth insulting her taste buds one last time.

But she couldn't delay it any longer. At the funeral, she'd asked Lauren to drop in for a chat, and if Lauren didn't go soon, it would be rude. There were a few reasons Lauren had been avoiding it, one of them being that she was expecting trouble, though Beth might go easy on her given the circumstances. She'd tried to keep in touch after Lauren had left for Boston, but she didn't want any more ties to home, nothing to have to come back for other than the expected holidays, and she'd avoided those calls wherever she could.

They kept in touch sporadically through Facebook, but every time Beth asked Lauren about coming home to see her, Lauren shut her down and changed the subject so fast she made herself dizzy. Lauren had suggested that Beth visit Boston, but that hadn't happened. Her unwillingness was just another example of the strange hold this damn town had on its residents. No one wanted to leave.

Lauren had considered it escaping more than leaving. She still couldn't see the appeal of the town. But it was the closest place to be with Kayla so right now, it was the only place on Earth she wanted to be. She leaned on the dresser and closed her eyes. No crying. She'd just re-applied her make-up. *Waterproof mascara, my ass.* She glanced in the mirror to check her overall appearance but couldn't look too long. Lately, she'd seen Kayla instead of her own reflection. Not in a weird, ghost kind of a way. More in the identical twin way as it had always been until she'd trained herself to see the minuscule differences only she knew. Their tastes in clothes, style, and hair had been as identical as their eyes, nose, and mouth. And it was too painful to see that right now. She had no idea when or if it would ever go away.

She wasn't sure she would want it to.

The keys to Kayla's apartment caught her eye. No, that was too painful right now too. She straightened, grabbed her tablet and slipped it into her tote bag along with her phone and wallet. She unlocked the door, still vaguely amused by the key's clunky wooden attachment, and opened it to find a guy outside looking like he was about to knock.

"Hi, Lauren. Nancy sent me up to clean your room." He raised the vacuum cleaner in his hand by way of further explanation.

Did he recognize her, or did Nancy simply encourage her staff to know their residents by their first names? The customer service here contrasted greatly with the faceless chain hotels she was used to staying in during work trips so regularly that she sometimes wondered why she bothered renting an apartment.

"It's Ethan."

Ah, he knew her and expected her to show him the same courtesy. Unfortunately, just as with Jamie Nelson yesterday, she drew a blank, and Ethan looked too young to have been through school with her. Perhaps she wasn't as good with faces and names as she thought she was. "Hi, Ethan, how are you?" While she was reluctant to act like she knew him, the forlorn look on Jamie's face yesterday hadn't left her, and she didn't want to upset more people.

"I'm good." He gestured beyond Lauren into her room. "So can I go in?"

"Of course. I'll leave the key with you." Lauren stepped aside and moved past him, glad he hadn't expected a longer interaction that would reveal her ignorance and relieved that he hadn't mentioned Kayla so that her mascara might be tested—and fail—again. She managed to make it outside with only a short conversation with Nancy, who threatened to send breakfast up to her room the next day at six a.m. to make sure she ate something. Not wanting to offend her, Lauren agreed to come down at seven to have a small waffle before she left for the cemetery. Nancy's smile—full of empathy, sympathy, or pity, Lauren couldn't decide which—made her bottom lip tremble. She'd have to go down to breakfast without makeup.

She turned right and headed up to Beth's, steeling herself and trying to flood her mind with thoughts of fluffy puppies, smart cats, and amazing animal rescue stories. She didn't have a problem with being emotional or vulnerable, but it had to be in an appropriate environment and with people she trusted and felt safe with. As a woman in a high-level position, controlling her emotions was all the more important. No one trusted a leader who couldn't maintain their cool under pressure. Lauren had trusted Beth in high school, but that was a long time ago. Lauren didn't know who Beth was anymore, and vice versa.

She was barely through the front door when Beth saw her and made her way around the counter.

"You made it." Beth hooked her arm through Lauren's and pulled her to a booth at the back of the diner.

"Of course. I promised I would." Lauren slid onto the leather-covered bench facing the door and placed her bag beside her. She didn't want to run into anybody else she knew or didn't recognize, or, most importantly, her parents, whom she still hadn't seen since the wake. Their frequent calls and texts were easy to ignore once she'd convinced herself she had work to do and that she'd visit on the weekend when she had more time.

"I wasn't sure you'd come." Beth sat opposite her and pushed the tray of condiments out of her way. "I didn't know how long you were going to stay in town after…"

Lauren smiled. Few people knew how to speak about death around those who were grieving. She wasn't one to judge. She wouldn't know what to say if the roles were reversed either. It was perhaps the one subject she found difficult to navigate. "I haven't made any plans to go home yet. I'm working remotely while I figure things out. I've got Kayla's apartment to sort out." She stopped abruptly and choked down the torrent of sadness that would have her breaking down and struggling to speak.

On one of Kayla's many visits to Lauren's place in Boston, they'd gotten more than a little drunk and the topic of death had arisen because Whit had recently lost her grandma to cancer. Whit talked about clearing out her grandma's apartment with her mom and how they'd found nude photos and sex toys. Whit said she wouldn't have been fazed by it but sharing the discovery with her mom and having to explain what certain things were had been mortifying. They'd gone out to buy latex gloves before they continued. She, Kayla, and Whit immediately made a morbid pact to clear out each other's places when they died, agreeing that no family member would be exposed to that knowledge.

The thought of Whit's grandma, whom Lauren had met many times, enjoying a *very* active sex life well into her eighties had always made her giggle, but the reality of their pact coming to fruition knocked that joy from her instantly. Her recurring thought that this shouldn't be happening echoed in her mind.

"If you need any help when you do that, you know you can call on me, don't you?"

Lauren nodded but had no intention of taking Beth up on the offer. That was something she wanted to do by herself so that she could be alone in her grief. "That's kind, thank you." The hassle she'd anticipated from Beth didn't look like it was forthcoming.

"Coffee or something stronger?"

Lauren frowned and looked to the counter. There was no sign of alcohol.

Beth tapped the side of her head and winked. "One of the perks of living above the place I work. We can go upstairs for lunch if you'd like."

"I'll stick to coffee, thanks." Going upstairs and out of the public eye might lead to tears over gin, and Lauren was trying to keep her sobbing to the confines of her rented room. Beth's smile faded, and Lauren feared she'd offended her. "Besides, I want to take in the ambience of this place. You've told me all about it, but this is the first time I've been able to visit. I want the full experience."

Beth's smile returned. She pointed to the small tablet in the center of the table. "The menu is all on there. You can even order from it using our app."

"Excellent." Lauren had seen the same technology in plenty of city restaurants and diners, but she hadn't expected to come across it in her hometown. She thought of the personal touches at the B&B, the café, and the florist. Wasn't small town supposed to be more about the relationships and not speed? "Do people around here like this?"

Beth tutted. "Just because it's a small town doesn't mean we don't like big ideas, Lauren."

She held up her hands. "I'm sorry, I didn't mean it like that. I'm staying at Nancy's and they're still using real keys. The convenience store still has price tags instead of barcodes. The town council won't allow chain stores to open up here. I'm just saying that people like their lives a little slower than city slickers, that's all."

Beth shrugged. "You're right." She pulled a leather-bound menu from the side of the booth. "And that's why we still have traditional options, but this caters to the tourists, see?"

"Ah, got it. That makes perfect sense. It's good to see the town is still popular."

A lot of the town, her parents included, didn't like the tourists, but they were necessary for the economy. Seeing all the visitors when she was a kid had been the first spark for Lauren that there was a big world beyond the boundaries of this town. It lit a fire in her, and she became desperate to leave. It never had the same effect on Kayla, and aside from college, she hadn't shown any interest in leaving. Now that Lauren thought about it, Kayla had hated being away for college too.

"It's a lot quieter from the end of November to March, but the resident population is high, so no one has to close. Income takes a dive though."

"I'll bet." Lauren flipped through the menu and chose the chicken salad with ranch. Beth relayed their order to a nearby waiter and returned with their coffees.

"How's everything else with you? How are Andrew and Millie?"

Beth rolled her eyes. "Andrew wants another kid."

"And that's a bad thing?"

"It is for my body." Beth leaned back and prodded her stomach. "Do you have any idea what it took to get back into shape after Millie?"

Lauren laughed. "You look great."

"And I wanted to stay that way for a while. But Mr. Stay-at-Home Dad says Millie needs a sibling. He was an only child. He says he was lonely, and he doesn't want that for Millie."

Lauren glanced away briefly, wishing the conversation hadn't taken this turn. For a moment, she'd managed to push aside her monumental loss and think about other people. "It's wonderful that he's such a family man though, isn't it? Who would've thought the high school quarterback would have made such a great father and husband—he is a good husband too, isn't he?"

"He is." She grinned and wiggled her eyebrows. "And I'm grateful to you every day for handing him off to me."

Lauren shuddered at the memory of her youthful make-out sessions with Andrew. "I'd like to say that was my plan all along, but I'd be lying."

"I don't think I ever told you that he was paranoid about me leaving him for at least the first five years of our relationship. He was certain he was responsible for putting you off guys." Beth laughed and shook her head. "He's the light of my life, but he's never been too bright."

"I'm glad you said that so I didn't have to. Though he should probably know that I wasn't into guys even before we dated. He was my cover for the sake of appearances."

The front door swung open, and Lauren glanced up to see Jamie enter. Lauren slid across the seat so that she was slightly out of view when Jamie approached the counter.

"What's wrong?" Beth turned briefly then leaned across the booth. "Ah," she said and raised her eyebrows. "I'm surprised you remember Jamie Nelson. She comes in every day. Never stays though. She still doesn't really socialize with anyone but her two friends from school."

"I ran into her at the cemetery yesterday." She flexed her leg and yep, that spot stung a little. When she'd gotten back to her room and removed Jamie's makeshift bandage, she hadn't been able to resist a smile. Jamie's reaction and the way she'd taken care of Lauren's leg had been incredibly sweet. She imagined herself talking about it with Kayla over a bottle of wine, and Kayla would have teased her mercilessly. Instead, she'd had to settle for a one-sided conversation about it at her graveside.

Beth pointed to a metal sculpture, about four feet long with maybe a twelve-foot wingspan suspended from the ceiling. "Do you see that phoenix over the bar?"

Lauren had noticed it earlier. "It's absolutely beautiful. I was going to ask you where you got it from but then you distracted me with food."

"Jamie made it."

Lauren raised her eyebrows. "Wow, that's amazing. Did you commission her to do it? Is she an artist?"

"Apparently, she is." Beth shrugged. "I had no idea until Kayla held a fundraiser a few years ago, and Jamie donated that. As soon as I saw it, I had to have it. I won it in the auction."

"Really?"

Beth nodded. "It was quite the bidding war between me, Simon, and a rich tourist who happened to be on vacation here at the time of the gala.

Simon's never forgiven me for beating him. Every time he comes in, he asks me if I'll sell it to him."

"The tortured artist, huh?" The artistry of the piece was something else. If asked, Lauren would've bet her last dollar that it had been brought in from a bespoke boutique store in the city. She'd been to the homes of many patrons and donors to LitLot who had similar art all over their mansions, and they'd paid five and six figure sums for them. "She's really talented. Why is she working at the cemetery when she's capable of creating something like that?"

Jamie was clearly wasting her talent, painting gates and digging holes at the graveyard. With the right connections, she could make a very profitable career and leave this unappreciative town behind.

"I honestly don't know. But she's good with her hands, huh?" Beth winked. "And you know she's gay, right?"

Lauren nodded. "I remembered when I saw her."

"Do you remember that folder she came into school with? The one that Michelle and her cronies stole from her and burned?"

Lauren frowned. She recalled the furor that surrounded it. Jamie had covered a regular binder with pictures of women: movie stars, bodybuilders, singers, writers, and politicians in various states of dress and undress. It had been her way of coming out to the world, and it had rocked the small-town mentality of the kids at school. Lauren was surprised how much detail she'd stored, but then she'd been struggling with her own sexuality at the time and seeing someone be so brave about their own had made a strong impression on her. "They burned it?"

"Yep. They knocked her around a bit too." Beth shook her head. "Made me glad I was always on the right side of them, but that was down to you."

Lauren clenched her jaw at the thought of that particular group of high school mean girls and their vicious campaign against Jamie and her friends. Bullying was something she abhorred, and she didn't stand for it as an adult. But as a young woman in *this* town, she hadn't been strong enough to challenge it, too afraid they might turn on her and see the difference she'd been hiding so well. It was something she regretted, even now. "I was lucky I was popular. I'm assuming Michelle and her buddies are still around here somewhere. I haven't had the misfortune to run into them yet."

"You assume correctly," said Beth, wrinkling her nose. "They all married young and had shotgun weddings. I'm sure you can imagine the story. Several kids, divorced, remarried, and keeping the local liquor store going between them. They're scattered across town, but I don't see them in here, thankfully."

Lauren knew the type. She'd seen plenty of that breed of parents in the schools she'd liaised with over the years. She glanced back at the counter just as Jamie reached the door to leave. Lauren almost called out but thought better of it. Jamie looked focused and purposeful, like she had just enough time to grab something to eat before she tackled her next task. "Has Jamie always worked at the cemetery?"

Beth raised her eyebrows and grinned. "Yes. And she's single, in case that was your next question."

Lauren blew out a belligerent breath. "That wasn't going to be my next question." As undeniably cute as Jamie was, hooking up with anyone, let alone someone from this damn town, wasn't on her agenda.

She didn't have the emotional capacity to cope with anything other than trying to get a handle on her new reality: a world without her sister.

CHAPTER SIX

JJAMIE EMPTIED THE GRASS cuttings onto the compost heap and got back on the ride-on lawnmower. She'd left the final area as long as she could, but she had a whole set of tasks on her to-do list to get to, and she couldn't leave it any longer. She'd thought Lauren would be gone by now—she usually was after two hours—but it'd already been three, and it was fast approaching noon. Jamie had to get the last section finished before lunch.

She drove as quietly as she could on what was essentially a 400cc tractor. When she was a hundred yards away from Lauren, who was sitting cross-legged on the floor with her back and head resting against her sister's gravestone, Jamie cut the engine and hesitantly walked toward her. As she got closer, she could hear Lauren talking. She could be on her phone chatting to a live person, but Jamie suspected she was deep in a one-person conversation with Kayla. It was the first thing Jamie did most days when she got to work. Her dad's grave was toward the back of the cemetery, and he'd been there a lot longer than Kayla, but like her, his residency had started too soon, and a quick check-in with him every morning prepared Jamie for a day of death and flowers.

"'Scuse me, Lauren," she said quietly. Lauren was completely caught up in her own world and seemed not to have seen Jamie walking toward her. After injuring her the last time she saw her, Jamie didn't want to risk giving her a heart attack this time.

Lauren looked up, her eyes bloodshot and heavy with bottomless sorrow. "Hi, Jamie."

Her words were barely a whisper, as though it had taken a huge effort to get them out. She looked at her watch then back up at Jamie.

"Do you close on a Wednesday?" she asked, a little louder now. "I'm sorry, I didn't realize."

Jamie held out her hands to stop Lauren when she moved to stand. "No, we're not closing." She motioned back toward her ride, instantly wishing she'd left this section until later and gotten on with the rest of her list. "I have to cut the grass…and I wanted to apologize again for hurting you the other day."

Lauren gave a small smile. "You didn't hurt me. It was the rock's fault."

Her joke relaxed Jamie a little. "Then I want to apologize for the rock. I'm supposed to keep them in line, along with the grass and the flowers."

Lauren's smile widened. "Oh yeah? Sounds like a difficult job. Do the flowers talk back?"

Jamie nodded. "You wouldn't believe the sass those tiger lilies give me some days. It's hard to take. I've lost count of the number of times I've thought about leaving this job. I think I'd get less hassle as a prison guard."

Lauren laughed, and Jamie swallowed hard. That sound, the look of momentary happiness on Lauren's face, and her movie star cheekbones brought back a rush of memories that left Jamie weak-kneed. *Long time to have a crush*, her mom had said. Damn her for being right again.

"Really? And what about the roses?"

Lauren's gentle gaze had Jamie looking away and gesturing toward the nearby circle of rose bushes just to catch her breath. If Medusa could turn a man to stone, Lauren could turn a person into a puddle of longing. So much for there being no attraction. "Don't even get me started on the roses. They love to gossip. They spread all kinds of rumors about the blackbirds." Jamie risked looking back at Lauren. Her smile was still the brightest part of Jamie's day so far, and she didn't think the sun could compete, no matter how high it rose in today's bluebird sky.

"I'd forgotten what a great sense of humor you had."

After that statement, one of the roses could've knocked her down. What did Lauren know of her sense of humor? "Really?"

"Really."

Oh crap, she'd said that out loud. "I didn't think you even knew I existed in school." What was she thinking, saying that? Fifteen years later, it shouldn't even matter.

Lauren smiled and almost looked a little shy, which made her even more adorable.

"Of course I did." Lauren stood and brushed off her trousers. "I was the student body president—I knew everybody."

The glimmer of hope that the most popular girl in school had actually *noticed* Jamie when she was an awkward, quiet, and socially stunted teenager was snuffed out with Lauren's last words. Yep, Jamie recalled how seriously Lauren took her role and how she'd canvas everyone to make sure they had a say in any student-led decisions. God, Jamie had been conflicted about the annual spring dances. On the one hand, she loathed the expectation for girls to don dresses and have dates, but on the other, she loved the opportunity to talk to Lauren in a small group when she was floating the themes for that year. And yes, Jamie had done her very best to be funny and charming, or what she'd thought was funny and charming as a teenager, just to get Lauren to look at her. For a moment there, she thought it might've worked.

"Jamie?"

Lauren's voice drifted into her awareness, and she realized she'd gone off in her head. "Sorry. I was just thinking about the school dances."

A sympathetic expression crossed Lauren's face. "You know, I've always regretted not doing anything about Michelle Yates and her gang."

Jamie took a step back and a deep breath to push down the memories that suddenly fought for attention at the mention of that name. She, Terri, and Fran had stopped being frightened of those girls long ago, but the emotions of that time were harder to forget. The three of them did take occasionally gleeful comfort in the disastrous path the lives of their bullies had taken.

Jamie felt the warmth of Lauren's grip around her wrist, and her touch chased away the fleeting pain.

"Are you okay?"

Jamie nodded and put her hand over Lauren's then immediately pulled it away. "I'm fine. School wasn't a great time for me, that's all."

Lauren's hand slipped away, leaving a trail of fire on Jamie's skin. God, she was being such a cliché. How could Lauren still affect her like this after all this time?

"I can't imagine," Lauren said.

Jamie glanced away, unable to take the pity in Lauren's eyes. That wasn't the emotion she wanted to see there. "How's your leg? No gangrene setting in?"

Lauren laughed and frowned at the same time, possibly confused by Jamie's less than seamless transition back to her original reason for approaching her.

Lauren shook her head and pressed her lips together. "It's touch and go. The doctor said I may have to have it amputated."

Jamie chuckled. Why wouldn't she still be attracted to Lauren now? She clearly hadn't changed at all. With that sense of humor, her intelligence, and her kindness, Lauren Gray was a perfect woman. And when that was topped off with good looks, it was hard not to fall at her feet right there.

Her wandering fantasies were sobered when she reminded herself where they were, and why Lauren was there… But this might be her only chance to talk to her before she left town again for another fifteen years, and Jamie had promised herself she'd try. "Could I take you for coffee?" *Go bigger!* "Or dinner even. To apologize."

Lauren bit her lip and looked to the sky briefly. "That's not necessary, honestly."

"Oh, sure. Of course." Jamie's limited bravado ebbed away like a receding tide. She gestured back to her ride-on mower. "I should get going."

"And I should get off," Lauren bent to retrieve her tote bag, "your grass."

Jamie scrunched her toes in her boots and tried not to visually react to the woefully timed pause in Lauren's sentence. It was neither the time nor the place to point it out, but God, did she want to say something smart. She didn't, of course. Whatever she might try to say while her brain was engaged in thinking about Lauren doing what she'd just said was bound to be incoherent nonsense. If she opened her mouth right now, she'd almost certainly be creating a winner for the weekly competition with her friends.

"I do need to eat later though," Lauren said.

Jamie snapped back into reality… Lauren was saying she *would* have dinner with her?

"I'm staying at Nancy's." Lauren hooked her bag over her shoulder and began to walk toward the path where Jamie had left the mower.

Jamie rubbed the back of her head. Could this really be happening? She fell in step with Lauren and ran through a series of responses. None of them made it out of her mouth.

"Were you thinking of anywhere in particular for dinner?" Lauren stopped at the mower and leaned against the seat.

Jamie's lack of words had become embarrassing. Her quick wit had gone AWOL at the worst possible time. "So you *do* want an apology dinner?"

Lauren shook her head. "No, but it'd be nice to have some company. I've been holed up in my room every night working and getting room service."

Lauren looked back toward Kayla's grave, and Jamie saw complete heartbreak, the kind it took years to recover from, and even then, it fundamentally changed a person. The kind of heartbreak Jamie had after her dad's death.

"Are you still a vegetarian?" Jamie asked.

Lauren's eyebrow quirked. "Yes."

"I know a great place a few towns over." Jamie had the feeling that Lauren didn't want to be seen around here any more than was necessary, and she also didn't want Lauren to be the subject of town gossip by going out with one of the town's few out lesbians. "I've got a truck."

"Of course you do." Lauren grinned. "Pick me up at seven."

Jamie suppressed a deep sigh at the instruction instead of a request. Strong-willed women were her kryptonite, but what else should she expect from a high-powered CEO? "Sure."

"How should I dress?" Lauren asked, pushing away from the seat.

Jamie missed a beat, trying not to think of how amazing Lauren would inevitably look tonight, and how she'd fantasized about Lauren sitting in the passenger seat of her truck for years back in high school. She reminded herself that she still had no idea who or what Lauren was into. And even if that preference was women, Jamie was unlikely to be high on her to-do list. "Casual elegant. It's a nice place." Like Jamie would take her to anything less.

"Great. I'll see you later." Lauren smiled and headed down the path to the exit.

Jamie dropped into the seat of her ride-on mower and watched Lauren walk away. Part of her was excited to finally be taking Lauren Gray out to dinner, but most of her felt Lauren's loss almost as if it were her own again. Outwardly, Lauren seemed to be coping admirably with her sister's death, but Jamie had seen the turmoil and despair swirling in her eyes. It made her want to take Lauren in her arms and hold her while she sobbed and released that misery. But Jamie knew all too well that letting go of the grief for someone you loved was a desperately long process. As Lauren went out of sight, Jamie looked across to her father's grave, not too far from Kayla's. It had been over twenty years since his death, and Jamie still longed for his presence, so solid and calm.

Going out with Lauren was the thing Jamie had craved most for years as a young adult. The passing time seemed not to have dampened that craving. She only wished it could have been under more favorable circumstances.

CHAPTER SEVEN

Lauren had planned to work from Beth's bar. It gave her a reason to dress in business attire, albeit casual, and made her feel less like she was somehow slacking off. At yesterday's meeting with Katie, she'd been told that the LitLot board had voted, and they were happy to give her full pay while she took whatever time she needed at home. Home had been an alien concept most of her life. As long as she could remember, she'd always wanted more than this town could offer, and she'd never felt like she belonged here. She'd always thought she was supposed to achieve something meaningful, leave a legacy, and certainly leave the world better than she'd found it.

The board's offer was incredibly generous, but Lauren couldn't see herself here much longer. She would get it together soon. She'd be able to push her key into Kayla's door and finally enter her apartment, sort everything out, and then get back to Boston. She ignored the reality that over a week had passed since the funeral, and all she'd managed to do was push the key around the top of the dresser in her room.

And she hadn't managed to find the motivation to leave her room after returning from her cemetery visit. She'd stayed at Kayla's grave longer than usual, though she hadn't really known why, and she might've stayed all day had it not been for Jamie's interruption. Cute, kind Jamie. Despite the depths of her grief reaching yet deeper into Lauren's soul today, she'd found it surprisingly easy to laugh at Jamie's wit. The short time they'd spent together had brightened Lauren's day and pulled her out of the funk she plummeted into the moment she laid today's flowers on Kayla's grave. And it had made her want more. So when Jamie offered to take her to dinner, Lauren had hesitated only briefly before deciding that it was *okay* to want more. It wouldn't stop her grieving, but it might remind her that she was still alive.

Her phone buzzed to indicate she had five minutes until her meeting with Whit. Lauren wanted to check in with her halfway through the three-day marathon of interviews for the New York City project manager. She had a quick bathroom break, poured herself another Tibetan Sky High chai, and freshened up to be camera ready, making her visit to the mirror as brief as possible.

She entered the Teams meeting, where Whit was already waiting.

"Hey, Number One. How're you doing?"

Whit leaned closer to the camera and narrowed her eyes. "*That's* for the geek reference. It was a geek reference, wasn't it?"

Lauren shook her head. "What are you talking about? You *are* my number one." She maintained a straight face for all of five seconds before laughing. "Sorry, I couldn't resist."

"I told you about that guy and his matching Kirk and Spock sex outfits in a moment of vulnerability." Whit moved back from the camera and shook her head. "I could sue you for emotional abuse in the workplace."

"And I'll countersue for the same—making me listen to your sexploits over lunch, Ms. Spock. There's bound to be a judge who'd call that cruel and unusual punishment. I take it you're alone?"

"Yep. I'm in my hotel room." Whit gestured around her. "I'd give you the one-dollar tour, but it'd only make you jealous." She flashed her cell at the screen. "I open my door with a QR code," she said in a sing-song voice.

Lauren glanced at the giant key hanging in the door lock. She had yet to get used to being forced into a conversation with Nancy or her daughter every time she wanted to leave or come back to her room. Conversely, she couldn't deny that the little chats had made her feel seen, and there was something cozy and comforting in that. "Enough bragging. How's everything going?"

"Good. We've interviewed fifty percent of the candidates, and I've got a favorite. She blew me away, actually. I'm glad that you weren't here, or you might've hired her to replace me."

Lauren raised her eyebrows. "You should know by now that you're irreplaceable. But it's great to hear that someone's even better than their résumé. Who is it?"

Whit's cheeks colored with the compliment. As confident and competent as she was, she still appreciated an ego stroke here and there. Who didn't?

"Stephanie Moss. She was one of your top picks when we were

selecting from the shortlist, but I'd discarded her because of lack of experience." Whit shook her head. "You're like a talent-diviner. You've taught me so much over the past few years, but I wish you could show me how to recognize that kind of potential."

Lauren smiled. "I wish I *could* teach that to people. There's so much talent out there that's passed over because they don't fit the boxes of regular recruitment."

"But how do you do it without even meeting them?" Whit shook her head. "You did the same with me. I didn't think I stood a chance of getting an interview. I just thought the experience of applying would be useful. But here I am."

"Yep, here you are." Lauren wrinkled her nose and tried to find the words to explain it to perhaps her greatest protégé. After a few moments of thinking, she blew out a breath. "I honestly don't know. There's something in the way their résumé reads, like there's hidden text calling to me." Lauren waved her hand at the screen. "It sounds ridiculous, doesn't it?"

"It does. Complete nonsense." Whit laughed. "But you *have* to show me what you mean. It feels like a superpower, and I have to have it."

"I will, I promise. But talking of hidden talent, how's Charlotte doing?"

"She's doing really well actually, so again, another addition to your talent-diviner collection," Whit said. "I thought she might be at least a little overwhelmed by the sheer scale of the project, but she hasn't been fazed by it. And she hasn't been afraid to ask questions, which is great."

Lauren nodded and smiled. The shift from operations to management wasn't for everyone, but she'd been sure Charlotte would embrace the challenge. Lauren did enjoy being right. "Do you see her becoming part of your team permanently?"

"Maybe. But I get the feeling that she really enjoys the face-to-face work with the kids too much to take a full-time spot with business development."

Lauren pointed to her screen. "I think you're right about that, but we could design a job role specifically playing to her strengths to give her the best of both worlds, and for us to get the most out of her… But we can talk to her more about that when I get back."

She saw Whit's expression change and registered the sympathy. She'd been getting that same look a lot over the past week, and it was beginning to bother her. She didn't want pity; *she* hadn't died in a fiery car crash. She shook the distressing images away and refocused on Whit.

"Have you been to Kayla's apartment yet?"

Lauren clenched her jaw. She'd been hoping their conversation wouldn't blow that direction, which was futile because Whit was her friend, not just her colleague. "No."

"You can't really think about coming back until you've faced that though, can you?"

Lauren raised her eyebrow. Nobody told her what to do or when to do it. But Whit's prod came from a place of love, she knew that. Having broken her own rules about developing friendships with colleagues, she had to suffer the consequences of someone caring for her. "I know. I just… wish I had more time." Not time here in this town. Not time to clear out an apartment which shouldn't need clearing out. But time with Kayla. *Thirty fucking three.* Lauren took a deep breath. "I could pay the mortgage on her place for the next six months and give myself some breathing space."

"You could." Whit nodded slowly. "I expect you'll be going back there more regularly now, won't you?"

Lauren frowned. She hadn't thought that far ahead. Taking one minute at a time had been her current strategy, which wasn't like her at all. But Whit was right. Kayla wouldn't be visiting Boston every other weekend anymore, so if Lauren wanted to be close to her sister, she'd have to come here. "I don't seem to be planning much beyond each day right now."

"That's understandable, Lauren. Have you got something else to focus on other than work while you're there?"

Almost instantly, Lauren thought of the project she and Kayla talked about often but had never moved into action. She also thought of Jamie briefly. "I suppose I could begin to seriously think about the literacy hub we always dreamed about creating."

"Bingo. And that'd give you something else to be there for. A kind of distraction."

Lauren sighed. "I don't know. It was our dream, and it never happened. Maybe it should stay that way. We were supposed to do it together."

Whit gave a small smile. "I get what you're saying, I do. But you'd be building a legacy in Kayla's memory. That town loved her, and if you made your dream happen, it'd be a place where everyone could always remember her."

Whit made a lot of sense. A physical building, visited every day by the children and young people Kayla had committed her life to teaching, would make a fitting tribute to her sister's passion. And if Lauren set it up right, it would be there long after she was gone too. Kayla deserved to be remembered, and it would give Lauren something positive to work on while she was there. It wasn't exactly a short-term project though. Unless she started it now and managed it from Boston. "Okay, I'll think about it." She remembered Kayla had drawn up rudimentary plans of what the building might look like. They'd be in her apartment, filed neatly along with the rest of the ideas they'd put together—on napkins, beer mats, and torn out sheets of paper. It was another good reason to finally face going to Kayla's apartment.

"Good. How are you finding remote working again?"

It wasn't a deft change of subject, but Lauren appreciated it anyway. Whit had a knack for knowing when and how far to push, and when to leave it alone. "I hate it. Like last time."

"Aw, come on. What's not to love about only wearing half a suit? You're wearing sweats, aren't you? You can tell me. Stand up. I promise not to screenshot you and post the picture to all of our employees."

"I trust you with the charity. I'm not sure I trust you with the knowledge of what I'm wearing out of view." Lauren laughed but really, she hated being cooped up alone in a room, unable to feed off the energy of her co-workers. She loved having an office and an open-door policy so that staff could drop in with their issues. Helping them find the solution for themselves was always such a thrill. Being away from all the action niggled and made her feel somewhat useless and out of the loop. Recruitment was also one of her favorite management pastimes, and she'd been looking forward to finding all the new project managers for this expansion. She didn't like not being at the core of things while she was this isolated. There was a question of being needed buried in there somewhere too, and she wasn't quite sure what to make of that revelation.

"Your lack of trust wounds me, boss."

"You'll get over it." Lauren winked. "I'll see you Friday afternoon. I'd like to see a—"

"Report of all the candidates and all our scored answer sheets plus their presentations by Thursday evening. I know. I've got you." Whit straightened the collar of her shirt and looked pleased with herself.

"Exactly. I said that you were irreplaceable and look at you, proving me right."

Whit's smile was almost shy. Honestly, Lauren probably didn't need to see the candidates. She was almost certain that Whit would select the perfect person for the job. The standard of applicants had been incredibly high, and the charity was in the enviable position where any one of the shortlisted people would be a good choice. But Whit was still learning, particularly about recognizing that X-factor, so Lauren wanted to see who'd she picked before offering her opinion.

"Do you have plans tonight? Or is it Nancy's room service again?" Whit asked. "Maybe you should mix it up and get takeout."

Lauren huffed. "I think Nancy might explode if I had food delivered. She seems to have decided I need looking after and has volunteered for the job."

"Judging by those breakfast photos you sent me, she's taking that role very seriously."

"She doesn't need to tonight. I'm going out for dinner."

"With Beth?"

Lauren pressed her lips together, suddenly wishing she hadn't mentioned it, which seemed illogical. It was just dinner. "No. With Jamie Nelson."

Whit frowned. "Is their last name important? Or is that how you announce everyone?"

"Hilarious." Lauren rolled her eyes. "She's someone from high school that I haven't seen for over a decade. She works at the cemetery. That's how I bumped into her." Lauren quickly retold the story of the gravel and her bleeding shin.

"This is her apology dinner?"

"I said I didn't need one, but she was being so sweet." And funny. And possibly even charming if Lauren stopped to analyze it.

Whit raised her eyebrow. "I know that look. Sweet, as in sweet and cute?"

"It's just dinner, Whit. I thought some company might be nice. I'm getting a little stir-crazy spending every night in this room." Which was her own fault. She could be at Kayla's apartment. But dinner with Jamie seemed far more appealing. She was a distraction, that was all.

Wasn't she?

CHAPTER EIGHT

JAMIE CHECKED HER REFLECTION in the just-cleaned window of her truck. She was comfortable in the outfit she'd chosen—the fifth one of the night—but she hadn't managed to achieve any level of confidence in it. Color choice, jeans or trousers, boots or tennis shoes, tie or not. She'd switched between all the options and settled on a gray and black striped shirt, dark blue jeans, and chunky black boots. She'd left the house with a tie but was halfway to Nancy's when she'd stripped it off at a stop light and stuffed it in the glove compartment. Casual elegant could mean something entirely different to Lauren, and this way, Jamie had it on standby if she needed it.

She turned from her truck to head inside when Lauren emerged from the B&B's front door. She wore a knee-length floral dress and heels, and her wavy hair bounced on her shoulders like she was slow-motion walking out of a commercial. Jamie swallowed hard and tried not to gulp out loud. She'd resolved to focus on building a friendship rather than feeding her crush, but the way Lauren looked in her version of casual elegant weakened that resolve.

"Hey." Jamie's words came out croaky. She cleared her throat. "Sorry, hi." She reached through the window of her truck and pulled out the bunch of sunflowers she'd grabbed from Simon just before he closed for the day. His hurry to close hadn't stopped the "Ooh, who's the lucky woman?" conversation because Jamie only ever bought flowers for her mom on her birthday and that was just over a week away.

Lauren took the flowers and smiled. "That's sweet. Let me take them in, and I'll be right back."

She turned away and treated Jamie to the rear version of her outfit. *Stop it*. Sweet? Was that the response Jamie had been looking for? Lauren hadn't stumbled, or looked surprised, or even aghast at the offering. That was a good start.

The blinds at the reception window shifted. Nancy peered through a gap and waved. Jamie thought she saw her wink too but dismissed it.

Nancy had no reason to act like Jamie's cheerleader. She waved back and opened the passenger door when Lauren returned.

"Good to see that chivalry is still alive and kicking in small town America," Lauren said as she climbed into the truck.

Jamie closed the door and came around to the driver's side not quite knowing how to take Lauren's comment. The small-town jibe didn't bother her. Lauren had made no secret of wanting out of Damarron for as long as Jamie had known her. She buckled her seatbelt, started the engine, and pulled away. "You'd rather open and close your own doors?" Upfront and honest was the only way Jamie knew how to be, and she wasn't about to disguise who she was even for her lifelong crush.

"Most of the time, yes. I don't expect people to do it just because I'm a woman, or even because I'm the boss." Lauren briefly touched Jamie's arm. "But I can't deny that it's nice when someone like you does it."

Someone like me. There was only one way to interpret that, wasn't there? Jamie kept her eyes on the road and took Main Street all the way out of town. "It's about an hour to the restaurant. Is that okay?"

"If I said no, do you have a bunch of candy in the glove box to keep me from gnawing on your leg?" Lauren opened the compartment, and Jamie's tie rolled out. Lauren lifted it up. "Were you wearing this?"

"Do I get more points for saying yes or for denying its existence completely? Like, someone must've broken into my car and planted it there."

"Because that's what the criminals are doing these days, breaking into cars and leaving fancy ties rather than stealing stuff?"

Jamie slapped the steering wheel. "That's exactly what they're doing. It's a new trend. And they're posting videos of them doing it all over TikTok. Perfectly law-abiding citizens are duetting the hell out of those videos."

Lauren laughed and raised her eyebrows. "You've seen them?"

"Yep, we have TikTok in *small town America*. This isn't Arkansas, you know? Not that there's anything wrong with Arkansas either."

Lauren shoved Jamie's shoulder gently and giggled. "I didn't mean that."

"Then you don't think that I could be down with the latest trends, is that it? Once a weirdo, always a weirdo, huh?" She grinned to show she was joking when Lauren's expression fell briefly.

"Actually, I meant that it's a lot of work, and you probably have more important things to do than scroll through a hundred videos a day. We employ someone full-time just for our social networking." She shook her head. "It's so time consuming."

Jamie harrumphed. "Okay, I'll give you that. But I've learned some of my best dance moves from those videos."

Lauren rolled her eyes. "No. I'm not falling into that one." She raised the tie again and held it to Jamie's shirt. "Looks like a perfect combination to me."

So far so good. This was going smoother than Jamie had expected. "Fine. Yes, I was wearing it, but I thought it might be too much. I haven't had dinner with someone as sophisticated as you since… Nope, I've never *known* anyone as sophisticated as you, let alone had dinner with them."

Lauren shifted and pulled her seatbelt away from her dress as if it was crushing her. Jamie made a mental note to do something about that for the next time Lauren got in her truck, *if* there was a next time.

"I don't know what strange tales you've heard, but I'm far from sophisticated. I'll happily eat a nut roast with a dessert fork and wipe my chin with a paper napkin."

Jamie laughed. "Thank you for painting that very vivid picture for me. But now I feel like I need to call ahead to make sure this place doesn't have cloth napkins. I don't want you to feel outclassed and out of place."

Lauren swatted Jamie's shoulder again. "Rude!"

"You look amazing, by the way. I didn't say. Back at Nancy's." And there was her tongue-tied self back to spoil her flow. Jamie wanted to kick herself. It was too much. Amazing? Why hadn't she just gone with nice? She never told Fran or Terri they looked amazing.

Lauren gave her a killer smile. "Thank you. I didn't say either. You look handsome, even without the tie." She wafted it in the air. "Should I put it back?"

Jamie didn't respond for a beat. She was still soaking in the warmth of Lauren calling her handsome. "Sure. Especially because I can't remember if this is a paper napkin kind of place or not. I don't want to overdress."

Lauren stuck out her bottom lip. "Shame." She returned the tie to the glove box and closed it. "Do you have a candy stash or not?"

"Huh?" Why would her not wearing the tie be a shame?

"You said the restaurant was an hour away, and I'm unusually hungry."

"I'm sorry, I don't." Jamie glanced sideways and caught a glimpse of Lauren pouting comically. "But if there's any chance that you'll be in my truck again, I'll make sure I stock up with your favorite treats. You still like Reese's peanut butter cups?"

"Okay." Lauren shuffled in her seat and sat sideways to look at Jamie. "Let's get serious. You remembered I was vegetarian, *and* you know my favorite candy. Are you one of those people who remembers *everything*, no matter how trivial or how long ago?"

Jamie sucked in her breath and pressed her lips together. What to say? Was now an appropriate time to reveal she'd had a crush on Lauren all through school? Maybe it was too soon in the evening for that, and she shouldn't tell Lauren that she remembered every minuscule detail about her because Jamie didn't take her eyes off her for thirteen years and it had all come rushing back. No, she'd probably pass out before she got to the end of that sentence because she wouldn't be able to take a breath. And that wouldn't be good for either of them. "Yep. That's it. I'm like a super elephant memory person. I should go on one of those TV shows and win millions of dollars with my brain."

"Mm, really?" Lauren narrowed her eyes. "Test time."

Jamie spent the rest of the drive answering trivia questions on Lauren, apparently Jamie's favorite subject. Ask her what she'd had for breakfast a week ago, and she drew a blank, but no matter how obscure the questions Lauren threw at her—What number did she wear for soccer? What swim stroke was her favorite? Which part of the frog did she throw across the room in biology?—Jamie knew the answers.

It made the drive entertaining and surprisingly quick. Jamie pulled up in the parking lot of Vixens and Vegans and cut the engine. "Question time is over. We're here." She scooted out of her seat and jogged around the front of her truck to open Lauren's door. Lauren gave her that same show-stopping smile, and Jamie melted a little. She closed the truck door and walked beside Lauren to the front doors, which opened automatically and saved Jamie the trouble of overthinking her chivalry.

They were greeted and shown to a booth.

"Do you like it?" Jamie gestured to the interior of the restaurant, which was lit entirely by candles, fairy lights, and giant Edison bulbs. She felt the need to impress Lauren though this was probably nothing compared to the elegance of Boston eateries.

"I do. It's really nice." Lauren pushed the table candle a few inches away further away from her. "It's a shame it wasn't here before. Fifteen years ago in Damarron, eating out as a vegetarian meant a baked potato or fries."

"Do you want me to blow that out?" Jamie pointed to the candle, thinking Lauren had pushed it away because it set a mood she wasn't in.

Lauren shook her head. "No. It's pretty. I can be clumsy, and I don't want to knock it over."

The waitress came over, and they ordered drinks and some spinach artichoke dip.

"Are *you* vegetarian?" Lauren asked after the waitress had returned quickly with a large bottle of water and a glass of Chardonnay.

Jamie looked away briefly and rubbed her forehead. "Do I get more points for being a vegetarian or for being a meat-eater prepared to put aside my carnivorous inclinations for a night?"

Lauren was just taking a sip of wine and almost spit it back into the glass. "There's a lot to unpack in that sentence. First, 'carnivorous inclinations?' Where did that come from? And second, what's with the point-scoring obsession? Do you think there's a minimum score you have to get to make tonight a success?" She tapped on Jamie's bottle with her nails. "Or are you just trying to impress me?" She frowned, as if she couldn't fathom why Jamie would do that.

Heat flamed up Jamie's back and neck, and she was sure her face was giving off more warmth than the table candle. She let out a long breath, because her first instinct was to ask if Lauren would think less of her if she admitted that she was trying to impress her. Jamie didn't want to be an asshole. Lauren was grieving, and romance was most likely the last thing on her mind. "I'm sorry. It's a bad habit, I guess. I don't spend a lot of time with anyone except my mom and a couple of friends. I'm a bit of a people-pleaser. I think it's a bit of baggage from school."

"Ah, I get it." Lauren reached across the table and placed her hand on Jamie's forearm. "You don't want to say the wrong thing and offend me."

Jamie nodded. She couldn't speak because...well, because Lauren Gray was touching her, and they were in a candle-lit restaurant. *Come on.*

"So just try answering the question honestly. Vegetarian or not?"

"Meat-eater?"

"Are you asking me or telling me?" Laura squeezed Jamie's arm before pulling back to pick up her glass.

"Meat-eater. Guilty. I tried to go vegetarian a few times, but God, I love chicken. And steak. And big, fat burgers." She held her fist to her mouth. "Sorry."

Lauren laughed and shook her head. "No need to apologize, especially since you've put your bloodlust aside for one night to bring me here. It's incredibly sweet of you."

She looked like she might say something else but took up her wine glass and sipped at it instead. Jamie sifted through her bank of questions to ask on a first date and dismissed them all given that this didn't qualify as a first date, and she knew the answers to most of them anyway.

The waitress brought their appetizer, and they dug in, not speaking for a little while. Jamie wondered if she might've blown it already. She heard Lauren's long intake of breath and readied herself for the worst. She'd never blown a date before the food had arrived. She reminded herself again that this wasn't a date; it was an apology dinner for nearly maiming Lauren. If anything, blowing that made it a little worse.

"Why *are* you being so sweet?" Lauren finally asked. "I don't deserve your kindness or your time. Not really."

Her forlorn expression made Jamie want to take Lauren in her arms and tell her she deserved everything in the world to make her happy. "Why would you say that? Everyone deserves kindness. And it's not like my time is super precious." And even if it were, Jamie had spent the formative years of her life wanting to give Lauren all of hers. That desire hadn't changed.

"Everyone's time is precious to them, Jamie. So why are you using yours to make me feel better?"

Jamie frowned. The steely look in Lauren's eyes was almost challenging, as if she was daring Jamie to pity her. But the ones left behind weren't to be pitied. They had the rest of their lives to enjoy, and there was nothing to pity in that. It had been a hard lesson to learn after losing her dad so early in her own life, but she greeted every morning with enthusiasm. Living was a privilege she had never taken for granted. "Why wouldn't I?"

"I don't know. It wasn't like we were buddies in high school." Lauren chased the last of the dip around the dish with the final tortilla chip. "Please don't misunderstand me though. I'm enjoying spending time with you. You're really easy to talk to, and it's been nice not to be fully focused on…on why I'm back in town." She shrugged and scooped the chip into her mouth.

Jamie let the silence simply be for a moment. "I spend every working day around grief and loss. I see what it can do to people." She thought about taking Lauren's hand in hers. Physical touch could sometimes be more comforting than any number of words. She gripped her bottle of water and shifted it from one hand to the other instead. "I see you at Kayla's grave every day, and I know how important it is to still feel close to someone who's passed."

"Do you still talk to your dad?"

Jamie raised her eyebrows. "Every day." She half-smiled. "Thank you for remembering."

Lauren pushed the appetizer bowl aside and took Jamie's hand in hers. "Of course." She smiled. "Even though she can't answer, it does feel like I'm staying close to her, you're right. I know she's gone, but her grave feels like… I don't know."

"The place where she picks up her messages from the people she left behind."

Lauren smiled. "Yeah, that's exactly it. Thanks for this." She flicked her gaze to their hands. "Thanks for tonight. And I guess I hadn't realized that talking to people was a good thing."

Jamie looked at her hand, enveloped in Lauren's smaller, far more delicate ones, and a rush of warmth flooded her body. The vulnerability of the moment took her breath away. They were mostly strangers, but she felt more connected to Lauren right now than she had to anyone in a long while. Which was crazy, and scary, and probably mostly her imagination. But it gave her courage. She'd promised herself that she would see if there could be anything between her and Lauren, and this was the time to tell her. To hold it back seemed underhanded and dishonest. "Do you still want to know why I'm being so sweet?"

"Yes, of course."

"I mean, it's only one of the reasons. Because, you know, there are plenty of reasons why I'd choose to spend my time with you. Who wouldn't, right? You're great company, for starters. And you've got a great sense of humor. And—"

Lauren squeezed Jamie's hand before she let go and picked up her wine. "You're rambling." She took a sip then tilted her head slightly. "You ramble when you're nervous. Just tell me."

"You really have no idea?" Jamie's courage retreated along with Lauren's hands. Maybe this wasn't such a good idea. *Just do it.* "I've always wanted to get to know you better. You were the most popular kid in school, and I was on the other end of the scale. Our paths barely crossed. But now they have. And I thought it'd be nice to talk to you, see if we had stuff in common, you know." It wasn't the all-out admission she had in mind, but it was better than nothing.

Lauren leaned forward. "I always wished that I'd talked to you in high school. It blew my mind when you brought that folder to school and came out to everyone." She shook her head and smiled. "It's still one of the bravest things I've ever seen."

"You remember that?" Jamie had done a lot of stupid things through school, things that earned her more beatings and mean names. The folder had topped them all, but she was proud to be called the name it resulted in. Well, the core of those names, anyway. Rug-muncher and muff-diver scrawled all over her locker hadn't been the best part of coming out.

Lauren glanced away and looked shy. When she returned her gaze to Jamie, it was as if Lauren's eyes pierced her soul.

"I remember that, because I wanted to study that folder with a magnifying glass." Lauren settled back in the booth and took another, much longer drink of her wine.

Jamie almost exploded as the waitress returned to their table with their food. Worst timing ever. Lauren had wanted to look at her folder with a magnifying glass. There was only one explanation for that. When the waitress asked if Jamie wanted anything else, she didn't ask for the barbeque sauce she always had with this dish because she was too desperate to get back to their conversation.

Lauren laughed. "You look cute when you're flabbergasted."

Jamie closed her mouth. "Good word."

"Thanks."

"So, you're… You wanted to look at my folder because you were…" *Please say the word.*

"Because I'm gay, yes."

Jamie looked up, tempted to fall on her knees and give thanks right there in the middle of the restaurant. The god of all things lesbian had finally set her gaze on Jamie.

CHAPTER NINE

Lauren opened her eyes slowly. Her brain felt like it was reverberating against the sides of her skull, and a none-too-subtle nausea called for her attention. Both were expected punishment for last night's excess. She'd considered switching to water after her second and third glasses of wine. But by the fourth, she would've fought a lion rather than relinquish the buzz the alcohol had given her.

She pushed her comforter down to discover she was still in her dress. *Jamie?* Lauren had a vague recollection of a short conversation with Rebekah, Nancy's daughter, to collect her room key. Lauren had joked about its size, saying she was too weak to get it upstairs and then... *Oh, Christ.* Jamie had *carried* her upstairs. Lauren searched her memory banks but couldn't recall anything beyond that. She'd been wildly aroused by Jamie's show of strength but hoped to God she'd kept that to herself.

And Jamie had stuck to water all night because she was driving. She wouldn't even have one beer which Lauren considered chivalrous and responsible. She got up, knocked back a couple of Tylenol, and headed to the bathroom to wash away the funk of the evening. She emerged, nicely refreshed, and her throbbing head had receded to a gentle tapping. She checked her phone to see two missed calls, both from her parents, and three texts, including one from her parents and one from Whit wanting all the details of her night out. The third was from Jamie, checking to see how she was feeling and recommending Patrick's breakfast stack to tackle her inevitable hangover. Lauren checked her watch. At eleven, it was already too late for breakfast. But she smiled, relieved she hadn't made such a fool of herself that Jamie wanted nothing more to do with her.

Her thoughts quickly shifted to her parents. It had been over a week since the funeral and despite them calling and texting multiple times to organize something, Lauren had avoided seeing them again. Her workday was light; Whit was busy with the final New York interviews, so there was little for Lauren to do until she received Whit's report that evening. She perched on the edge of the bed, called her parents, and arranged to go over. Her mom insisted on her coming immediately for brunch after hearing Lauren hadn't had breakfast.

Less than an hour later, Lauren stepped onto the narrow pathway that led to the front door of her parents' house. She faltered for the briefest of moments when the memory of playing hopscotch on this concrete hit her. There would be no more games with her sister.

"Hi, sweetheart."

Lauren looked up to see her mom at the door and smiled. "Hey, Mom." She hurried up the path and gave her a brief hug. Her mom held on when Lauren moved to end the embrace, so she stayed, wrapped in her arms, for longer than she was comfortable.

"Welcome home, honey," her dad said as he enveloped them both in a bear hug.

Lauren couldn't pinpoint the exact time she'd created the emotional barrier between herself and her parents, nor what had caused her to do it, but it was around the middle of high school. They'd been nothing but loving throughout her childhood, but Lauren's yearning to leave Damarron behind as soon as possible meant she'd excluded everything else around her except for Kayla. As the hug went on, her thoughts inexplicably drifted to Jamie losing her father when she was only nine. Lauren relaxed into her parents' embrace. One day, they wouldn't be here to come home to either.

"Thanks for coming." Her mom drew back, her red-rimmed eyes brimmed with tears yet unshed. "I hope you don't mind eating in the kitchen?" she asked, walking toward the back of house.

Lauren frowned. Why would she mind? She'd eaten most of her meals when she'd lived there on the table her dad had made. "Of course not." She and her dad followed and seated themselves at the table that separated the main area of the kitchen from their den-like spot and its two over-sized couches. The food her mom had prepared covered the table, like she'd catered for ten rather than just the three of them. "You got all this ready since we spoke, or are you expecting more people?"

Her mom shook her head. "You know what it's like around here. Practically the whole town brought us food. I don't think I'll have to cook for a month." Her vague smile fell, and she sighed. "Not that I feel like eating."

Her dad placed his hand over her mom's. "You need to eat, darling. I don't want you to waste away."

Her mom gave a mirthless laugh. "Waste."

Lauren waited for the context or the rest of the sentence, but her mom added nothing else.

Her dad tapped her mom's hand before releasing it. "I know, darling." He looked at Lauren and gestured toward the bounty on the table. "Dig in."

Lauren scooped some strawberries, granola, and yogurt into a bowl. If she was eating, she didn't have to talk, but the air was oppressive with its expectation for conversation. Her parents wanted to say something, that much was clear. An obscure quote from the 1900s popped into her head about brunch sweeping away the worries and cobwebs of the week. There was no food on earth that could do that right now.

"The flowers you're taking to Kayla's grave are beautiful, sweetheart." Her dad plucked a bagel from a pile and covered it with cream cheese before dropping a few blueberries and strawberries on it.

"You've seen them?" she asked.

Her mom scoffed. "Of course we've seen them. We're going to the grave every day too."

Her dad placed his hand over her mom's again and squeezed. "She knows that, sweetheart."

Her mom harrumphed. "Does she? You mean, she doesn't think she's the only one who's grieving?"

Lauren clenched her jaw. She hadn't seen her mom aggressive like this before, but then she hadn't had to bury one of her daughters before either. Her mom's comment wasn't too far from the reality. Lauren had been so engrossed in her own grief that she hadn't stopped to think about how her parents were coping. Her parents would probably have been better off if she'd been the one to die. She was hardly ever around anyway, but Kayla visited them at least twice a week and always went over for dinner on Sundays.

"Have you thought about staying?"

Her mom's attitude change made Lauren dizzy. "Why would I stay?" The words were out of her mouth before she could engage her brain. There was nothing for her in this town except her parents. There never had been, but saying it right now was helpful to no one. Their relationship wasn't great, but that didn't mean Lauren wanted to hurt their feelings.

Her mom's mouth fell open, and she looked like she wanted to say something but couldn't find the words. Her dad closed his eyes and shook his head. Clearly, this wasn't how they'd hoped the brunch would go. All the wordless meals she'd had at this table came flooding back, reminding her why she'd always been so desperate to leave. Without Kayla to act as a buffer between them, what hope did they have to get through a family meal that necessitated conversation?

"How long are you staying for?" her dad asked.

He'd obviously decided he'd have to step up in Kayla's absence, but it wasn't as if Lauren found him any easier to talk to. She chased the granola around in the yogurt to mix it. Why was this so hard? She spent her whole work life talking to complete strangers. Why did she find it so hard to talk to the people who brought her into this world? There was no easy answer. "I don't know yet. The board has said I can take as much time as I need."

"Have you been to…" Her mom's chest heaved, and her breathing quickened. "Have you…" She shook her head. "I can't, David. Please."

Her dad rubbed her mom's back gently. "Are you okay, darling?" He waited until she'd nodded slowly before he turned back to Lauren. He took a deep breath and blew it out through his mouth like he was practicing yoga. "Have you been to Kayla's apartment?"

His words came out in rapid fire, as if they wouldn't make it out of his mouth if he took his time. Lauren sighed. He was hit just as hard by Kayla's death but was expected to be the strong one and handle everything. *This* was one of the many reasons she'd had to get out of this town. The archaic gender expectations were suffocating. Would her mom even let him cry for his own loss? She briefly thought about Jamie and wondered why she had never escaped this town. How could she be herself in this town and be comfortable? Unless she stayed simply to be close to her father's grave. Jamie's mom was still alive, and Lauren thought they'd have a far closer relationship than she had with her mom. They'd only had each other as Jamie grew up, bullied and ostracized for being different. She probably relied on and needed her mom more than Lauren ever had.

But independence was a good thing, wasn't it?

"Lauren?"

"Sorry, Dad." She'd retreated into her thoughts too long and left his question unanswered. "No, I haven't been yet. I'm not ready."

"If you don't want to do it…" Her dad shrugged. "We have a key."

Lauren shook her head. "Kayla wanted me to do it. We made a pact." It hadn't been so her parents didn't see anything. It was supposed to have been so Kayla's kids didn't stumble on anything their eyes couldn't unsee. It was supposed to have been in sixty fucking years. She slammed her spoon on the table, making her parents jump. "Sorry, Mom. Dad."

Her mom's hands shook as she raised her glass to her lips. She probably should see the doctor to increase the medication that calmed her nerves. That affliction had skipped a generation, thankfully.

"We could help."

Her dad gave a hopeful smile. The reason he wanted to go to Kayla's apartment was the same reason Lauren was avoiding it. He wanted memories. He wanted to touch the same things Kayla had touched every day when she was alive. He wanted to hold her clothes to his nose and breathe in her scent, as if she were still right there in the same room. He wanted to play whatever TV show she'd recorded and sit on her sofa as if she were sitting beside him. He wanted to flip through the clothes in her closet and remember all the times he'd seen her in those outfits.

Lauren pushed away from the table and rushed to the bathroom. She turned on the faucet and splashed cold water on her face. Her mouth filled with liquid, and she switched to the toilet, certain she was about to be sick. She didn't fool herself that it might be the wine from last night disagreeing with the yogurt. She was grieving, she wasn't delusional.

She opened her mouth and spat out the watery bile, but nothing followed. How was she ever going to open Kayla's apartment if this was her reaction to just the thought of what she would encounter behind that door? Maybe Jamie would act as moral support and accompany her, though that might be a big ask. It was one thing to want to take Lauren out to dinner, it was another to take Sobbing Mess Lauren to help clear out Kayla's home.

Lauren wiped her face and mouth with a wet washcloth and glanced up at the mirror. It had to start with being able to face herself again. She studied the lines around her eyes. She had less of those than Kayla did but only because she was prepared to spend a hundred dollars a pop on night cream. Kayla had thought her frivolous for that but had also said she deserved it because of how hard she worked, and that people in big cities were far more judgmental and beauty-oriented than small town folk. Lauren had disagreed with her on that one.

Their lips were the same but for a small scar just to the right of Lauren's lip where she'd fallen from the monkey bars with a lollipop in her mouth and the stick had jammed into her face. Lauren's gym and salad lifestyle contrasted to Kayla's pasta, wine, and walking existence, and the difference showed in their faces, though they shared the same high cheekbones.

A gentle knock on the bathroom door jolted Lauren from her self-guided therapy.

"Sweetheart, are you okay?"

"Sure, Dad. I'll be out in a minute." She flushed the toilet and rinsed her hands. She took one last look in the mirror while she towel-dried and then she opened the door.

Her dad pulled her into another hug. "You're still our baby, Lauren, even when you don't want to be." He released her and headed back to the kitchen.

She followed him and retook her seat at the table. "Is that what you think?"

"About what?" her mom asked.

Her dad shook his head and widened his eyes in her direction. Clearly, he didn't want to talk about the bomb he'd just casually dropped. Lauren did, but she respected that her mom wasn't in the best headspace to have a deep discussion about their relationship with their only remaining daughter. What was her dad supposed to think? She hardly ever visited, and it was brief when she did, and she couldn't wait to get back to Boston. Was she afraid she'd grow roots and never be able to escape again? "I've been thinking about the project Kayla and I always talked about setting up here."

Her mom looked up, and her eyes brightened. "Really?"

"Did Kayla ever mention it to you?" Lauren asked.

Her parents nodded. "Oh, goodness, yes." Her mom tapped her dad's forearm repeatedly. "She talked about it all the time, didn't she, David?"

Her dad smiled and sighed deeply. "She did. We even drew up some plans for the furniture, you know, the desks, and bookshelves, and computer stations."

Her dad was a carpenter, and a damned good one. He'd often tried to teach them the basics. Lauren had never been interested—she couldn't cut wood straight even with a table saw—but Kayla had loved working with him on all manner of projects on the weekends. Lauren had loved the end result, like their treehouse, the bunkbeds, and the climbing frame, and she'd been happy to watch them work while she did extra homework and extra reading. She gazed past him out the back windows at the treehouse, still standing and perfectly maintained with a fresh coat of paint. What she would give to see Kayla climbing down the knotted rope and running into the kitchen right now. "Would you show me?"

Her dad's lip trembled so slightly that she could've easily missed it. "I'd love that."

Lauren dropped her spoon into her bowl and pushed it away. "Would now be a good time?"

Her dad exchanged a quick look with her mom, and she rolled her eyes but nodded. "You two go. I'll bring a plate of sandwiches in."

Her dad practically jumped off his chair. He went behind Lauren and gave her shoulders a quick squeeze. "I can't wait for you to see these."

Lauren smiled at her mom and excused herself to follow her dad into his den. An unfamiliar feeling of comfort began to settle in her mind, almost unnoticed. She hadn't looked at her watch, or checked her emails, or scrolled social media, nor had she wanted to. She had no place to be or other pressing engagement that would cut her visit short, and she was contentedly, and unusually, ignorant of the time.

Maybe she hadn't had the best relationship with her parents, but their grief united them now. And perhaps in working together to realize a legacy for Kayla, they might forge a relationship that she'd never thought herself capable of and one that she'd never realized she needed. Until now.

CHAPTER TEN

JAMIE SHOVED THE PRUNING shears in her tool belt and picked up the bucket of dead headed flowers. She made her way to the composting hole, lifted the doors, and tossed the flowers in. The bright yellows, reds, and purples added some color to the slowly browning grass clippings from earlier in the week. She quickly closed it before the noxious smell settled in her nose and then knelt to inhale the perfumed scent of the rose bush by Mr. Johnson's grave. Jamie had helped his widow plant it before she took residence in her adjacent plot less than two months later. The people in town said that losing her husband of fifty-seven years broke Mrs. Johnson's heart, and she simply gave up. Jamie thought it was both sweet and sad at the same time. Of course, it was tremendously romantic and had the makings of an epic love story, but Jamie also wondered about the children and grandchildren they left behind. What would they have given for more time with her?

She checked her watch. The morning had zoomed by, as it often did at this time of year when there was so much gardening and repair work to do. She headed out of the grounds to the café to grab her usual lunch. She was halfway there when her mom pulled up beside her and rolled down her window. Olly went berserk and jumped into the front seat onto her mom's lap.

"Olly!"

"Hey, boy." Jamie ruffled his fur and gave him a good neck rub before her mom managed to wrangle him back onto the passenger seat. "How're you doing, Mom?"

"I'm heading back to work once I've dropped your naughty mutt at home. Do you want me to bring takeout over tonight?"

Jamie laughed and shook her head. Olly was only ever *her* dog when he'd done something bad. "Don't you have a hot date?"

Her mom shook her head. "No date with a man will ever be as important as spending time with my amazing daughter."

Jamie raised her eyebrow. "You want to know if there's anything happening with Lauren, don't you?"

"Simon told me you brought flowers."

"Simon would know."

"You only buy flowers for me, and my birthday is a week away," her mom said. "I put the pieces together and—"

"And made a pretty picture of me and Lauren?"

Her mom nodded. "Sooo pretty."

Jamie chuckled. Sharing the status of her dating life had always been part of their relationship, though Jamie's was far less interesting and varied than her mom's. "I can do an early dinner at six, or you could come to the bar with me. Olly would need his walk before we went out if you were coming drinking with us."

Olly bounced on the seat as if he understood their plans.

"Ooh, so there is something to tell," her mom said. "Let's do early burgers, and maybe I'll join you and your friends for a couple of beers. See you later, honey. Love you."

Jamie patted the roof of her mom's car. "Love you too, Mom."

Her mom drove away, and Jamie crossed the street. She was tempted to drop in on Simon and tease him about customer confidentiality, but her rumbling stomach persuaded her to go straight to lunch.

She opened the café door and stepped back to let a man with a stroller exit.

Beth greeted her at the counter. "Hey, Jamie. You're running late today."

"Yep, sorry." She pulled her wallet from her pocket and was about to pay when movement caught her eye. She looked up to see Lauren waving from a booth in the center of the restaurant. Jamie waved back. She'd been hoping to run into Lauren somewhere other than the cemetery, because she didn't want to keep encroaching on her time with Kayla. She also wanted to see if she could summon the courage to ask Lauren on a real date now that she knew she was gay.

Beth held up the brown bag containing her steak and cheese sandwich. "Do you want me to plate this up so you can join Lauren?"

Had Simon told everyone in town that she'd brought flowers for Lauren? Jamie looked over at Lauren, her laptop, and the mass of paperwork covering the table she sat at. She looked way too busy to stop to talk.

"I was about to take her lunch over," Beth said, as if she'd read Jamie's mind.

She glanced over to Lauren, who was now gesturing for her to come over. "I guess I'll see if she's got time."

Beth smiled and pulled Jamie's lunch back. "Great."

Jamie made her way over to Lauren. Her stomach tingled for reasons other than hunger. They'd exchanged a few texts since Wednesday night but hadn't made any more plans, and Jamie was beginning to think she'd blown it. After Lauren had said she was gay, they'd spent the rest of the night talking about high school, and Lauren had gotten pretty wasted. Jamie had often fantasized about carrying Lauren upstairs to her bed, but her being practically unconscious had never been part of that dream.

"Do you have time to join me for lunch?" Lauren gestured to the seat opposite and began to clear some space. She stacked the pages neatly in a nice-looking leather folder and closed it. "You've got perfect timing. I needed a break."

She figured her dad wouldn't mind her not leaning against his headstone for one lunch break. "Yeah, I'd love to." She scooted into the booth just as Beth brought out their lunch and a bottle of water.

"Thanks, Beth."

"No problem." Beth winked and left them alone again.

"It's my turn to apologize to you with a meal anyway," Lauren said. "I'm sorry I got so drunk that you had to carry me to my room."

Jamie smiled at Lauren's adorable look of shame mixed with something else she couldn't quite figure out. "No need for an apology. It saved me a workout the next day. Not that you were heavy, and it was hard. You're not. And it wasn't." Jamie clamped her jaw shut before she said anything else potentially offensive.

Lauren laughed. "There you go again, rambling when you're nervous."

Jamie closed her eyes briefly and shook her head. "It's *your* fault."

"Ha! How do you figure that?"

Jamie opened the bottle of water and was about to take a swig when Lauren caught her wrist gently.

"How is it my fault?"

Jamie lowered the bottle and took a deep breath. Despite her promise to herself, she hadn't managed to tell Lauren about her crush. Their

Wednesday night conversation had twisted this way and that, never allowing for Jamie to bring it up without it sounding completely out of left field. *No regrets.* "You make me nervous. You always have."

Lauren looked puzzled, but maybe there was a hint of something else in her expression, as if she thought she might know what Jamie was about to say.

"Why do I make you nervous?"

Jamie couldn't hold Lauren's intense gaze, so she scanned the rest of the bar. "Because I had a crush on you all through school." Nope, she didn't feel any lighter with the weight of that silent burden lifted. She should feel different now, braver, but it wasn't like she was telling her in high school when the crush was at its height. She'd chickened out for the last decade and a half.

Lauren leaned back and tilted her head to the side. "Are you playing with me?"

From the moment Jamie knew it was possible to *play* with another woman, Lauren had been her first pick. She took a bite of her sandwich.

"Really?" Lauren asked after Jamie answered by *not* answering. "Why didn't you ever tell me?"

Jamie laughed hard, and Beth looked over, smiling conspiratorially. When had Lauren's best friend become Jamie's cheerleader? "Now you're playing with me. I couldn't have even dreamed that you were gay, let alone deluded myself into thinking you might be interested in me, the school weirdo."

"I never thought you were weird."

"You probably never thought of me at all." Jamie held up her hand when Lauren looked mildly upset. "I don't mean that in a mean way. But in the school's social status, you were here," Jamie raised her hand high above her head, "and I was here." She dropped her hand below the table. "We weren't breathing the same air."

Lauren smoothed a napkin before opening it out over her lap. "We're breathing the same air now."

Jamie swallowed and gave a small smile. She didn't have a response that would come out in anything other than more rambling nonsense.

"But it's been a long time." Lauren stuck her fork in a chunk of cheese. "No doubt you stopped crushing on me when I left for college."

Lauren grinned, and Jamie's heart raced. She had nothing to lose by telling the truth. "I don't think anyone ever gets over their first love."

"I was your first love?"

Lauren's grin grew wider, and it was clear she was enjoying Jamie's embarrassing confession.

"First and only. So far. I mean, I've got plenty of time." Jamie gestured around the bar at the wholly heterosexual clientele. "And there are *so* many options around here for someone like me."

Lauren chuckled. "I'll bet."

The moment was slipping away. Jamie pulled on her big butch pants and cleared her throat. "Hypothetically, if seeing you *had* reignited that years-old crush, would you consider going on an actual date with me now that I'm a little bit less of a weirdo? Emphasis on little bit and hypothetically."

"Look at you controlling your nerves to get a whole sentence out."

Jamie raised her index finger at Lauren. "A *hypothetical* sentence." She winked. Oh god, an actual wink. Where did that ridiculous thing come from? She'd never winked at anyone in her life.

Lauren clapped lightly, and Jamie bowed her head before they both laughed.

"Okay, I have to be serious for a moment. This is a horrible time for me right now."

Crap. She'd completely misjudged the situation and gotten carried away. Of course Lauren wouldn't be thinking about dating right now.

"But I really enjoyed spending time with you the other night, so if you were, *hypothetically,* interested in asking me on an actual date, then my answer would be yes. But it wouldn't be yes because you were less weird, it'd be because you'd finally gotten around to asking a question that I would've answered yes to in high school."

If Jamie's mind could've exploded, it would have. "I wasn't ready for a woman like you in high school. I would've totally messed it up." Who was she kidding? There was no way she would have gotten anything like the courage needed to even ask Lauren on a date when they were seventeen. She was struggling now.

"Are you ready now, or are you going to leave it in the realms of the hypothetical?"

Should she? Was it enough to know that the most beautiful woman, inside and out, that Jamie had ever seen would go out on a date with her *if* she asked? *No regrets, remember.* "I'm going to hope that I am ready, yes."

"Perfect. Pick me up at seven tomorrow night. You can choose the restaurant again, because the last one was really nice."

Jamie nodded, a little dumbfounded. That had been easier than she'd thought it would be. Lauren continued to eat her salad, and Jamie had to stop herself from running to the hospital and the grocery store to see Fran and Terri. She'd wait until tonight, but with news like this, Jamie had no chance of winning their weekly game.

"You looked deep in thought when you came in," Lauren said. "Busy afternoon of work ahead?"

"Did I?" Jamie shifted the vase on the table with its single rose. The scent reminded her of what had been on her mind while she was walking to lunch. "Do you remember the Johnsons?"

"Yeah. They live on Caletho Drive overlooking the lake, don't they?"

Jamie tilted her head. "They did. They both died a little over five years ago."

"Oh. I'm sorry, I didn't know," Lauren said. "Were you close to them?"

"No. But I was by their graves today, and I ended up thinking about how Mrs. Johnson gave up on life after her husband died."

Lauren frowned. "Is that what happened?"

"That's what people say. There was no clear cause of death. She had a clean bill of health, and they used to walk all the way around the lake every morning and every night. She was probably fitter than me."

Lauren laughed. "I find that hard to believe. You look like your job keeps you in good shape, and you're on your feet all day, aren't you?"

"Okay, bad example." Jamie enjoyed the way Lauren's gaze drifted over her upper body though. Her work at the cemetery was strenuous enough that she didn't need a gym membership. She had a punching bag hanging in the barn, but that was as much to work out minor frustrations and excess energy as it was to keep her in shape. "But anyway, she and I planted a rose bush by his headstone. Six weeks later, she was dead too."

"Okay, so if she gave up on life like people say, is that what's bothering you today—after five years?"

Jamie shrugged. "Kind of."

"Now that I think about seeing them when I was a kid, I would've expected them to die close together." Lauren gave a small smile and looked beyond Jamie, like she could almost see them in the distance.

"Really? What makes you say that?"

"They were always together, don't you remember? They ran that little boating and fishing business that meant they worked side-by-side every day." Lauren's smile widened. "It was obvious how in love they were. They were adorable."

"They had three kids, three grandkids, and four great grandchildren." Jamie counted them off on her fingers. She didn't feel the need to mention that she'd known Maren, one of their forty-something-year-old kids, on a more intimate level briefly. "Don't you think they were worth staying alive for?"

Lauren tsked. "That's not for us to judge, Jamie. Did any of the children live with them?"

"No."

"Do they live close by?" Lauren asked.

Jamie gestured around them. "Most of them live either here or in a neighboring town."

"Did they visit all the time?"

"I don't know." This was beginning to feel like an interrogation. "I think she saw them every couple of weeks or so, some not so often. But I spoke to the three kids at the funeral, and they loved their parents. Why?"

Lauren took a sip of her coffee. "Because that's only a few hours in every month. What about the rest of her day? Her week?" She tapped on the table as if to reinforce her point. "She was with her husband almost 24-7. Can you imagine loving someone so much that you wanted to be around them that often? Where it felt like you couldn't really breathe unless they were around?"

Jamie swallowed. "When you put it like that, I think I'd like to."

"Okay. So, imagine you've had that for fifty years, and then, poof, it's gone, taken away from you faster than you could blink. Imagine the loneliness and devastation." Lauren shook her head. "The kids were being selfish if they wanted her to stick around just for them when they only saw her a few hours out of all the ones she had to live without him every week."

Jamie could see Lauren's point, but it still didn't sit right. "Don't you think that life is too precious to let it go so easily, if not for everyone around you, then for yourself?"

Lauren ran her finger along the rim of her mug and seemed to consider the question deeply. "I think that everyone is entitled to value their own existence as they see fit, and you can't judge someone for making a decision that they believe is right for them."

Jamie opened her mouth to respond, but Lauren held up her finger.

"I also think this is way too heavy a conversation to address over a quick lunch and without a glass of wine—though not as many as the other night."

"You're right, I'm sorry." Talking about death with someone who'd just lost their sister probably wasn't the most sensitive topic for Jamie to have chosen.

"That's okay. You don't have to tiptoe around me, conversation-wise. If I'm not comfortable talking about something for the obvious reason, I'll let you know. But I like talking about things like this."

"Cool." Jamie checked her watch. "I've got ten more minutes before I have to be back. How about we stick to small talk?"

Lauren laughed. "If we must." She motioned to the pile of papers she'd stacked to make room for Jamie. "Or you could look at this recruitment report and tell me who you'd hire."

"I'm far better at small talk than anything like that." Jamie took another bite of her sandwich. Beth's steak and cheese sandwich had never lasted her so long. "Why do you think I work in a cemetery? Not much paperwork there."

Lauren flicked her gaze to the bar. "Tell me about that."

Jamie followed Lauren's eyes to her sculpture hanging above the bar. "Nothing much to tell."

Lauren arched her eyebrow. "I doubt that, but I'll file it away as something to follow up on when we've got more time to talk."

"If we must." Her regret at ever letting her hobby out into the world was tempered only slightly by the knowledge of how much it had earned for Kayla's fundraiser, doubling her total and smashing her target. Jamie had been certain it was headed out of town when a well-heeled tourist joined the auction, which would have been preferable, but it hadn't worked out that way.

Jamie returned her attention to her rapidly disappearing lunch break and asked about Lauren's work to draw focus away from her. A small bubble of excitement fizzed in her stomach at the prospect of Saturday's date, and she couldn't wait to tell Fran and Terri tonight. It didn't matter that Lauren was only in town temporarily and that even if things went really well, there was probably no real prospect of a future together. It would have to be enough that she'd asked Lauren out after all these years.

CHAPTER ELEVEN

Rebekah grinned as Lauren handed her the room key. "Will I be giving this to Jamie again tonight?"

Lauren huffed. She missed the discretion and silent judgment of the staff at faceless, chain hotels. "I don't plan on getting into that state again, no."

Rebekah looked over her shoulder to the back office before she whispered, "Can't say that I would mind Jamie carrying me to bed."

Rebekah had been a few years ahead of her in high school, and Lauren remembered her having quite the reputation with the guys. Still, she hadn't expected the sharp sting of jealousy that registered with someone else's interest in Jamie. "Really? I didn't think she'd be on your radar."

Rebekah winked and leaned over the counter. The low-cut top she wore struggled to contain her breasts, and Lauren struggled to look away. It was little wonder she'd been so popular in school. No doubt that popularity hadn't dwindled with the passage of time, considering how good she looked.

"You haven't been around for a while. I'm not the same person I was in high school," Rebekah whispered.

"Have you and Jamie…" Lauren made an expression she hoped would complete her sentence.

Before Rebekah answered, Jamie pulled up to the curb.

"Speak of the devil," Rebekah said and didn't answer Lauren's question.

Lauren smiled as sweetly as she could and tamped down her sudden desire to swipe her nails across Rebekah's face. "See you later." She headed out, sure that her strange surge of aggression would disappear in the warm summer air.

Jamie got out of the truck with a beautiful bunch of flowers in her hand. Roses, not sunflowers: a far more traditional flower for a date. The heads were huge, and the red so vibrant it was almost unreal.

"Hey there." Jamie held out the bouquet.

Lauren took them and kissed Jamie's cheek. "They're stunning. Thank you."

Jamie's face flushed, and she grinned as she touched her cheek. "I might never wash my face again." She gestured toward the B&B. "Are you taking them in?"

Lauren looked back to see Rebekah wave. She was still leaning across the counter and her breasts looked impossibly perfect. She didn't want Jamie going in and seeing that while Lauren took the flowers up to her room. "No, I want to keep them with me."

Jamie frowned and shrugged. "Okay." She walked around the truck and opened the passenger door. "Your carriage awaits, miss."

Lauren got in, and Jamie closed the door gently. She reached for the seatbelt and saw the clip attached to it.

Jamie slid into the driver's seat and responded to Lauren's questioning look. "So you don't crush your dress."

Lauren fixed it into place and pushed her seatbelt in. The clip hadn't been installed the last time she'd rode in Jamie's truck, which meant that Jamie had seen her holding it away from her dress. But Jamie hadn't just seen it, she'd done something about it. It was a small but incredibly thoughtful gesture. "If you're still adding up points on how successful our time together is," she tapped the seatbelt attachment, "this just scored you a bucket of bonus ones."

Jamie grinned and swung the truck around. "Now you're just encouraging my bad habits, but I'll take 'em."

"Different direction? Where are we headed?"

"My mom told me about a restaurant in Rock Lake with an extensive vegetarian menu. I haven't been but I trust her judgment." She glanced across to Lauren. "And if it sucks, I can blame her and not lose any hard-earned points."

"Noted. How is your mom?"

"Working her way through all the eligible men within a hundred-mile radius." Jamie shifted back in her seat and smiled at Lauren. "I don't mean that in a bad way. Like, she isn't *sleeping* her way through those men."

Lauren rolled her eyes. "What would it matter if she was? I hate those double standards that dictate a woman can't be as sexually active as a man without getting herself a bad name. It's bullshit." She bit her lip. Maybe her politics shouldn't be her priority topic of conversation on a first date. "Sorry. That's one of my pet peeves."

Jamie lifted her hand from the steering wheel. "No need to apologize for being passionate about women's rights. I just worry about her. This is a small town, and you know what people are like."

Lauren looked out the window, trying to spot deer in the dense trees of the forest they'd entered. "I do. And they were another good reason for leaving."

"I remember you being so desperate to get out of here." Jamie gave a small smile. "You were always too big for this place."

She'd never thought of it that way. It made her sound too big for her boots, as if she thought she was better than everyone else in the town. It hadn't been like that, and she didn't want Jamie thinking that it was. "I was desperate, but it wasn't that. I just never felt comfortable here." Lauren and Kayla had shared countless conversations about Lauren's desire to leave compared to Kayla's embracing of the small-town culture. They'd been identical in many ways, but so different in others it would be easy to think they'd been raised separately. "I had things to prove to myself."

"Mm. Did you parents put pressure on you to succeed?" Jamie slowed at a stop sign and turned left, going deeper into the forest. "You were the number one student in school. I always admired your drive."

"Really?" She took the time to really look at Jamie. She had been right for the most part; Lauren hadn't noticed her in school until the infamous folder incident. She'd seen her, of course. Jamie had always been front and center at any student council meeting Lauren had run, but she hadn't *seen* her. And now that she was looking at her properly, Jamie was all things good. Short hair, strong jaw, kind eyes, sexy lips, and a good body from what Lauren had seen. But she was so much more than that. There was so much about her that was impossible to see and could only be felt, be experienced by spending time with her. She was sweet, caring, generous, and tremendously thoughtful. She had such gentle energy and a sensitivity that was rare. Lauren could never imagine her raising her voice or getting aggressive, unlike far too many of the women Lauren had known. She was beginning to think there was something about her that attracted those kinds of people, ones who felt the need to compete with her powerful position at work by being overbearing at home. It was refreshing to be in the company of a woman as emotionally stable as Jamie appeared to be.

"It's just the way I'm built, I guess. My parents encouraged us both, of course, but they never made me feel like I had to do any of the things I got involved in. I drove myself."

Jamie shook her head. "I'm not sure that drive is a big enough word for it. You never stopped. I never saw you kicking back and relaxing with your friends. If there were pictures of people in dictionaries, you'd be the one for ambition."

Seeing herself through someone else's lens was interesting and good for her ego. "I've never liked wasting time. The world is so big, and there are so many problems with it. People suffering in war-torn countries, kids living in poverty, our community being persecuted. I need to be doing important things with the time I have." She swallowed. Time was too strict a master, and it was impossible to know how much time you had on the planet. She'd thought she would have enough to build the hub with Kayla, but her time was cut short. She looked up, unblinking, to stave away the threatening tears and was grateful for the tender silence that followed.

"So, did you?" Jamie asked gently after a few moments.

"Did I what?"

"Prove things to yourself? Are you happy with where you are and what you've achieved?"

"There's always more we could all be doing, isn't there? The accolades, awards, and acknowledgments are temporary. If I stopped now and moved back here to work in Beth's bar, I'd be wasting my potential to enact more change and help more people." Lauren pushed her hair behind her ear and sat up straighter in her seat. "I'm happy with what I'm doing and where I'm doing it, but I don't think I'll ever be satisfied with what I've achieved."

She looked out the window again. The forest had gone, and green and yellow fields stretched out for miles. She missed Boston and its tall glass and concrete structures, each one built higher than its predecessor, always striving to be bigger and better, always reaching toward the stars. That's what she was doing. Each of her achievements were mere building blocks to stack on top of each other, to raise her higher so that she could reach and complete the next task, help the next group of people. Kayla's death, though, made her wonder how she was going to stay on her feet, let alone climb those lofty ladders.

"That's got to be tough on you. Do you ever have time for yourself?"

Lauren looked at Jamie. "What do you mean?"

"Like, what do you do for fun? Something that's just for you and not for the good of a hundred other people."

"I drink." Lauren laughed. "But I think perhaps I drink a little too much, so I might have to think about stopping that when I get back to Boston."

"So, it's all or nothing for you? No in between, no gray or compromise?"

Lauren turned in her seat so she could face Jamie's profile better. A deep-dive therapy session on her professional lifestyle hadn't been on her list of things to do tonight. "These are very intense questions for a first date. Have you heard of small talk?"

Jamie laughed. "The problem we've got here is that I already know a lot about you. You seem to be forgetting that you were my favorite subject in school, so I can't ask about that time in your life. And the town grapevine kept me up to date on what you've done career-wise since you left, so the deep stuff is all I've got." She grinned and glanced sideways. "Unless you want to talk about your past girlfriends, because the rumor mill had nothing on that little gem, and I'd love to know all about the many women whose hearts you've broken."

Lauren smiled at the completely unrealistic picture Jamie seemed to have painted of her. "How do you know I broke *their* hearts?"

"Come on, look at you. No one in their right mind would leave you. But I guess I don't know for sure, which is what makes it a good subject." Jamie wiggled her eyebrows. "Unless you want to go back to deconstructing your workaholic lifestyle?"

Lauren had been called worse things than a workaholic before, and in a far less gently challenging manner. Her commitment to her work had often been the bone of contention in relationships that made it beyond a few months. Lovers complained of her never having enough time for them. *They* weren't the ones who were fifteen with the reading ability of a five-year-old and no prospects in life. Those were the people she was helping, but the women she'd dated didn't get it. People could be so selfish.

She rolled the window down and breathed in deeply. "The clean air here is about the only thing I miss by living in the city."

Jamie laughed and slapped the steering wheel. "Epic change of topic, and so smoothly navigated." She rubbed her neck. "I could sue you for giving me whiplash."

Lauren swatted Jamie's shoulder. "You know, for the town weirdo, you have a smart mouth."

Jamie grinned. "It was my mouth that used to get me in all that trouble. You don't miss your friends?"

"Kayla was my best friend, and she used to visit Boston all the time." She took a beat to steady herself. Kayla wouldn't be able to spend the weekend in Lauren's apartment and go out with her and Whit ever again. Lauren had begun to wonder how often she'd come back. Part of her wished she could've had Kayla buried in Boston, so she could spend time with her every day, just like Jamie did with her dad. "I've lost touch with almost everyone else except Beth, and we're not that close anymore. I know she's there for me, and she knows I'm there for her, but we don't have that closeness that we used to have when we were in high school." Lauren rested her hand on the window's edge and let the wind rush through her fingers. She didn't drive in Boston very often, but when she did, she couldn't have her window open without choking on fumes. "And if that's gone, I don't really see the point of pretending to stay in touch on a regular basis. Occasional messages, birthday cards, and Facebook likes—those things are superficial, and they don't make a real friendship. Beth's grandma died, and she'd practically raised her. They were really close, and it must've hit her hard, but she didn't reach out to me. I found out from Kayla."

"You don't sound happy about it," Jamie said as she joined the Interstate and accelerated into traffic. "Maybe the friendship still means more to you than you want it to."

Lauren shook her head. "No. It's a time thing again. If we're not close, that's okay. People come onto your path, and they stay as long as they need to, for you and for them. But you can't be half on and half off my path. If you're in my life, I'll make time for you, but if you're not fully on my path, then I don't have the time to waste. It's like you said at lunch yesterday; life is too precious to waste a moment of it."

"Haven't you been working from her bar most days? Aren't you talking?"

"Of course we are. And when we get together, conversation comes easily enough, but it's mostly about the past. It's not philosophical discussions about judging an old woman who chooses to let herself die after her husband is gone."

"Mrs. Johnson. We have to get back to that." Jamie smiled. "So, I'm scoring more points on the conversation scale and would make a good friend then?"

Lauren nodded but didn't say that Jamie's riveting conversation and her physical appearance, coupled with her stunningly sweet personality made her more than good friend material. There was no harm in getting to know Jamie better, but Lauren couldn't allow it to be more than that. As soon as she'd cleared out Kayla's apartment, she'd be heading back to Boston. Sure, she was tentatively planning the hub building, but that didn't include moving back to her hometown. "Beth said you always go out with your Musketeer friends on Saturday night, so I guess I should be honored that you're taking me out instead."

"I'm the one who's feeling honored that you're going out with me on a Saturday night," Jamie said. "But we're meeting for lunch tomorrow instead, so you shouldn't feel bad that I'm missing out. I told them about your Musketeer nickname—they liked it a lot. We all wish that everyone at school had called us that rather than all the other names they used."

Lauren remembered some of the unkind group names the bullies had for the three friends. Where did kids learn to be so cruel so early? "How are Francesca and Teresa? What are they doing now?"

"Fran's a nurse at an ER in Rock Lake, and Terri's an associate in a grocery store near Camden Forest. They both love what they do."

Associate? Wasn't that just a fancy name for shelf-stocker and cashier? Teresa's SATs were some of the highest in the school. She'd always been one of Lauren's academic competitors, though Teresa probably never knew it. She could've had her pick of top colleges *and* gotten a full ride scholarship. Why had she stayed in Damarron and wasted her potential? "Did Teresa not go to college?"

Jamie gave Lauren a look she couldn't decipher. "She chose to stay and look after her family. Her brother's a handful, and her parents had them both when they were in their forties. She stuck around to help."

"That's a shame. She won the science fair every year, didn't she? She would've had a successful career in STEM." Lauren saw Jamie's questioning look. "Science, technology, engineering, and math. It's an industry that has a severe lack of women in it."

"Got it. Well, she enjoys what she does, so that counts for something, doesn't it?"

Lauren shrugged. "I guess, if she's not bitter that she gave up her future for her family." She'd often thought the same of Kayla, but it hadn't been the case. Kayla simply lacked the same ambition and drive that Lauren had. It seemed she'd picked up the whole family's quota.

"You don't think looking after a family is an acceptable life choice?"

Lauren didn't miss the slight challenge in Jamie's tone. It wasn't aggressive though and sounded more like a prompt for further discussion. "Just like your Mrs. Johnson, everybody should be free to make their own choices. I just worry when it's not someone's first choice."

Jamie smiled. "You put other people's needs ahead of your own all the time. Isn't that the same thing?"

"No, because it's always been my choice to work in the non-profit sector." Lauren shrugged. "It's my calling, if you like. I've never wanted to do anything else other than help people. It was my first choice, and no one tried to influence me to do anything else."

"Then you were lucky," Jamie said. "Not everyone gets that freedom."

"Yeah, you're right about that." Lauren went quiet. She liked the gentle way Jamie challenged her beliefs and stimulated conversation. She had the emotional intellect that Lauren always looked for when she recruited management…and potential love interests.

"Is it okay if I swing by my house to pick up Olly after we've eaten? I need to take him for a walk around the lake."

"Only if you'll let me have a look at your studio."

Jamie laughed. "Studio is a bit of a stretch. It's a barn with a work bench. But there's not much to see. I just dabble, that's all. You won't be impressed."

Jamie's nerves were evident in the way she rambled. Her open and easy to read nature were yet another thing to like about her. The non-profit sector wasn't quite as cutthroat as commercial business, but people could be cagey about their motives and agendas, and they often played their cards close to their chest. Lauren preferred uncomplicated people who were honest and even-keeled, people like Jamie. "I'd still like to see it. And if you've got more pieces like the phoenix at Beth's place, I can assure you I'll be impressed."

Jamie grumbled but said nothing else.

"How come you don't sell your work?" Lauren asked.

Jamie glanced at her and looked incredulous. "Because it's not that good. And even if it was, I'm not interested in making money from it. I do it because I enjoy it. No one would've seen that phoenix if your sister hadn't harried me into donating it for her cause."

Lauren smiled. "She did have a way of getting what she wanted when she set her mind to it." She thought of all the times Kayla had twisted their dad around her little finger to get him to take them horseback riding, or to the library, or even better, the bookshop.

"She really did." Jamie pulled into the inside lane and took the exit to Rock Lake. "She happened to be jogging past my house when I was welding the wings. She just strolled down the drive and asked if I'd donate it to her next auction."

Lauren could practically see Kayla doing it, and she pushed away the thought that she'd never see Kayla doing anything ever again. Instead, she focused on how wonderful it was to share memories of her with someone else. "And you couldn't say no?"

Jamie glanced at Lauren then looked away. "She reminded me too much of you to deny her anything."

It suddenly occurred to Lauren that Jamie might've had a crush on both of them, and she shuddered. It wouldn't be the first time. She lost count of the number of people, mostly men, who had approached them on nights out in Boston. Regardless of the fact that Lauren would never want to have sex with anyone in front of her sister, she'd never wanted to have sex with a man. But Kayla was less gender-oriented in her desires. Did Jamie know that? And if she did, had she ever thought to ask her out?

Jamie touched Lauren's arm lightly. "If you're thinking what I think you're thinking, the answer is no. I never had a crush on your sister. It was only ever you."

Lauren couldn't suppress a smile at Jamie's heartfelt declaration. "Most people couldn't tell the difference between—"

"I could. And it's not just about subtle differences like the scar you've got, it was the way you acted that was different. Your personalities were vaguely similar, sure, but if anyone bothered to really pay attention, it was obvious."

Lauren looked out the window and nibbled the inside of her top lip to keep her grin from turning into a full-blown smile. Jamie sure knew how to say the right things. How on Earth was she single when there were vamps like Rebekah around to tie her down, probably literally? "So, you'll let me see your barn studio because you can't say no to a Gray girl?"

Jamie shook her head. "Apparently."

"Great." All the wasted talent in this town. Kayla could have been a professor in English Literature, Teresa could've been an engineer or scientist, and if the phoenix was any indication, Jamie could be carving a lucrative career from her art. It was as if there was some spell cast on the population, keeping almost everyone with a gift within the town limits.

Lauren was enjoying this date immensely and was in no hurry for it to be over, but she was already looking forward to seeing Jamie's art. Maybe Jamie didn't have to stay under this town's spell like everyone else.

CHAPTER TWELVE

"TELL ME AGAIN WHY we're not at Beth's place?" Fran wrinkled her nose and took another sip of her coffee. "This is an insult to the coffee bean. How is it possible to make it taste this bad?"

"You're being dramatic. It's not that bad," Jamie said.

Fran arched her eyebrows. "Then why are you drinking bottled water?"

"Because I've had my morning cup of java, and that's all I need. You know I only drink water through the day."

"Normally, yes." Fran placed her mug on the table and pushed it away. "But this is our displaced Saturday night get together, so we should all be drinking beer and downing shots."

Terri tapped her watch. "It's 1:13 p.m."

Fran tapped her watch and stuck her tongue out. "Then it's 5:13 p.m. somewhere else."

"We can go to Beth's if you don't want to hear about my date with Lauren Gray last night."

"What are you, twelve? Shouldn't she just be Lauren since everyone knows *exactly* who you're talking about?" Fran rolled her eyes and stood up. "Of course we want to hear all the details—"

"Unless it gets sexy," Terri said and stuck her fingers in her ears.

"Unless it gets sexy, then Terri can go and sit in the kids' play area while you tell *me* all the details. But if we're staying here, I'm switching to OJ so I can imagine there's some champagne in it." Fran motioned to the remaining drinks on the table. "Any refills?"

Jamie and Terri shook their heads and sipped at their drinks.

Fran returned a few moments later with her juice and dropped some menus onto the table. "I'm hoping the food might be better than the coffee. I don't see this place surviving long."

"They're out-of-towners hoping to make a quick buck on the tourism here. What do you expect?" Terri handed out the menus, placing each one perfectly straight in front of her friends before looking at her own. "They better have steak and eggs, or we're going somewhere else."

"What made you choose this place anyway?" Fran asked as she scanned the food options.

"Let it go, Fran." Jamie didn't say that Lauren had told her how bad the coffee was, and Jamie had come here precisely because Lauren wouldn't. It'd be hard to talk about her if she was in the same place and could overhear Jamie gushing about her. "Mom wanted me to try it out and see what the new owners were like." That wasn't a complete lie. Her mom had seen a guy around her age watering the planters outside the diner and wanted to know if he was single.

Fran narrowed her eyes but didn't say anything else. Terri waved someone over, and he took their order.

"Who's going first?" Terri asked.

"First for what?" Jamie looked at Fran, but she shrugged and focused on Terri.

"Our weekly game." Terri slapped her five dollars on the table, so Jamie and Fran did the same.

Jamie ran her hand across the back of her head. She'd been so focused on Lauren that she could barely recall what she'd done all week. "It's been a slow one. I've got nothing other than dropping a can of black paint all over one of the lion's heads at the cemetery gate." That had been partly about Lauren too, because Jamie had been so distracted when she'd run into—and maimed—her. "Damn stuff got everywhere. I'm still trying to get it out of his nostrils and off the pavement."

Fran laughed. "That's a good one. Terri, do you have something to put you in the running for a two-in-a-row win?"

"I've got a ten-year-old kid sent to the shop on his own to get an avocado. He picked one up and pressed the top of it—all okay so far because that's how you find out if it's ready to eat or not. He obviously wasn't happy with that one, but did he put it back in with the avocados? No, he did not. He put it on top of the cherry tomatoes. And I thought, actually, that's good thinking because if he puts it back into the box and keeps at this, trying to find the perfect avocado, how's he supposed to tell which ones he's checked and which ones he hasn't checked? So, I busy myself rearranging a stack of apples and figure that I'll sort it out when he's gone. No big deal. He's just a kid. The next one he grabs, he squeezes around the middle, but he didn't stop squeezing, and it basically explodes in his hand. Does he look around and think, oh crap? No, he does not. He takes another one and does exactly the same thing. Splat, green goo everywhere. By the time I got to him, he'd squished enough avocados to make guacamole for ten people."

"What did you do with him?" Jamie asked.

Terri shrugged. "Nothing I could do. His parents weren't in the store, so I couldn't talk to them. I wiped his grubby little hands and sent him off to the register with two perfectly ripe avocados."

Fran shook her head. "That's a letdown after last week's story."

Terri held up her hands. "Like Jamie says, it was a slow week. I suppose you've got something to blow us all out of the water?" She tapped the table. "It's little wonder you invented this game. With your job, you were bound to win most weeks." Terri knocked on the table a little more forcefully. "I think we should have a new weekly game."

"Agreed. I said so last week, but you disagreed because you finally won. Now you just want to go out on a high. Change the game, I say." Jamie joined the mutiny just for the exasperated expression on Fran's face.

Fran crossed her arms and leaned back in her seat. "Screw the both of you. My stories are great."

Jamie grinned. "That's not in dispute. We're just saying it's hard to compete. It's not every day a giant deer runs into a grocery store and knocks itself out. But you work in the ER, and that's where people go after they've gotten up to some strange stuff. Am I right?" She held up her hand, and Terri high-fived her.

"Fine. I won't tell you about the cyst then." Fran looked around the diner at the very few customers.

Jamie nudged her. "Come on, you know you want to." She nodded toward the fifteen dollars on the table. "The money's down. You may as well win it."

Fran huffed. "A kid with a cyst the size of a golf ball, but that's not the worst of it." She leaned in and beckoned Jamie and Terri to join her. "Guess where it was?"

Jamie and Terri shrugged. "Hand?" Jamie asked.

Fran shook her head and pointed downward. "On the poor girl's labia."

Jamie squeezed her thighs together and grimaced. "Oh, no, tell me you're kidding."

"Nope. Some sort of climbing harness trapped her lips when someone dropped her thirty feet from a wall for a laugh."

Terri pushed the stack of bills toward Fran as she shook her head and squeezed her eyes closed. "Take it, and never tell us that story again."

Fran laughed and shoved her winnings into her pocket. "You should've seen the p—"

"No! No, we shouldn't." Jamie pressed her hand over Fran's mouth.

She batted Jamie away. "Okay, no more details, I promise. But we want details from you. How did your date go?"

Jamie waited until the server placed all their plates and silverware. "We should eat first. You know how Terri hates cold food."

Fran cut off a piece of pancake and wafted it around on her fork. "I'm beginning to think you're playing for time because you didn't really go out with Lauren." She popped the food into her mouth.

Jamie ignored the accusatory look and concentrated on her grits and biscuits. They ate in relative silence, only stopping to comment that the food *was* better than the coffee. Jamie didn't see the guy her mom had told her about though. Other than their young waiter and server, the rest of the staff were women.

After they'd all finished, Terri gathered their plates and placed them on the table behind them.

Jamie washed the last mouthful of her biscuit down with a swallow of water and waited for her friends' attention. "It was amazing. From the moment I picked her up, we hardly stopped talking."

"Did she like the roses?" Terri asked. "Simon said they were from Ecuador, but I had no idea why that should impress me."

Jamie coughed. "Because they're the best roses in the world, apparently." And they should be for the price, but they were worth every cent for the look on Lauren's face. "She loved them. She even took one into the restaurant, and the waitress put it in a vase for our table."

"Ooh, classy."

"What did you talk about?" Terri asked.

"Deep stuff. Ambition, hopes, future plans, families. We didn't have to bother with all the small talk you usually get bogged down with on first dates because we already know each other so well."

Fran coughed. "How so? You knew everything about her when she was living here, but she hardly knew you existed. And people change a lot in fifteen years. I'd say there should've been plenty of small talk."

"I'm thinking family stuff, where you grew up, schools you went to." Jamie sighed at Fran's reaction, but she knew where it came from. They were either not acknowledged at all or sought out for the wrong kind of attention. "I know we don't *know* each other."

"But you want to get to know the older Lauren?" Terri asked.

Jamie nodded. "I really do. She's so smart and funny. We laughed a lot, but we talked about serious things too, including you guys, actually." She told them about their conversation, and that Lauren had expected Terri to have gone off to become a famous scientist. Jamie registered the change in Terri's expression. Had Lauren been right about the choice Terri had made?

"That would've been nice," Terri said and looked beyond Jamie like she was thinking.

"Did you want to go to college? You always said you could never see yourself leaving this town." As soon as she said the words, Jamie saw the difference in bright neon. Terri not seeing herself leaving wasn't the same as not *wanting* to leave. "You wanted to go to college, didn't you?"

Terri moved her fork a little to the right and stared at the table. "If I didn't say it out loud, I hoped my desire to do it might fade away."

"I wish you had." Jamie's heart fell into her guts. She'd never seen that her best friend wanted something entirely different from the life she'd chosen. Terri looked up, her eyes full of tears. Jamie hadn't seen her cry since they were in school. That had been so frequently that, as adults, they'd made a pact to limit their tears to funerals and weddings. "We never asked."

Terri gave a sad smile and tears tracked down her cheeks. "It wasn't meant to be."

Fran pulled a tissue from her bag and offered it to Terri. "Family, huh?"

Terri tilted her head to the side. "It meant The Three Musketeers stayed together."

Jamie laughed lightly at the use of Lauren's nickname for them, but she felt far from joyful. What would Terri have achieved if she'd followed her dreams and gone to college? A Nobel prize? Discovered the cure for cancer? Become a NASA scientist? "Hey, we would've stayed in touch." She thought about Lauren and Beth, but they were different, and the physical distance had developed into an emotional one. But nothing tore Jamie and her friends apart in school, and nothing in the world would tear them apart now. "It's not too late, you know. People go back to college as mature students all the time. And you're still young. Some of the best scientists are in their sixties."

Maybe Lauren had some contacts in Boston. Her NPO was in education, so maybe they could sponsor Terri to attend college. She was the most intelligent person Jamie knew. She could do anything if she decided that's what she wanted.

"That's right." Fran bounced forward in her seat. "And Ethan's got a job now. He can look after himself. Your parents are healthy for their age. Now would be the perfect time to retrain."

Terri fiddled with her coffee cup. "Maybe."

Jamie picked up her phone and fired off a quick text to Lauren about scholarships for older students then stuck it back in her pocket.

"So, what else? Was your mom right about the restaurant?" Terri asked, signaling an end to the discussion about her future.

"I think so. The food was great, but we didn't stay as long as I thought we might."

Fran wiggled her eyebrows. "A-ha! Time for you to hit the kids' play area while the grown-ups talk about bumping uglies, Tezza."

"Smoke break." Terri made to get up, but Jamie put her hand on her arm.

"No need. We rushed back to pick up Olly for a walk around the lake—but not before Lauren had appraised my tinkering in my barn."

Terri's eyes widened, and she settled back into her seat. "You showed her your art? Wow, you must be serious."

"It's not art, and I didn't have much choice." There was that word again. She hadn't been one hundred percent comfortable with showing Lauren the inside of the barn, but Lauren had seemed so excited about it that it had been impossible to say no. She could've made a choice to be an ass about it, she supposed, but she liked Lauren too much for that. She also thought it might've been about being close to something that Kayla had seen, like a shared experience Lauren could hang onto now that Kayla was gone. "Beth told her about the phoenix at her place and Kayla's fundraiser, and that was all the encouragement she needed."

Terri moved her fork out of the way, put her forearms on the table, and adopted her serious pose. Jamie suppressed a smile. She was so lucky to have such great friends. Lauren seemed so lonely.

"What did she think of your work?" Terri asked.

"She got really excited and couldn't believe I wasn't selling any of it." Jamie shrugged. "I've been doing it for a long time. There are a lot of pieces in my barn."

Fran and Terri nodded.

"We've been telling you that you should be selling your art for years," Fran said. "Now that the great and powerful Lauren Gray has said the same, are you finally going to do something about it?"

Jamie huffed. "No. I do that stuff just for me. I don't need external validation by getting money for it. Just because Lauren is obsessed with awards and achievements doesn't mean everyone else is." She picked up her glass and drained the last of the water to avoid the intense eye contact she knew her friends would be throwing her way. Her overreaction smacked of self-doubt. It was one thing to raise a few thousand dollars for a local cause, it was another thing entirely to stock a shop with her work and expect people to part with their hard-earned cash for her metal wrangling.

"That's a bit unfair, isn't it?" Terri asked when Jamie set her bottle down. "It seems to me Lauren's always been under a lot of pressure. She was the smart twin, *and* she looks the way she does. She had to work three times as hard to make people take her seriously."

"Kayla was no slouch academically either," Jamie said. "She went to Harvard too."

"We're not talking about Kayla though, are we? She was always a homebody, and she cruised through school doing the minimum. She wasn't class president, or captain of the cheerleading team, or high school swim champion. Lauren learned that awards and achievement equaled recognition." Terri relaxed back into her seat as if she'd finished making her point.

She had. The more someone achieved, the more everyone else around them expected. No one had ever expected anything from Jamie. Her mom was happy as long as Jamie was happy, and that had been okay her whole life. But it had also bred an apathy toward ambition. She had none and she wished for nothing greater. Her art—if she could bring herself to call it that—had always been important to her, and occasionally, she had wondered what it might be like to sell her work or even have her own store. And despite acting to the contrary, Jamie had been thrilled at Kayla's auction when the phoenix had been the star of the show.

But at what cost? Lauren was doing great things for a lot of people, but from what Jamie could see, her personal life was nothing to covet. Her only friend was her work colleague, and she'd lost any true connection to her old friends. Maybe there was a balance, and maybe they could learn from each other. It was obvious Lauren wouldn't be in town any longer than was absolutely necessary, but that didn't mean Jamie couldn't make the most of being with her now. And maybe all that self-confidence and ambition might rub off on Jamie, and her quiet, latent fantasies about doing something with her metalwork might turn into something real, something exciting.

CHAPTER THIRTEEN

"AND EVERYTHING IS RESOLVED now?" Lauren stopped pacing and dropped back into her chair. She was glad she'd taken this meeting in her room and not been working at Beth's, though Rebekah knocking on her door to make sure she was all right after hearing her shout hadn't been optimal.

"Yes. It's all been taken care off," Kate said. "Whitney calmed them down and renegotiated the terms. It was a knee jerk reaction to a media story, that's all."

"Great job, Whit." Lauren looked at her on-screen and smiled. "But it's crazy that they think it's okay to pull the plug in the middle of a project."

Kate nodded. "You're right, but we all know that government funding is a law unto itself. Jenna wants to sue for breach of contract, but given that Whit has managed to settle everything, that's not an avenue I want to go down."

"No, that's not a good idea. As much as I'd love to, we're too reliant on that income stream for our core costs." Lauren hated being beholden to a fund managed by a guy who let his emotions rule his decision-making process. This wasn't the first time he'd caused them problems by withholding payments, and it probably wouldn't be the last. They had to get away from any dependence on public funding, and their current focus would help them do exactly that by diversifying their income streams across school boards.

"Anyway, I have to go. Little Jim is screaming for his next feed."

"Okay, thanks for coming on the call, Kate." Lauren waited until Kate had disappeared from the screen. "That was definitely something you could've done without."

Whit shrugged. "I'm just glad it happened today when I had the time to deal with it. I'm traveling to Albany late tonight, and I won't be back in the office until Friday morning. God knows what would've gone down if it had been tomorrow."

"I would've flown back and dealt with it," Lauren said.

"You're on official leave, boss. That's why Kate didn't bother you with it until we had it under control."

Lauren nodded. She understood but being kept out of the loop in such a potentially huge crisis smarted, and more than a little. She needed to suck it up, clear Kayla's apartment, and get back to Boston. *Why? When Whit can handle everything without me?* There was no rush. The point of employing a perfectly capable team was so that they could take care of business when called upon. And Lauren had built that perfect team, with Whit as her perfect successor. But she hadn't planned on being surplus to requirements just yet.

She blew out a breath. That was her ego talking. *Rein it in.* "Is Charlotte ready for Albany?"

"She sure is. I think her hubby is a little pissed that she's spending more time away from home, but he's supposed to be the stay-at-home dad, so I don't think it's going to be a problem for her."

"Mm." Lauren wasn't so sure. She'd met Charlotte's husband a few times, and he always seemed a little uncomfortable with his wife providing for their family. She thought he was more or less unemployable, mainly because of his temperament, and had settled for the home dad position rather than actively wanting it. And she was sure Charlotte could do better, but maybe she'd settled too. "Keep an eye on that situation. They've got a special needs kid. If the husband leaves, Charlotte will have to take some time off until she can get a suitable babysitter. And that'll leave you flying solo."

"Do you want me to line someone else up to help me out just in case?" Whit frowned. "Though it seems like a leap to go from a little pissed to leaving the wife and kid, but you know her better than I do."

Lauren clenched her jaw. Yes, she did know Charlotte better than Whit. She knew her whole team inside out, personal lives included. No one could come to work and leave their home life at the office front door. She took a deep breath. What was with her ego today? "Talk to Danielle in Human Resources. I think she'd like the opportunity to accompany you."

"Okay, will do." Whit looked off-screen, presumably at a checklist. "Stephanie Moss has accepted our offer, and she's happy with the salary offered. You were right on both counts about those phone calls. The yes ones are amazing, and the no thank yous stink."

Lauren laughed. "You have to take the rough with the smooth, Number

One."

Whit pouted. "You could get HR to call the unsuccessful candidates. Why don't you?"

"Because it wasn't HR who spent an hour getting to know them." Lauren noticed her hair looked a little unruly. She smoothed it down. All this remote working was playing havoc with her daily regime. It was so much easier to stay perfectly groomed for work when she had to go into the office every day. "Think of it as a courtesy thing. Applying for a big job is an emotional exercise, and you build a relationship with the people interviewing you. You're trying to sell yourself, and when you don't get the job, it feels like a failure. I think it's important to be the one to talk to them after and to answer any questions they've got about how they did. HR can't know that. All they'd have was a no, and you can't learn much from a simple no."

Whit put her hands together and bowed her head. "You know you can't go anywhere for a long time yet, don't you? You've still got so much to teach me, sensei."

Lauren laughed. She hadn't planned on going anywhere, but it was always nice to be appreciated and needed. Her ego was slightly mollified. "You've got nothing to worry about on that score."

Whit took a deep breath. "Are you any closer to doing what you've got to do there?"

"I'm going tomorrow," Lauren said, making a spur of the moment decision. "My dad showed me some plans he and Kayla had made, and he says she had more in her apartment."

"Is your dad going with you?"

"Of course not. I remember the pact, Whit."

Whit laughed. "Kayla did seem really eager to get that in place."

Lauren half-laughed. Kayla *had* been the one to suggest it and had gotten them both to agree. She closed her eyes briefly, hoping to all that was holy that she wouldn't find any homemade sex tapes.

"So, you're going on your own?"

Lauren shrugged. "I was thinking of asking Jamie to come with me, but I'm not sure. It doesn't seem like good second date material."

Whit leaned closer to the screen. "Meaning the first date went well enough to warrant a follow-up?"

"Yes." Strangely, Lauren didn't feel like sharing the intimate details of her date with Whit, and she wasn't sure quite how to unpack the meaning of her reticence. Since they'd become fast friends, Lauren had discussed her private life with Whit freely, and vice versa. So, why was she reluctant to talk about Jamie now? "Jamie's a metal sculptor. She let me go into her studio on Saturday night, and she's got so many great pieces cooped up in there that she won't let anyone see. I don't understand." Lauren shook her head. "She could have her own boutique, or distribute them to houseware stores across the country, or sell them online. Or all three. Instead, she's working in a cemetery."

"Not everyone has the same ambition and drive as you, Lauren," Whit said.

"It's more likely to be a self-confidence thing. She was bullied at school, and I don't think she's ever had people tell her she's talented or that she could put her work out into the world."

"Who could tell her if she doesn't let anyone see it?"

Whit raised a good point. Maybe some critical feedback from a few art experts would be just the nudge Jamie needed. No doubt her mom and friends had told her that her sculptures were great, but who really believed family and friends? It was their job to build you up. Lauren looked at her phone and flicked to the gallery app. She'd taken some photos of a few sculptures when Jamie went to get her dog from the house. "I'm sending you a few pictures now. Tell me what you think."

"Okay. Let me get my phone." Whit left the screen.

Lauren selected five shots of different pieces and forwarded them.

When Whit returned, she nodded. "Wow, you weren't kidding. I wasn't expecting that kind of quality. I thought you were just talking junkyard metal made into robots for holding wine bottles. I'm no art critic, but this looks like real art, if there is such a thing."

Lauren laughed. "Hey, if you can sell a dead shark for twelve million dollars, who knows what real art is now?"

"Exactly." Whit looked back to the screen. "I know you love nurturing talent, Lauren, but if she doesn't want to show anybody, is there anything you can do for her?"

Lauren continued to flip through her photos. "Of course there is. I'm going to send the best of these photos to some people in Boston and New York and ask for their opinion."

"Shall I get you the contacts for the stores and galleries we use for auction donations?"

Lauren nodded. "Please."

"Let me make a note, then I'll get Sally to do it as soon as we're done on this call." Whit scribbled something then glanced back at the screen. "I love how you're always looking for ways to help people."

"Thanks, Whit." Lauren had always been that way. She enjoyed helping people achieve their potential or giving them a boost when they needed it. It was why she was in the non-profit sector instead of working for a blue-chip company. "On that note, there's something else I need to do. Could you also get Sally to pull together some information on full-ride scholarships for mature students with an aptitude for STEM? Preferably for colleges within a five-hundred-mile radius from Damarron."

Whit frowned. "Sure. Who's this for?"

"Teresa Caddy, one of Jamie's friends. She's a genius, but she didn't go to college because of her family. Jamie and I talked about her on Saturday night and then I got a text from Jamie on Sunday to see if there was any way I could help."

The text had surprised Lauren. Jamie had seemed adamant that Teresa was happy with her decision not to go to college and to work in a grocery store. She guessed they must've talked about it, and Teresa wasn't so content after all. It meant that Jamie had listened and processed rather than just ignored what Lauren had said. Maybe she was already coming around about her own potential too. This town may have kept its vines wrapped around Kayla, but if Lauren could free Jamie and Teresa…

She didn't finish the odd train of thought. Jamie and Teresa's futures had nothing to do with Kayla. And if people wanted to stay in this tourist trap of a town, that was their choice. But if she *could* help, she was all but obligated to. The world outside this town needed more successful women in it, in the creative sector and especially the STEM industry.

And if that meant Jamie left Damarron to live in a big city to be closer to a thriving art community, maybe the sparks that had ignited on their date could turn into a long-burning fire.

CHAPTER FOURTEEN

"Do you want some company?" Jamie held out one of the two brown bags from Beth's. "You've been here a while. I thought you might be hungry. I brought you a falafel and sweet chili wrap."

Lauren shifted against Kayla's tombstone, smiled, and nodded. "That would be great. Thank you." She took the bag and patted the ground beside her. "I don't have a blanket."

Jamie squatted down and sat cross-legged opposite Lauren. "This grass is better than a blanket."

Lauren ran her hands along it, and the strands of grass slipped between her fingers. Jamie swallowed, imagining Lauren's hands slipping through her hair the same way.

"It *is* really soft. You keep these grounds beautifully."

"Thanks." Heat rushed up Jamie's spine. She was glad of the light summer breeze that drifted up the back of her T-shirt to counteract it. She pulled out her roast beef and mustard sandwich and tried to think of anything else other than Lauren's lips on hers. Since Lauren's quick goodnight kiss on Saturday night, that had been pretty much impossible.

"Can I ask you a question?" Lauren carefully ripped her bag open and made it into a plate.

"Is it really personal?"

"Why? Do you want to avoid personal questions in case you reveal too much of yourself to me?"

Jamie laughed. "That ship has sailed. I'm an open book for you, and you can know me as well as you want to."

"So, I can ask you a question then?"

Jamie shrugged at her inability to deny Lauren anything. She still couldn't believe she'd let Lauren spend time in her barn, waxing lyrical about her sculptures. "Apparently."

"You don't have to answer if you don't want to." Lauren gently touched Jamie's knee before she pulled back and took a bite of her wrap.

"Like I said, you can know me inside out, if you're interested. I mean, you know, what's in my head. And my heart. Not…you know." Jamie closed her eyes briefly. When she opened them, Lauren simply smiled at her with that knowing expression.

"Do you work at the cemetery so that you're close to your dad every day, or is this what you want to do with your life?"

"I should record these conversations. Fran thinks we need to indulge in some small talk to get to know each other, but I think conversations like this—"

"Tell us much more about each other than any small talk ever could?" Jamie nodded. "Yeah."

"You should know that I'm really enjoying getting to know you this way." Lauren put her wrap down on her makeshift plate and leaned closer to Jamie. She placed her hand around the back of Jamie's neck and pulled her in. Her gaze flicked up to Jamie's eyes, as if checking for absolute permission, before she returned her attention to Jamie's lips and kissed her softly. She released her grip and rocked back on her butt.

Jamie bit her bottom lip and gave a deep sigh. It hadn't been the passionate kiss Jamie had often imagined, but given their location, she was surprised to get any kind of kiss at all. And this gentle one nestled deep into her most cherished memories, registering as so much more important than any kiss before it. She could only hope that it might be joined by many more, but Lauren's inevitable departure limited that possibility. "What was your question again?"

Lauren laughed. "I don't think for a second that you've forgotten, but I'll humor you. Do you work here to be close to your dad?"

Jamie looked around the cemetery. She could see his grave from here, and she pointed toward it. "He's over there, in front of those bushes and to the left of the willow tree." Her mom had chosen the spot specifically because of the proximity of the tree. She'd said it was just like the one they'd gotten married under. She'd also said they'd made Jamie under the same tree, which was information Jamie wished she didn't have.

Lauren twisted around to see. "Willows are my favorite trees. They're so graceful. It's like they dance in the wind," she said, returning to her original position. "It's a beautiful spot."

Jamie's heart skipped. Of all the tens of thousands of tree species… what were the odds? "It's one of the reasons I work here, yeah. I started a year after high school. I tried a couple of jobs, but nothing stuck. No matter what I was doing though, I visited Dad most days, and I'd pull weeds and trim the bushes behind his headstone." Jamie plucked a blade of grass and smoothed it between her fingers. "One day, the groundskeeper came up and offered me an apprenticeship. I didn't recognize him because I was just a kid when he'd been around, but he was Dad's best friend, Mick. He taught me everything I needed to know about grass, trees, bushes, and plants—and digging holes, of course."

Lauren wrinkled her nose but said nothing. Jamie didn't expand on the hole-digging, especially since Kayla's was one of the last ones she'd dug, and with four in the family scheduled for the same plot, it had been a deep one. It was morose to think that Jamie had dug the original hole that Lauren might end up in one day.

"I found that I liked the solitude and the peace and quiet. I get to work outside, which is another good thing. I couldn't stand being in an office all day, every day. It'd just be too claustrophobic." Jamie picked at her sandwich. "So, my dad isn't the only reason I work here. I like what I do. Why do you ask?"

Lauren indicated to her mouth and finished chewing. "I like to know why people do the things they do. Whether it's choice or circumstance, desire or necessity. Some people work to live, and others live to work."

Jamie jutted her chin toward Lauren. "Which one applies to you?" She thought she knew the answer but maybe she was wrong.

Lauren arched her eyebrow. "I said that I like to know about other people. I didn't say I liked other people knowing about me," she said and winked.

"Huh, it's like that?"

"No, not at all." Lauren nudged Jamie's knee with her own and rested back against Kayla's gravestone. "I choose to do what I do, but I'm not sure I have an actual choice. Does that make sense?"

Jamie nodded. "For you, it makes perfect sense. You could choose to work in an industry that's not all about helping people, but you'd be completely miserable and lost in a sea of selfishness."

"Ooh, alliteration. Nice."

"I have no idea what that means, but I'm glad you liked it." She'd google the word later. English had never been her favorite subject. She could communicate with just about anybody, and that was good enough.

"You've got me," Lauren said. "I don't know what it is, or where I got it from, but I have a desire deep down in my bones to help people. I could earn a lot more money with my skill set in the private sector, but I'm happy with my life."

"Some of those CEO positions pull in crazy money," Jamie said. "What would you do with your first six-figure bonus check?"

Lauren pulled out her phone. "That's easy." She swiped the screen then held it up for Jamie to see. "Isn't it gorgeous?"

Jamie looked at the picture of a sports car on Lauren's phone briefly, then looked past it into Lauren's eyes. "Absolutely stunning."

Lauren huffed. "You're not even looking at it."

Jamie chuckled. "I looked. It's nice."

"Nice? That's British engineering at its best. 007 drives an Aston Martin."

Jamie laughed at Lauren's sudden switch into a gearhead. "It's not a truck. And what do you care what James Bond drives? I thought you were all about the powerful women?"

"I didn't say James Bond. 007 *is* a woman in the last movie. You haven't seen it?"

Jamie shook her head. Another thing to google.

"They do an SUV. Maybe you'd like that, you redneck."

"Wow, you're resorting to insults now." Jamie shielded herself when Lauren swatted at her. "And that's six figures worth of car?" She shook her head and munched her sandwich.

Lauren sighed and looked at her phone. "Over two hundred thousand dollars' worth."

Jamie nearly choked on a piece of beef. "For a car? And a British one? What do they even know about cars? Their roads are barely wide enough for a motorbike."

"Ha! And you'd know because you've traveled to the UK extensively?"

"I had to go once for my grandma's funeral. It was terrifying; the speed limit increases as the roads narrow and the streetlights decrease. It makes zero sense."

"Whatever." Lauren slipped her phone back into her bag. "If your dad wasn't here, what other job might you do?"

Jamie frowned. Was this about Lauren's visit to her barn? "Are you asking if I'd like to be a professional artist?"

"I wasn't, but since that's where your mind has immediately gone, maybe that's your answer." Lauren blinked and smiled.

Damn, her smile was a showstopper. "I haven't given much thought to what else I might do because I'm happy doing what I'm doing."

"Happy like Teresa is happy at the grocery store, or actually happy?"

"Actually happy." Her response was immediate, but she wasn't as convinced as she sounded. "Speaking of Terri, thanks for saying you'd look into the options for her. You got me thinking on Saturday night, and when I spoke to her about it the next day, it was obvious that you were right." Jamie rolled her eyes. "What's that like, always being right? Does it get boring?"

"No, it does not." Lauren smiled widely, and her eyes sparkled. "I should have something for you by tonight. Do you think Teresa will apply to a college and move away?"

Jamie shrugged. "I think she's seriously considering it. She didn't dismiss the idea on Sunday, and she's texted me since to see if you'd come up with anything. But she probably doesn't want to get her hopes up. A brand-new future is a very scary thing." Jamie went quiet for a moment. Was she still talking about Terri, or was she thinking about her own future and how she was too frightened to even dream it, let alone try to live it?

"You'd miss her, huh?"

Jamie nodded. "She's my best friend."

Lauren reached behind herself and touched the grass over Kayla's grave. "I miss my best friend."

The light in Lauren's eyes dimmed and tears rimmed her eyes. Jamie tossed the rest of her sandwich aside, got to her knees, and pulled Lauren into a hug. Lauren wrapped her arms around Jamie's waist, and a few seconds passed before she buried her face against Jamie's chest and sobs racked her body. Jamie held her tighter. No words were necessary; none would offer comfort or solace. Jamie knew this pain well. It had lived inside her since she was nine, and it had eaten away at her for just as long, slowly distancing her from the possibility of letting anyone else into her heart to keep it from breaking still further.

But Lauren already had a place in there. She'd been a resident since Jamie first laid eyes on her at five, before she even knew the lexicon for love. And as Lauren cried for the loss of her sister, Jamie grieved for the loss yet to come. Lauren would leave, and Jamie would go back to her regular life. So she had to make the most of the here and now. "I've got you, baby," she said softly. And she did.

For now.

CHAPTER FIFTEEN

"Thanks for being willing to do this with me." Lauren squeezed Jamie's hand as they stood at the foot of the driveway to Kayla's second-floor apartment.

Jamie lifted Lauren's hand and kissed her knuckles. "Of course. Why wouldn't I?"

Lauren let out a small laugh. "Because it doesn't seem like a fun thing to do on a second date."

"Then let's not call it that. Honestly, it's fine. Whatever you need." Jamie gestured toward the front entrance of the three-story house. "Is there a code, or do you have a key?"

Lauren thought of the giant key at the B&B. As if this place was far enough into the twenty-first century to have a coded entrance. She put her hand in her pocket and pulled out the set of keys Kayla had given her. "Here."

"Ready?"

Lauren had definitely made the right decision in asking Jamie to come with her to do this, at least for the first time. There was no hint of impatience or hurry, and she felt safe enough to take this at her own pace. "I'm not sure that's what I am, but let's see." She released her grip on Jamie to hold the keys with both hands and walked steadily toward the front door.

It opened when they were halfway down the path, and Kayla's elderly neighbor, Edith, emerged with her white toy poodle trotting beside her.

Edith clasped her hand to her chest. "Kayla!" She stumbled back slightly, and the dog began yapping.

Lauren stepped back. Words wouldn't come, and the world spun so that she had to brace herself against a post.

Jamie held out her hand to steady Edith. "It's Lauren, Edith. Kayla's twin sister."

Panic flashed through Edith's eyes then she seemed to settle into a hazy recognition. "Kayla has a twin sister?" She nodded slowly. "Of course she does. I forgot." She gave a gentle tug on the dog's lead. "It's okay, Troy. Everything's okay."

All Lauren really heard was Edith using present tense as if Kayla was still here. But Kayla had been forced into the past tense, her future snatched away from her, with no present to live in. She shook from deep inside her chest, despair threatening to tear her open.

"We're here to sort out Kayla's apartment." Jamie helped Edith down the two stone steps to the pathway.

"Oh, I see." Edith placed her hand on Lauren's forearm and squeezed lightly. "Kayla is a lovely girl. She's been a wonderful neighbor for me, helping with my shopping and walking little Troy when I was in the hospital on more than one occasion."

Lauren nodded, still unable to speak, and still taken with Edith talking about Kayla as if she was still around. She closed her eyes briefly and took a deep breath. "She told me all about you, Edith."

"All good, I hope. She really is one of those special people."

"She was." Lauren didn't know why she felt the need to correct Edith. Maybe because she wasn't sure if there were memory issues or something more serious. In the next few days of clearing the apartment, Lauren didn't think she could handle it if Edith continued to mistake her for Kayla or if she kept asking when she was coming home.

She was never coming home.

Lauren pushed back the ball of anger that rose to the surface and bobbed about for attention, not quite ready for that stage yet. Moving along the guided path of grief felt like she might be moving farther away from Kayla, and she definitely wasn't ready for that.

Edith rubbed Lauren's arm. "No, sweetheart, she *is* one of those special people. She's still here. *Was* infers Kayla is in the past, but she isn't. She's all around you and all around this town." Edith released Lauren's arm and pressed her hand against Lauren's chest. "She lives on in here too, still working away and keeping you company. That means she's never in your past. Don't forget that."

Edith stepped around Lauren, and she and Troy set off on their walk.

Jamie came up beside Lauren. "Are you okay?"

Lauren took Jamie's hand, needing someone to help ground her, to keep her from dissolving into a mist of tears. "Yeah. I'm fine." She held up the keys and approached the door. "Let's get inside before I change my mind." She opened the main door and took the stairs to the second floor. She pressed her hand against Kayla's door for a moment before she pushed the key in and unlocked it. She waited there, on the threshold of entering all that remained of Kayla's life. "What did Edith mean?"

Jamie placed her hand on the small of Lauren's back. "Mean about what?"

"When she said that Kayla was working in my heart. What does that mean?"

Jamie leaned against the doorjamb and rested her head against the wood. "Edith is a spiritual woman, and she's got an interesting take on death. People often go to her for comfort when they've lost someone. I don't know if you want to hear that sort of thing."

"Have you spoken to her…about your dad?"

Jamie nodded. "Not until I was older, but yeah."

"Did it help?"

"Yeah, it did."

Lauren leaned against Kayla's door and sighed. "I'd like to hear anything that might help with this constricted feeling." She wrapped her arms around herself. "It's like there's a belt around my chest. It's hard to breathe. I want to scream, but it won't come out. I want to beat my fists against walls until it brings her back, and yet I can't seem to move, like losing her has solidified parts of me and trapped them under the concrete of my soul." She swallowed hard. "So, anything you can share…"

"Okay," Jamie said. "Edith says that your heart is built by the people you love. And that's where they go when they die, and they watch you live out your life. You carry them with you, and they're always there for you, helping you make decisions, helping you face the dark times."

Lauren smiled. "That's a nice way of thinking about it." She pushed away from the door, opened it, and went in. "I mean, I don't know that there's a little ecosystem inside me, where everyone's got their own little house and viewing deck to see what I'm up to, but I get it metaphorically."

Jamie laughed and followed her in. "That would be cool, though."

"Wouldn't it? Especially if they had an internal communication system that went directly to my brain. Kayla could send messages to tell me not to do stupid things." Lauren stepped closer to Jamie and caressed her cheek. "Or she could tell me to do the things that scared me when I hesitated."

She pulled Jamie into a long kiss, ignoring her own fear that she was doing the wrong thing and shouldn't be letting herself feel what she was beginning to feel for Jamie. She let herself go, ignoring the possibility that she was using Jamie to distract herself from the pain of loss. The taste, the feel, the softness of Jamie's response surprised her. There was such tender hesitancy, almost as if Jamie was unsure that they should be kissing at all. Lauren's stomach flipped at the profound emotion that swamped her mind, while her core throbbed at the promise of more than a kiss. She pulled away and hooked her finger in the V of Jamie's shirt. "Thank you again for coming with me to do this."

"Um, no problem. Really. It's fine. Happy to do it."

Lauren smiled. "You're rambling."

"You're beautiful."

Lauren sighed and turned away to finally face what she'd been avoiding. She inhaled deeply, and Kayla's scent filled her nose. She couldn't describe it, couldn't put words to the feelings it evoked, except that it was extremely comforting.

Kayla's place was messy-tidy in that way where Kayla would've known exactly where everything was even though none of it was ordered in any logical manner. Stacks of books covered the carpet in front of the TV and the main window, while her bookcase was stocked with DVDs, terrible crafty things by her young students, and souvenirs of her trips, mainly to Boston. The walls were covered with paintings and photos of the family. Lauren picked up the Red Sox baseball and turned it over and over in her palm.

Jamie wandered past Lauren toward the kitchen. She took off her backpack and pulled a carton of milk from it. "Shall I make coffee?"

A simple yes should have been easy to say, but Lauren wanted to look around the apartment properly one time before anyone began to move anything.

Jamie crossed the room and put her hand on Lauren's waist. "Are you sure you want me to stay with you? It's okay if you need me to leave."

Lauren shook her head. "I just want to walk around for a little while."

"Okay. Just talk to me, Lauren. If it gets too much, or if you need me to leave, you can say anything to me, I promise. I understand." Jamie gestured outside. "I'll go and get the flatpack boxes and tape, and then I'll wait on the sofa, if that's okay?"

"Sure. Thank you." Of course Jamie understood. She'd experienced an unimaginable loss at a young age, and she'd coped with it. She dealt with grieving people every day at work. She really did understand. Lauren straightened. She could do this.

She spent the next twenty minutes slowly circling the apartment, starting with the kitchen, then moving onto the living room, the bathroom, and the guest room. She appreciated Jamie staying silent the whole time, though once she'd returned with the boxes and parked herself on Kayla's sofa, Lauren didn't miss her regular glances of concern, as if she was ready to swoop to the rescue if Lauren faltered. She hovered in front of the shelving where their childhood copies of the Dr. Seuss books sat. *Don't cry because it's over. Smile because it happened.* It would be a long, long time before she could heed that advice.

Lauren repeated her circuit three times before she finally opened the door to Kayla's bedroom and walked in. She approached the modest two-door closet in the corner of the room—Kayla had never been interested in fashion. She'd marveled at the number of shoes, boots, sandals, and tennis shoes Lauren had, while Kayla only owned two pairs of boots, brown and black, and the same in shoes and sandals. When Lauren opened the closet door, it was as if Kayla had walked in, her scent was that strong. It made Lauren want to seal the clothes in airtight containers to preserve it, so that when she was missing her in the weeks, months, and years to come, she could open one and take a hit. She could revel in the memories it brought forth and be comforted by Kayla's presence.

She lifted a jacket sleeve to her nose and pressed it to her nose. It was Kayla's favorite jacket, a DKNY one she'd gotten for fifteen dollars, down from four hundred, in a Macy's sale nearly ten years ago. Lauren had offered numerous times since to replace it with the latest version, but Kayla said the threadbare sleeve edges and tiny holes from excessive wear gave it character.

Lauren wiped away the escaping tears and closed the closet door. She sat on the edge of the double bed and flopped back onto it. She pulled a pillow to her chest, spooning it like it was a real person, like it was Kayla. They'd slept like that so many times as kids when they camped out in the backyard on cool spring evenings. Lauren squeezed the pillow tighter and buried her face in another one. "I miss you, Kayla," she whispered. "We still had so much to do together."

Their hub plans popped into her head. A legacy. It was a chance to be all over this town, just like Edith had said. It would be a fitting memorial to a woman who'd dedicated her life to improving the education of the kids here. Kayla would want that rather than Lauren sobbing into her bedsheets.

"Hey," Jamie said gently.

Lauren uncurled herself from around the pillow and patted the bed. Jamie came over and sat beside her. "I need to find something."

"Okay."

"Kayla and I talked about building a literacy hub in town, something big enough to cater to the kids here and to get them here from all the small towns within driving distance." Lauren took a tissue from the box on Kayla's bedside and dabbed the tears from her eyes and cheeks.

"That sounds amazing. The young people around here would have really benefited from something like that." Jamie tucked her leg under her butt and scooted around to face Lauren properly. "It's a shame you didn't get to do it."

"I'm thinking of adding a play area and game fields so it would appeal to kids who express themselves through sports and don't read much. Initially, the game time would be a reward, but slowly they'd read and write without that incentive."

"Wow. You're actually thinking of going through with it?"

Lauren propped herself up on the pillow. "I am. We talked about it so much…" The weight of what she was thinking of doing caught her unawares. "I kept putting her off. I always had a project with work that I thought was more important." She let the tears continue to fall. "I never made the time, and now Kayla doesn't have any time at all. Do you think it's too late?"

Jamie grasped her hand. "No, I don't. If you believe old Edith, then Kayla will still see you building your dream." She rubbed her thumb along the back of Lauren's hand. "Seems like it would be a huge project. Is that something you'd be here for, or would you be able to manage it from Boston?"

Jamie didn't make eye contact, and Lauren thought she might know why. They hadn't spent much time together, but when they had, it had been intense and laden with possibilities. Jamie wanted more, and Lauren couldn't deny that she felt the same. What she was proposing was a huge project, Jamie was right. She'd need six months of fundraising before she could even break ground, and that's if the permits were all in place. Six to twelve months to build, and then furnishing and decorating would take another couple of months. Meetings, recruitment, long-term planning. There was so much to it—which was why she'd never gotten around to doing it with Kayla. The size of the project didn't worry her, nor did the cost. She was sure she could pull it off and get the financing in place. But would it tie her to Damarron in a new way that she wasn't comfortable with? Kayla was supposed to run it once it was completed, and Lauren was supposed to return to work in Boston or whichever city the next big challenge resided. But if she created something fresh and exciting here, would she want to stay for a few years to watch it flourish? And in the time it would take to get the project completed, traveling between Boston and Damarron, how would that change her relationship with Jamie?

"What makes you ask that?" Lauren asked.

Jamie glanced up at her. "You're going to make me say it?"

"Saves any embarrassing misunderstandings, doesn't it?" Lauren screwed up the damp tissue and tossed it aside.

Jamie sighed. "I'm asking because I'd like to know if I can get excited about the possibility of you sticking around here for a while longer."

"You'd be excited by that prospect, would you?" It appealed to Lauren too, but she was just beginning the implementation of the biggest project of LitLot's history. Now wasn't the best time to leave them rudderless and looking for a replacement. She looked around the room and saw Kayla in every design choice, every stick of furniture, every photo on the wall. Kayla's time was up, and she never saw it coming. If she'd known, what would she have wanted to achieve before she was gone? Would their dream of the literacy project have been on that list? Was there ever a best time for anything? Or was life best lived by simply *doing* and not waiting for the perfect time that might never come? Lauren had spent her life planning, doing, and achieving, and making sure everything fit into neat little packages of managed time.

She looked deep into Jamie's eyes and saw hope, desire, and need. Jamie had crushed on Lauren all her school life and the timing had never been right for her to tell Lauren how she felt. Fifteen years later, they were tentatively getting to know each other, but it was as if they'd been friends for years. Their time together was easy and stimulating, fun and challenging. What if Lauren had died before she'd had the chance to go on a date with a woman she'd known all her life and yet not known at all? It was all about timing. It was everything and nothing at all. It could be wasted or spent wisely. What choice was Lauren supposed to make? If she chose to live as if she were dying, the only time to concentrate on was the here and now. No time frittered away. No putting off the important stuff. Kayla dying was beginning to affect her in ways she hadn't anticipated.

Lauren had recruited Whit to be her successor, and she was ready to take that step up even if she didn't realize it herself. That would leave Lauren free to make the literacy hub happen.

But if there was one thing Lauren didn't do, it was make life-changing decisions without careful consideration. Sitting in her sister's apartment with grief filling every aspect of her being wasn't the time for something so pivotal. "I'd probably have to be here sometimes, yes. But I could also recruit a project manager to take care of everything on this end and run the financing from Boston. I suppose it would depend."

"On whether or not you could stand to be confined to this town for a large chunk of time?" Jamie smiled, but it looked a little rueful.

"There are lots of things to consider." Lauren sat up as the organizer part of her brain overrode the despairing side that wanted to wrap herself in Kayla's comforter and lay there all evening reminiscing about all the wonderful adventures they'd had together. "My dad said that Kayla had a file full of plans, and drawings, and permits details. I want to find that first."

Jamie smiled. "And everything else?"

Lauren scooted off the end of the bed and got up. She didn't want to think about packing Kayla's world into crappy cardboard boxes when she was focused on their dream project, which of course was also a distraction from *having* to think about packing up Kayla's apartment. "One thing at a time."

Jamie smiled and nodded, again lacking judgment or comment and seeming to understand that Lauren needed to do this at her own pace. Lauren came around from the bottom of the bed and pulled Jamie to her feet. "How about you start making up the boxes while I find what I'm looking for, then we'll have a few hours packing." She checked her watch. "Or maybe just a couple of hours."

"Remember I have coffee. And Mom's walking Olly tonight, so I'm happy to be here until midnight if that's what you need."

Lauren ran her finger across Jamie's lips. She didn't expect Jamie's guttural groan and half-lidded eyes in response, and she clenched her thighs. "You're so wonderful. Thank you again for doing this," she whispered.

Jamie bit her bottom lip. "It's no problem, honestly."

Lauren refocused on what they were supposed to be doing. Her emotions and hormones were all over the place; one minute she wanted to break down and cry, and the next she wanted to push Jamie onto her back and see what other sounds she could get her to make. She supposed it was a good sign that she wasn't disconnecting from the world, which had been her first response when she'd gotten the news of Kayla's death.

She tilted her head toward the kitchen. "Coffee."

Jamie snapped her eyes wide and saluted. "Yes, ma'am."

Lauren tapped Jamie's chest lightly. "Less of the ma'am. I'm not old enough for that title, thank you very much."

Jamie grinned. "My apologies, miss."

Lauren leaned closer and kissed Jamie softly. "Get in that kitchen. I'm thirsty."

"No problem."

Lauren watched her walk away. Specifically, she watched Jamie's ass as she walked away. She never had been able to resist that butchy swagger. She looked around the bedroom again and dismissed the possibility that the paperwork might be in here. More likely, it was in the living room around Kayla's desk area. She went back in, pulled out Kayla's office chair, and sat down. Kayla's favorite coconut wood fountain pen sat neatly on a legal pad. Lauren picked it up and held it tightly in both hands. The pen had been Lauren's gift to Kayla when she got her first teaching job, and it had cost Lauren half a week's paycheck. She'd miss searching for things that Kayla would love. Christmas wouldn't be the same. And celebrating their birthday might never be possible again.

Jamie placed a steaming cup of divine-smelling coffee on a glass coaster beside her. She put her hands on Lauren's shoulders and kissed the top of her head. Lauren closed her eyes and allowed herself a small smile. Losing Kayla had broken her heart. But finding Jamie gave her some hope that it might one day be whole again.

CHAPTER SIXTEEN

JAMIE SOLDERED THE FINAL leaf into place and stepped back. She'd been working on the sculpture for two weeks and was relatively happy with the final product. It was the first time she'd attempted a tree, but her mom had specifically asked for it as her fiftieth birthday gift. Jamie looked over at the giant photograph she'd taken of the willow tree at the cemetery and then back at her creation. It was pretty accurate, right down to the gnarly bend in the trunk. Her mom had to see it now so she could decide if she wanted it painted or left natural.

Jamie pulled out her phone, fired off a quick text to her mom, and walked around the protective shield to where Olly sat on the threadbare old armchair from her dad's den. She tickled him behind his ear, and he rubbed against her hand appreciatively. Jamie had covered the armchair with a blanket to protect it, but it had been nearing a trip to the junkyard even before her dad's death. After he'd passed, there was no way Jamie would throw it away. He'd spent hours in that chair, and she'd spent hours on his knee as he read her stories of mythical beasts and furies in faraway lands. She thought he might've hoped those books would inspire her, and she would leave this town, go to college, and do something different, but that had been his dream, never hers. She was third-generation Nelson in Damarron, and she was happy there. She liked this community, liked knowing the names of all the shop owners on Main Street, and she loved the fairs, and farmer's markets, and fundraisers that brought everyone together. She couldn't—and didn't want to—imagine living in a big, anonymous city where people were too busy with their own lives to spare the time for a conversation with a stranger. There *were* no strangers in Damarron, and that's how Jamie liked it.

And even if she'd wanted to leave, there was the fact that she wasn't intelligent enough to go to college. Jamie had struggled through school and only scraped by with Terri's help and patient tutoring. She smiled when she thought about Terri and the bright new future she'd been presented with. Lauren had given Jamie a whole pack of information on mature students and scholarships, and when Jamie had dropped it off with Terri that morning, the glee and excitement in her expression were clear. She'd stuffed the folder into her bag and said she'd read it at work. It was less than two hours later before Jamie received a text, detailing the colleges Terri had been applying for and something about early action by November.

Jamie squatted on an upside-down paint can and stroked Olly's back. He promptly shifted around so she could tickle his belly. "You're so easy." Jamie had to admit to being a little envious of Terri's prospects, but if anyone should be making use of their potential and talent, it was Terri. Now that she had revealed she had aspirations beyond Damarron, Jamie was sorry that Terri had wasted over ten years of her life stuck in a grocery store. She'd sacrificed her own dreams for the benefit of her family and had lost so much time.

Jamie glanced around the barn and the many pieces she'd created over the past decade. Everything before that had been stowed in the adjacent shed because she'd run out of room in here. Was this her dream? "This is just junk, Olly."

He whined and hooked his paw over her arm to keep her in prime tickling position. She loved this place. It had everything she needed, and she'd never felt the desire to leave, but there was a subtle stirring in the back of her mind that was challenging those beliefs. Jamie didn't need to have Terri's IQ to understand what was going on.

Lauren Gray.

She'd swept back into town, glamorous even in grief, and a shining example of life beyond Damarron, of all that could be had and achieved in the wider world. She was a whirlwind. She'd shaken things up for Terri, and she'd gotten Jamie thinking about the useless collection of metal around her and what she should be doing with it. But Jamie liked her work at the cemetery. It was safe and comforting, and it kept her close to her dad. The stuff she messed around with in the barn was exactly that—stuff she messed around with and nothing more.

Yesterday, Lauren had talked about bringing her entourage to Damarron to build the dream she and her sister had shared. Jamie had to use all of her self-restraint not to jump up and down on Kayla's bed. What had started as her having the courage to finally act on her high school crush had developed into some of the best times of her life. And she'd been trying hard to be okay with knowing that the Lauren Gray show would swing out of town in a couple of weeks and leave Jamie to return to her reality. She wanted to enjoy the time she was having, time she never thought she'd get.

But this new possibility of Lauren staying for longer, for more conversation, more kisses, and hopefully, the whole nine yards, was something Jamie wanted more than anything she could ever remember wanting. She rubbed Olly's belly harder, and his leg began to kick in response. He jumped up and ran out the door. "Something I said?"

A few seconds later, her mom's heels clicked down the driveway. Olly had heard her way before she had. The barn door opened wider, and her mom came in, followed by their mutt.

"Is it finished?" Her mom clasped her hands together and grinned.

Jamie pushed up from her makeshift seat. "It's complete, but it might not be finished."

Her mom frowned. "That's not cryptic at all. Can I see it or not? I know it's not my birthday until Friday, but I promise I'll act surprised when I unwrap it in front of everyone."

Jamie wagged her finger. "No way are you opening this in front of anyone."

Her mom rolled her eyes. "It's *my* gift. I'll show it to anyone who'll look. I think your art is amazing." She peered over Jamie's shoulder. "Come on, let me see it."

Jamie moved into her mom's eyeline. "I've finished putting it together, but I need to know if you'd like it painted." She wrinkled her nose. "I know how much you like your bling." She'd do it, even though the idea of spraying it gold was beyond bad taste. Her mom liked what she liked, and it *was* her half-century birthday.

Her mom clapped her hands. "Come on, daughter, let me see."

"Follow me." Jamie turned and beckoned her mom around the heavyweight tarpaulin hanging from the ceiling. "Here you go." She didn't know what reaction she was expecting from her mom, but it hadn't been silence. Her mom and silence were distant friends, at best. Jamie closed her eyes and blew out a long breath. She was stupid to think she could create something her mom would be happy with. Maybe Simon had some more of those crazy-expensive roses in.

Jamie slowly turned to face her mom. She'd clasped her hands over her mouth and tears streamed down her cheeks. "I'm sorry, Mom. I tried my best." She shrugged. "Now you know why I didn't want anyone else to see it. I'm not an artist."

Her mom shook her head, dropped her hands from her mouth, and pulled Jamie into a hug. "Jamie, it's absolutely beautiful. How can you not see that?" Her mom gave her a tight squeeze then released her and moved Jamie aside. She leaned closer to the sculpture and gently ran her fingers along its trunk. "It almost feels like the bark, baby."

Her mom circled the table it sat on, and more tears fell to the ground. Olly wound himself around her feet and whined quietly. Jamie dropped to her knees and ruffled his collar. "It's okay, Olly. Everything's okay."

Her mom grasped a handful of Jamie's T-shirt and pulled her up. She wrapped her arms around Jamie again and squeezed so tight, Jamie coughed. "Christ, Mom, you're going to break my ribs."

Her mom released her and slapped her shoulder. "Don't be so dramatic." She cupped Jamie's cheek. "I love it, honey. It's perfect. I've got so many great memories of willow trees. It'll be like having your dad back in the house."

Jamie stuck her fingers in her ears. "Don't tell me that story again, please. I don't want my ears to melt."

"For a young woman, you're such a prude."

"Trust me, Mom, *no one* wants to know about their parents' sex life. No. One."

Her mom shook her head. "Well, anyway, it's stunning." She wiped away the last of her tears. "Your dad would've been so proud of you."

Jamie picked up a pair of snub-nosed pliers to occupy her hands. "Do you think so?"

"I know so. You're a wonderfully kind and generous person, Jamie. And you *are* an artist, I don't care what you say."

Jamie picked at the edge of the table with the pliers and avoided her mom's intense stare. "You don't think he would've been disappointed that I'm just a gardening grave-digger?"

"You could never have disappointed him, honey. You were his sunshine." Her mom narrowed her eyes as she put her fingers underneath Jamie's chin and tilted her head up to face her. "What's making you think such things after all this time? Has someone said something? Whose ass do I have to kick?"

Jamie laughed. "No one has said anything. What's going on with Terri has gotten me thinking about my own life, that's all."

"What *is* going on with Terri? Has that brother of hers gotten the family in debt again?" Her mom walked back around the tarp and dropped into the armchair. "That boy was born a menace and just grew bigger."

Olly trotted with her and put his head on her lap. Jamie dropped the pliers on her bench and followed. She took up her paint bucket seat again and brought her mom up to speed on Terri applying for college.

"That's good news…isn't it?"

"It absolutely is. I mean, obviously, I'm going to miss her. She's been one of my best friends since I was five, and we've been through a lot together." Like years of bullying, Jamie's dad's death, her coming out, and all the crazy shit Terri's brother had put their family through.

"But it'll be like breaking up the band," her mom said. "Are *you* thinking about college?"

Jamie laughed at the unmissable disbelief in her mom's voice. "To do what? Manicure their lawns and bushes?" Though some of the country's colleges had gorgeous gardens that she'd love to tend.

"No need to be a smart ass." Her mom examined her nails. "Speaking of manicures, I need to get mine done before Friday's little party." She gestured to the metal work all around her. "People go to college for more than brainiac stuff, you know. You could study art."

Jamie shook her head. "I have zero desire to sit in a classroom ever again. I had enough of that at school." She looked around at her work. "I'm happy playing around like I do. It's nothing serious."

"But it could be, couldn't it? Has Lauren got you thinking about doing something with all of this? I heard her cooing all over it the other night."

Jamie frowned. "You could hear her?"

"I live next door, of course I could hear her. She wasn't exactly being quiet."

Jamie thought back to the previous Saturday. Sure, Lauren had been vocal in her praise, but she hadn't exactly been shouting from the barn's rooftop. "What else do you hear, bat ears?"

Her mom grinned and stroked Olly's ears. He smacked his chops and nuzzled in closer. "Don't worry. It's not like I listen in when you've got gentlelady callers. I just happened to be outside having a smoke."

"Oh god, Mom! Now I'm glad I don't bring people home that often."

"You know that's weird, don't you? What do you even say to them? 'Let's go to your place because I don't want my mom to hear us?' I could keep my windows closed. You just have to warn me."

"Mom! Can we stop talking about my non-existent sex life, please?"

Her mom laughed. "Speaking of which, have you invited Lauren to my party?"

Jamie rubbed the back of her neck. "No. I wanted to check it was okay with you first."

"It's more than okay with me, and you didn't have to check. You can bring whoever you want. I'm looking forward to talking to Lauren."

"Why?"

"Because I want to know what her intentions are toward my daughter, what do you think?" Her mom rolled her eyes. "Because it'll be nice to talk to someone new, that's why. Invite her parents too, if they're ready for the community again. It might still be too soon, but distraction can help a little with the daily grief."

Jamie wrinkled her nose, unconvinced, and wondered if she should put Lauren through a mom interrogation. She was even less sure about Lauren's parents being interested in coming. But Jamie didn't want to miss any opportunity to see Lauren, so she reasoned that her mom would probably be too caught up with her own friends to terrorize Lauren much. "She's still a little shaky about her sister, so maybe don't talk about Kayla."

"Honey, I've been on this ball of dirt for nearly fifty years. I know how to conduct myself around people who are grieving."

Jamie held up her hands. Of course she did. Losing the love of her life was good practice. "Okay, okay, I'm sorry. I know you do."

"Terri and Fran are coming, aren't they?"

Jamie nodded.

"Good. I'll try really hard not to embarrass you at my own party." Her mom patted Olly's head and stood up. "Come on, boy. Let's go for a walk."

"Mom, what about the tree? If you want it painted, I need to know now so I can get it started tonight."

Her mom ruffled Jamie's hair. "I want it just the way it is. Like I said, it's perfect, honey."

"You're still not opening it in front of everyone."

Her mom shook her head. "So many rules." She pointed to Jamie's phone on another paint can beside her dad's armchair. "Text Lauren and ask her to come on Friday. See you later, honey."

"Night, Mom." Jamie waited until her mom was out of sight before she switched seats and flopped back in the armchair. A spring prodded her butt cheek, reminding her she needed to get some fresh stuffing. She picked up her phone and began to text Lauren before deciding she wanted to hear her voice instead. She pressed the call button and waited. And waited. She was about to give up when Lauren answered, sounding breathless.

"Have you been running?" Jamie retrieved a piece of stray metal wire from the floor and began to wind it around her finger.

"Yeah. I was downstairs with Edith when you called."

"You heard your phone from two floors down? How loud is your ringtone?"

"My watch buzzed to let me know so I ran upstairs. Lucky I'm in flats."

"Would you still have run up if you were wearing heels?" Jamie had a mental picture of Lauren tearing up the stairs in four-inch stilettos.

"Maybe. You'd be surprised what I can do in heels."

The image in Jamie's mind quickly degraded into something else when she thought of Lauren naked but for heels. "Uh, yeah? I bet. Listen, I'm sorry I couldn't help earlier, but I'm free for the rest of the night."

"You're all done with your mom's gift?"

Jamie unwound the wire from her thumb and began to fashion it into a heart. *Oh my god.* "Yep. She doesn't want it to be painted, which I'm relieved about."

"Why? Don't you like painting? Do you prefer to keep the metal raw?"

"It's not that. My mom's got strange taste. She likes things sparkly and gold…and glittery. It would've broken my heart to do it, but if that's what she wanted—"

"You would've done it. You're so sweet."

Jamie's cheeks flushed, making her glad she wasn't face-to-face with Lauren. "So, would you like my help, or are you done for the night?" Jamie glanced at one of the wall clocks she'd made. It was nearly eight. "Haven't you been there since you left the cemetery at noon?"

"I have, but I've made really good progress. I'm going to give it another couple of hours. If you're sure you don't mind, I'd like the help *and* the company. And maybe that special coffee brew you made too."

Jamie smiled. "I really don't mind. I can be there in twenty minutes.

But I have something to ask you before I forget."

"Ask away."

"Would you come to my mom's birthday bash with me on Friday? I understand if it's not your thing. It's very low-key. And Mom will probably be embarrassing and ask you all sorts of questions you don't want to answer. So, you can say no. That would be fine."

Lauren laughed. "Have you finished rambling, Nervous Nellie?"

Jamie smacked her palm to her forehead. She was sure she'd been at least a little smooth with women before Lauren came back into her life. Where was that hiding? "I have."

"I'll come with you if you come with me to Boston on Saturday. I want to take you to a special steak restaurant you'll love."

Boston was over seven hundred miles away. Even by US standards, that was pushing it, no matter how good the steak was. "You want to fly me to your city?"

"Yes. I thought we might stay overnight and fly back Sunday afternoon."

Jamie leaned back in her armchair and tried to process Lauren's words. "You mean, in a hotel? Like separate rooms, or twin beds? What am I thinking? You've got a place in Boston. I'd be happy on the couch, or I could get a hotel room. You probably don't want me drooling on your couch."

"I mean, let's stay together in the same room *and* the same bed."

Jamie's mouth filled with imaginary cotton, making it impossible to speak. *The same bed.* That's what she heard. It couldn't have been anything else. Lauren always spoke clearly, though her voice had gone a little huskier and quieter when she'd delivered that line, though it was less of a line and more of a knockout punch.

"Jamie? Are you still there?"

Jamie cleared her throat. "Uh, yeah. I'm here. I think. Or I could be in a dream and don't realize I'm asleep, because it sounded like you just asked me on a date that will definitely end in us sleeping together, no matter how many stupid things I say."

"Oh, I don't know. If you said something *really* stupid, I could just leave you at the hotel and go to my apartment." Lauren laughed gently. "But you've got nothing to worry about. Almost everything that comes out of your mouth is charming and adorable."

"I guess." Jamie blew out a breath. Lauren befuddled her. That's exactly what Lauren did, befuddled her. Her chances of getting through her first sexual encounter with Lauren smoothly were impossible. Some stupid, inappropriate, or misplaced quip was inevitable.

"I could always gag you, if you're that worried, but that seems like an awful waste of your sweet mouth."

Jamie pulled the phone away from her ear and looked at the display. Yep, it was Lauren. Talking dirty to her. Despite being seated, her legs went rubbery. And a hotel? Somehow, that made the whole trip sexier than if Lauren had invited her to her home. *Say something.* "That sounds great, I'd love to. Come to Boston and stay, I mean. Not the gag."

Lauren chuckled softly. "You're so easy."

Easy? Nothing about this was going to be easy. When they'd been in school, how many nights had Jamie's sleep been plagued with dreams of Lauren? How many times as a teen in her sexual awakening had she touched herself while thinking of Lauren? And now it was actually going to happen? She imagined her head cartoon-exploding. "Apparently I am if I'm going to bed with you on the third date." *There you go. You can perform under pressure. Oh Christ, the pressure.*

"Technically, it'd be our second date, so yeah, you are easy," Lauren said. "Do I need to bring anything on Friday?"

"No, just you is gift enough." *For me.*

"I'll bring wine. It's not good form to show up to a party empty-handed."

"There's no need. I've got everything covered." Jamie slapped her palm against her forehead. "Damn, I nearly forgot. Mom asked me to see if your parents might want to come too, you know, if they wanted. No obligation, of course. Only if they were ready for something like that."

"I'll ask, but I'm not sure what they'll say."

Lauren's hesitancy was clear, and Jamie regretted extending the invitation. She should've just told her mom she'd asked, and they'd politely declined. But in a town this tight, the truth would eventually come out, and her mom wouldn't be impressed. "It's okay. Mom understands what they're going through... what you're all going through." Jamie swallowed hard. "So do I," she whispered and ran her hand over the arm of her dad's chair the way she'd watched him do hundreds of times. But not enough times.

"Are you still coming over?" Lauren asked after a small silence.

Jamie pushed up from the chair and glanced at herself in one of her handmade mirrors. Denim shirt over white tank, faded jeans, and Converse boots. She didn't look too scruffy, and she was helping pack, not taking Lauren for dinner. "I can be over in ten if I don't change, twenty if I grab a quick shower and clean myself up."

"Don't change," Lauren said and hung up.

Don't change. She felt herself changing more every second she spent with Lauren. Her general disenchantment with finding love, with finding *the one*, began to change the moment Lauren said yes to going out with her. Jamie had tried to find someone she could live with over the years, but if she was truly honest, she'd compared them all to Lauren and none of them had measured up. Which was a stupid concept since she and Lauren had never even been together, and Jamie had built an idea of who Lauren was based on a young woman she hadn't seen for over a decade. Strange thing though, Lauren was showing herself to be everything Jamie had imagined and more.

Don't change. Her tidy, safe life in the boundaries of her small hometown had begun to morph with possibilities. Big, scary possibilities she didn't feel ready for. She couldn't possibly be enough for someone as dynamic and ambitious as Lauren, the same woman who'd left this town in her dust as soon as she was old enough.

Jamie flicked off the barn light and strode up the driveway. She wasn't ready for any of it, but she wasn't about to run away from it either.

CHAPTER SEVENTEEN

"YOU CAN STILL BACK out if you don't feel like coming, Mom. Jamie's mom would understand." Lauren fixed her dad's tie properly and smoothed it down. Years of dating smart-looking butches had turned her into quite the necktie expert. She drifted briefly into wondering what Jamie might be wearing this evening and dared to hope that her outfit would include a neatly ironed button-down shirt and tie to give her a dashing look. The one she'd secreted in her glove compartment the first time they'd gone out would do just fine. Lauren made a mental note to tell Jamie what the dress code for the restaurant tomorrow was, and then she'd be guaranteed a shirt and tie combination at least once. Undressing a woman in that kind of outfit had always been a hotspot for Lauren. And she hadn't waited this long to sleep with anyone since…ever.

Sex hadn't been at the top of her priority list of feelings for almost three weeks now. Honestly, she hadn't thought about it at all and probably wouldn't have now if it hadn't been for Jamie's presence. She was beginning to complicate things—immensely—but Lauren didn't want to contemplate those things right now. She just wanted a little distance from the grieving and a project to occupy her mind. She'd get the first tonight at Jamie's mom's party, and the second one tomorrow after the restaurant, if everything went according to plan. Morten Thomz had seemed as excited about Jamie's work as she was when they'd Zoomed a few days ago, and he'd cleared his schedule to meet them for drinks. All Lauren had to do was keep the surprise a secret. *All* she had to do. It was a big ask. She was energized with the possibilities for Jamie's art and her future, and she wanted desperately to share it with her. Lauren couldn't wait to see Jamie's face when they met with Morten. And with Teresa leaving in a few months, Lauren hoped Jamie would be able to see how her own life could change.

"Where did you learn how to tie a Windsor knot?" her dad asked.

Lauren focused on him again. "I've had lots of practice. You should see me with a bow tie. I bet I could beat Simon in a speed tie race."

Her dad chuckled. "I'm sure you could. How many bowties can one guy own?"

"Right?" Every day she'd been in for flowers, he wore a different one. "You haven't said anything. You don't have to come to this if you're not ready, you know?"

He nodded. "I know that. And you know that you wouldn't be able to force your mother to do anything she didn't want to do. She wants to show a brave face. And she wants to take any opportunities you give us to spend time with you."

Lauren clenched her jaw. She had no idea her continued absence had been such a strain on them both. With Kayla staying close by, she'd thought they were happy with their own company and glad she was living the life she'd always dreamed of. She was doing good work. Weren't they proud of all she'd achieved? Weren't they proud of her?

Her dad put his hands on her shoulders and looked at her seriously. "That's not a guilt trip, Lauren. Don't ever think that. We just miss you, and when you're here, we want to squeeze every last drop from the visit."

She wanted to say that this wasn't a visit. It wasn't her choice. There was no way she would've stayed here for three days, let alone three weeks, if given an option. But her sister had died. And that had hit her in unimaginable ways, wrecked her in ways she was struggling to comprehend, and it had ruined her in ways she had yet to face. The way-too-familiar sting of tears assaulted her eyes, and she looked at the ceiling and tried to blink them away. Her makeup was waterproof, not floodproof, and she wanted to make it through one night without another box of Kleenex.

"Is Mom angry with me?" She shouldn't have asked. She might not like the answer. And it would make the car ride over to Jamie's and the ensuing evening more than awkward.

"Why would you think such a thing?" He rubbed her shoulders and shook his head. "Losing her youngest… Parents shouldn't have to bury their children, sweetheart. This is hard on all of us, but it's hardest on your mom."

Lauren took a deep breath. Grieving wasn't a competition. It wasn't measured in the gallons of tears shed or the highest decibel scream of agony. "We're together in this though, Dad. There's no hierarchy of pain.

We can't compare the sense of loss we all feel." She stepped back. This wasn't the best conversation to be having considering she was hoping for a little reprieve this evening. "Let's not talk about this now."

"Okay. Another time, but soon. Maybe we could come over and help at Kayla's apartment?"

She nodded and headed upstairs to her old room to breathe. She'd done the incriminating evidence sweep she, Whit, and Kayla had promised each other. There was nothing for her parents to find. Lauren had even giggled a little when she found Kayla's collection of sex toys. *They* weren't something she could box up for Goodwill. A retirement home for older lesbians, maybe, but not Goodwill. And she could use the help with Kayla's more personal stuff. She'd been struggling with separating things into piles. What to donate, what to keep, what to throw away. All the things Kayla had collected in her three short decades on this Earth— how was Lauren supposed to make those choices? So many mementoes, special books, photo albums, and music. So many memories that Lauren had to put in a landfill, give to someone else to use, or store in a unit she'd barely visit because she wasn't sure she'd be able to face the onslaught of emotion. Jamie being there had helped keep her sane, and she'd held her through the many bouts of sobbing.

And she was still here, seemingly unfazed by Lauren's breakdowns and totally able to cope with the outpouring of emotion. Jamie Nelson was someone special, and she was better than this backwater. She deserved more. She deserved to *be* more. And sticking around this one-horse town was to deny the world a special talent. Okay, so she was exaggerating slightly, but Jamie's art had so much potential commercially. High-end buyers would eat it up, and Lauren was convinced that Jamie would struggle to keep up with commissions, such would be the demand. Morten shared her belief, and that was as good as a presidential seal of approval.

There was a knock on the door, and Lauren turned to see her mom looking lovely in a light summer dress and heeled sandals.

"Ready when you are, honey."

"You look beautiful, Mom."

Her mom shooed her away with a wave. "This old thing," she said and gave a twirl.

Lauren approached her mom and took her hand. "*Are* you ready?"

Her mom withdrew her hand and cupped Lauren's face. "I might never be ready, Lauren. But I wouldn't miss Val's big birthday."

"I didn't know you two were close." If they'd been close when Lauren was a kid, maybe she and Jamie would've been thrust together earlier and become fast friends. Lauren regretted the comment when her mom raised her eyebrows. Thankfully, she didn't accompany the gesture with a reprimand, though Lauren knew exactly what she was thinking: how could she know they were close when she never came home? If she was going to change one thing after all this settled down and normal life resumed, it would be visiting home on more than just the holidays…or maybe she'd start with sticking around a little longer on holidays to begin with and ease into it.

"Val tells me you and her daughter have been spending quite a lot of time together."

Lauren pressed her lips together to suppress a smile. The mere mention of Jamie's name seemed to get that reaction, but her mom's gentle prod for more information amused her too. The same question twenty years earlier and Lauren would've had a fit, slammed the door, and jumped onto the bed, bemoaning the parental intrusion. Why did she have such a contentious relationship with her parents when Kayla had always been such a good daughter? It was as though Lauren had never really grown out of her sulky teenage phase.

She pulled her mom into a hug. Her mom was a little stiff at first, probably with shock, but she quickly softened and returned the embrace.

"What did I do to deserve that?" she asked when Lauren released her and stepped away.

"What *haven't* you done?" Lauren was strangely overcome with gratitude that she'd never shown and guilt for not showing it before. Her parents had sacrificed so much to make her dreams come true, and she'd repaid them with petulance and continued absence. She became aware of her dad hovering at the top of the stairs.

"Are you ladies ready to go?"

The warmth in his expression indicated that he'd witnessed Lauren's uncharacteristic show of emotion, and she decided to go one step further, hoping her makeup would be up to the task. "Thank you both, for everything you've done for me."

Her mom's lip trembled, and she caressed Lauren's cheek. "We love you, honey."

Her dad stepped closer and put his hands on her mom's shoulders. "I thought we'd lost you, sweetheart."

Lauren frowned. That seemed a strange thing to say. "Lost me?"

"Lost you to the world," he said. "You're doing such wonderful things, and we're so very proud of you. But selfishly, we wish we could have a little more of you and the world had a little less."

Her mom patted his hand. "We miss you, that's all. But we don't want you to change anything. You've got your own life to lead, and you should do what makes you happy. Your dreams have always been too big for this town to have ever been enough for you." She turned her head to Lauren's dad. "We've always known that, and we've always been proud of you for following your heart." She straightened and tapped her watch. "Now, come on, I don't want to be late." She took Lauren's hand. "And you can tell me all about what you and Jamie have been up to."

Lauren sighed, thankful the car journey and thus the interrogation, would take less than ten minutes. It was a beautiful evening, and they could've walked, but she'd worn a pair of her highest heels to impress Jamie. They were far from conducive to a route march across town.

Dutifully and patiently, Lauren answered all of her mom's questions about Jamie and their friendship. She wasn't sure what to call it. She wasn't a fan of labels. They'd only kissed a few times, and that had been all too brief. The first kiss had buzzed with potential, but her mind had been on how she would feel walking into Kayla's apartment for the first time. She hadn't had the mental capacity to process what her growing fondness for Jamie's company might mean.

Her dad dropped her at Jamie's front door after discovering the road was packed with cars, and there were no spaces close by.

"I'll stay with your dad, honey."

"Okay, Mom. See you both in there." Lauren waved them off, a little unsure as to whether they'd just continue driving and go home. In their place, she certainly would have. She admired their fortitude. Facing the community at a celebration less than a month after they'd buried their daughter was going to be hard, she was sure of that. *Parents shouldn't have to bury their children.* Her dad's words echoed in her mind. They'd pull through. Together, they were stronger than platinum.

"Hey, you."

Lauren turned to see Jamie walking up the driveway. Her outfit of shiny brogues, dress pants, button down shirt, and tie didn't disappoint. "You look very handsome."

"And you look stunning." Jamie bit her lip and gestured toward Lauren's heels. "They're gorgeous."

Lauren smiled at the blatant desire in Jamie's eyes and voice. So predictably easy to please. In her experience, the quickest way to a butch's heart had always been a killer pair of heels. *Heart?* Is that what she was aiming for? When had Cupid ridden town and strung up his bow? "Dad's parking the car." She held out the basket her mom had prepared, and Jamie took it.

"I said you didn't need to bring anything other than your," Jamie swallowed hard, "very beautiful self." She scanned the contents. "Wine, cheese, fancy bath products, *and* chocolate? Your mom knows my mom well."

"Right? When did that even happen? And why didn't it happen when we were kids?"

Jamie grinned. "We still wouldn't have had playdates. You would've outgrown me by third grade."

Lauren swatted Jamie's shoulder, and a bolt of desire coursed through her when she registered Jamie's hardness. "You don't know that."

Jamie motioned to the house and held out her other arm. Lauren put her arm in and liked the way holding onto Jamie felt.

"It doesn't matter. I wasn't ready for you back then," Jamie said. "I definitely would've blown it, and you wouldn't entertain talking to me now."

Lauren tugged Jamie's arm gently. "And you're ready for me now?"

A flush colored Jamie's cheeks. "God, I hope so, or tomorrow's going to be a bust."

Lauren stopped. "We don't have to do anything, you know?"

Jamie slipped her hand around the back of Lauren's neck, and a shiver of need pulsed through to Lauren's core.

"Oh, I want to, *and* I have to," Jamie said, looking deep into Lauren's eyes. "Otherwise I might explode."

Jamie pressed Lauren against the doorjamb and kissed her hard, delivering a show-stopping, movie-worthy, breathtaking kiss. Lauren's whole body softened between the immovable brick wall and the incendiary insistence of Jamie's body pressed against her. She needed to sit down before her legs gave way. The sudden shift from Jamie's usual light and airy demeanor to a lustful yearning melted Lauren. Judging by that kiss and the passionate promise in Jamie's words, she couldn't help thinking that when they finally did get to sleep together, *she* might be the one to explode.

CHAPTER EIGHTEEN

"THIS IS THE BEGINNING of the end," Fran said and sat on the rocking chair closest to the firepit.

Jamie gave her a look of disbelief. Terri didn't need additional pressure, given that she was already conflicted about her decision to leave. "I'm thinking of it as the beginning of a new chapter for her." Jamie put her arm around Terri's shoulders and pulled her in for a bro-hug. She released her after the maximum two seconds of body contact Terri tolerated. Jamie grabbed an Adirondack chair, lifted it closer to the fire, and sat. Terri opted for the porch swing a few feet away.

"Still, we should enjoy tonight. It could be the last time we're together like this." Fran raised her wine glass. "To new beginnings."

"That's more like it." Jamie clinked her beer to Fran's and stretched to do the same with Terri. Terri went through the motions, but it was clear she was troubled about the whole situation. "How did your mom and dad take the news?"

"Not great." Terri twisted her beer bottle around and around in her grip and avoided eye contact. "They're worried about Ethan."

"But they're happy for you?" Fran asked.

Terri shook her head. "I don't think I've seen my parents happy for a long time…if ever." She took a long pull on her beer. "At least, not since before the first time they had to declare Chapter 13 bankruptcy."

Jamie recalled the incident and sighed. Terri's parents had remortgaged their house and maxed out their credit cards to finance Ethan's big idea even though Terri had advised them against it. But he was their golden boy and could do no wrong, so they ignored her and backed him. That pattern had continued for the last decade and resulted in Terri not going to college so she could earn a wage and help keep the family from becoming homeless. Jamie had thought about Terri's situation a lot since Lauren had set everything in motion. She wasn't happy with her complete lack of awareness that Terri had buried her academic ambitions so deep that

Jamie had considered her content with her life. She'd been a bad friend and wanted to make up for it by fully supporting her now. Terri would need it, because her parents clearly weren't excited that their main breadwinner would soon stop contributing to clearing up the mess they'd made.

"You're not wavering, are you?" Jamie watched closely for Terri's reaction. She wasn't about to let Terri waste any more of her life and was fully prepared to step in.

Terri pushed herself back and forth on the swing. "I wouldn't call it wavering as much as considering a complete turnaround." She looked at Jamie and shrugged. "It's my family, buddy. You know how important they are."

"I do." Jamie nodded. "I feel the loss of my dad almost every day but, and you're going to think this is harsh, I don't live my life to please my mom, and if Dad was alive, he wouldn't want me to either."

Fran made a cautious mumbling noise, but Jamie ignored her and shifted forward in her seat. "I wished that I'd known earlier that you wanted to go to college and to do something bigger in the world. I can't turn back time, as much as I'd like to for myself as well as you, but I'm not about to let you keep wasting your genius in a grocery store." Jamie leaned back a little, aware she was encroaching on Terri's comfort bubble. "Your Friday night stories are hilarious, of course they are, but, Jesus, someone with your IQ shouldn't be clearing up used diapers behind oats in the cereal aisle."

"To be fair, *no one* should have to clear up used diapers from a cereal aisle," Fran said, and Terri nodded.

"Whatever." Jamie waved her off, slightly irked that Fran had little of use to contribute. She'd always wanted to be a nurse, she'd trained for it, and she'd achieved her goal. She should have more empathy. "I'm saying that you and your brain were made for bigger things than this town could ever give you. Think about all the discoveries and tech advances in the past few decades—what if all those people had stayed in their hometown and not gone to college? All of those people probably had families, Terri. You've sacrificed nearly fifteen years to help them get out of the messes Ethan keeps getting into. Nothing's changed. Nothing will change. They're all going to have to be responsible for themselves now." Jamie took a breath. She could see Terri was taking it onboard, and that's all she could ask. It wasn't like she could dictate anyone's life choices, and she wouldn't want to. But it would be such a waste for Terri not to follow through on her dreams when she'd been given a second chance.

Terri nodded slowly. "I might need you around a little more than usual."

Jamie relaxed back into her chair and smiled. Terri's simple statement was as good as confirmation that Jamie had hit her target, and she didn't have to say anymore.

"What about you?" Fran asked. "When will you be following Lauren Gray to the big city?"

Jamie frowned. She hadn't told them about Lauren's invite for tomorrow. "What are you talking about?"

"Your art, dummy. We've been telling you for years that you were talented, and you've done as much with that as Terri had done with her giant brain. You can't sit there and tell Terri not to waste her genius and then do the same thing yourself." Fran raised her eyebrows and looked to Terri.

Terri tilted her head and raised her beer. "I'll drink to that."

Jamie scoffed. "I wouldn't compare me messing about in my barn to the brilliant things Terri will do."

"No one's saying it's the same," Terri said. "We're just saying that maybe you could do more than you're doing right now too."

Jamie turned her attention to the firepit. "I'm happy doing what I do, where I do it. Some people are made for greatness, but most of us are average, and that's okay."

"Hey."

Jamie looked up to see Lauren standing in the kitchen doorway.

"Saved by the belle," Fran said and laughed. "Come on, that was a good one."

Terri smiled and nodded. "You've got to give her that one. It was sharp."

Lauren stepped out onto the deck. "What do you need to be saved from?"

Jamie joined Lauren and kissed her briefly. "Well-intentioned but overbearing friends."

Terri snickered. "I think you're describing yourself there." She gestured toward Lauren. "Although I could put that down to Ms. Gray's influence."

Lauren brought her hands to her chest. "I won't apologize for wanting people to achieve their potential, especially when their brains have the potential to improve the world for everyone, *Ms. Caddy*."

Terri grinned widely, and Jamie smiled too. It was like a weight had been lifted from Terri's shoulders, and she was lighter, breezier, happier. The thought of someone relying on Jamie to change the world terrified her, but Terri seemed energized and excited by the prospect. They were such different people, it was a wonder they were friends. But wasn't the world a better place because of that variety? Jamie was certain she wouldn't have survived high school if it hadn't been for Terri and Fran. They'd been on her path for a reason, regardless of their incompatibilities.

Jamie looked at Lauren, and her smile grew. Dreams did come true, and this had been hers for a long time. To be standing beside Lauren as…as whatever they were to each other gave her a buzz no alcohol could match. She clenched her thighs together when she thought of their impending night together in Boston. As much as she wasn't interested in big cities, bright lights, and bustling streets, the idea of being away with Lauren made her heart jump and her head explode.

"Oh my god, Jamie, get a room." Fran flicked wine at her.

Lauren wiggled her eyebrows but said nothing.

"As a matter of fact, we've got one—tomorrow night. Lauren's taking me to Boston to a special restaurant." Jamie put her arm around Lauren's shoulder and pulled her close, hoping it wasn't too showy or out of line. Lauren didn't move, and Jamie allowed herself a mental fist pump. "I may even wear a full three-piece suit."

Lauren bumped her hip against Jamie. "You *better* wear a three-piece suit."

Terri and Fran oohed and made way too many other immature noises. Lauren smiled through it all and seemed happy to take Jamie's friends' joking around.

"Anyway," Lauren said and tugged lightly on Jamie's tie. "I came to tell you that your mom is hungry for sugar, and she wants the surprise cake she doesn't know about."

Jamie laughed. "The surprise cake she laid out very specific instructions for, right down to the icing color and decorations? That surprise cake?"

Lauren shrugged. "Could be."

Jamie gestured toward the back door. "After you."

Lauren kissed her gently then smoothed Jamie's tie. "I'm hungry for your sugar," she whispered in Jamie's ear.

Jamie sputtered the beer she'd just taken a drink of. "Wow, that's super corny."

Lauren wrinkled her nose. "Is it though? Or is it super smooth?"

Jamie shook her head. "Not smooth, no. Cute. But not smooth." Jamie was barely through the door when her mom came around the corner into the kitchen and grabbed her hand.

"I've been looking everywhere for you."

Jamie chuckled. "That must've taken you all of thirty seconds in this massive two-bed house."

Her mom squeezed Jamie's hand. "Don't be a smart ass, or I'll open your gift in front of everyone."

"Okay, okay." Jamie released her hand and shooed her mom back out of the kitchen. "Go back to your friends. I'll be out with your surprise cake in a few minutes."

Her mom grabbed a fork from the counter and hurried away. "I'll be waiting with my surprised face," she said, brandishing the fork in the air.

Lauren, Terri, and Fran waited in the doorway.

"Anything we can do to help?" Fran asked.

"Definitely. Could you take those plates and forks in?" Jamie looked at Lauren. "Would you help me carry the cake? Beth might've gone a little overboard, but it *is* for nearly fifty people. Follow me." Jamie walked through to the pantry and opened the door. She breathed a small sigh of relief when she saw the three-tier cake still sitting, pristine and intact on the wheeled-table in the center of the room. Olly had been overly interested when Beth and her chef delivered the cake earlier that afternoon, and he'd patrolled the kitchen as if on sentry duty until Jamie had taken him for a walk. As soon they got back, he returned to lay against the door like a door draft stopper. It was only when one of her mom's friends showed up for the party with her own dog that Olly reluctantly left his post.

Lauren touched the small of Jamie's back. "That could be the biggest cake I've seen outside of a wedding reception."

Jamie caught her breath at her response to Lauren's innocent touch. She was beginning to feel like a desperate, horny teenager. She pushed the resulting images of them in bed together to the back of her mind. This party had been weeks in the making, and Jamie wanted to make sure her mom had the best time. Being distracted with thoughts of having sex with Lauren wasn't the way to stay focused. "What can I say? My mom has a sweet tooth. Her instructions were to get a cake that was big enough for everyone to have a good slice *and* to have half left over for breakfast and dinner for the next two weeks."

"Cake for breakfast? Is there a twelve-year-old stuck in your mom's body?"

Jamie laughed as she began to roll out the table. "Could be."

"I thought you needed help carrying it?"

Jamie grinned. "I just wanted to keep you close."

Lauren shook her head and patted Jamie on the ass. "Are you afraid I'm going to disappear?"

More than you know. Jamie turned and caressed Lauren's cheek. "Maybe. This *is* all feeling a little dream-like. I could wake up or turn into a pumpkin any time now, and you'll be gone. Poof. Smoke. Lauren back to Boston."

Lauren laughed and pulled Jamie close. "*Poof?*"

Jamie's gaze drifted to Lauren's lips, and she swallowed hard. "Yeah, *poof*," she whispered and pressed her mouth to Lauren's. Her heart pounded, and other parts of her pounded harder.

"Have you gone to Beth's to get the cake or what?"

Fran's shout made Jamie jump. She broke away slowly and looked into Lauren's eyes. It was too early to search for *that*, to search for anything other than lust, probably, but Lauren's eyes were breathtaking. So many colors and shades. They were the most unusual eyes Jamie had ever seen, and she couldn't wait to see them drowsy with sated desire.

Jamie gestured to the five boxes of candles and the box of sparklers. "I need your help putting those on." She guided the table from the pantry, and Lauren pushed from the other side.

"I don't think you're going to need matches to light those," Terri said as they went back into the kitchen.

Fran smiled widely. "The whole thing might spontaneously combust."

"Don't be assholes." Jamie rolled her eyes but really, she agreed with them. She'd kept her libido under strict control for the past few weeks, acutely aware of Lauren's vulnerable emotional state. But tomorrow's date was Lauren's idea, meaning she was ready for something more, something physical. Jamie had been ready for that with Lauren since she'd gone through puberty and discovered that girls made her feel funny inside. She was grown now, and while she wouldn't describe what was going on inside as "funny," her stomach was performing quadruple somersaults and triple back pullover twists in anticipation of what was to come. She couldn't ever remember feeling this nervous in her life.

She looked up and met Lauren's gaze over the cake as all four of them emptied a box of candles each and began to carefully place them around the "Happy Half Century" lettering in the center. Lauren smiled softly, and Jamie wanted to know what was going on in her head. She seemed to be fitting in back home so easily, but it was also clear that she was too big for this town, too full of ambition and drive. She was a wild Mustang who needed endless possibilities and no boundaries. The opposite of what Damarron could offer.

When her mom blew out these candles—which she bet would take at least four puffs—Jamie would be making a wish of her own: that tomorrow night would be as perfect as she'd always imagined it could be. Because it might be the only night they'd ever have.

CHAPTER NINETEEN

LAUREN DIDN'T EXACTLY KNOW how she'd expected Jamie to react to her personal tour of Boston's highlights, but she'd hoped for more. She wanted Jamie to be blown away by the place and to already be talking about how she could see herself living there. Lauren hung over the bridge and looked at all the boats wrapped in a white protective coating, like they were waiting for new owners. That's what Jamie seemed to be wrapped in, making herself immune to the city's charms. Lauren was being ridiculous, of course, to think that a Damarron stalwart like Jamie would be so easily swayed to the temptations of the sprawling metropolis, and even more ridiculous for her to be thinking of Jamie living here. Added to that, she was putting way too much pressure on their relationship, which was barely in its embryonic stage. Christ, they hadn't even slept together yet, and she was beginning to plan Jamie's move. In the three weeks Lauren had been back in her hometown, she'd somehow managed to morph into a lesbian cliché. Whit wouldn't be impressed. Hell, Lauren wasn't impressed with herself. Maybe being back on familiar ground would flush out the crazy, and she could go back to being her normal self. She began to think she should've come back a day earlier and spent some time in the office, remembering what it was to be in that high-pressure, quick-fire environment. She had a breakfast meeting with Whit the next morning, but it might not be enough to plug her back into her life fully. With her work on Kayla's apartment almost complete though, it wouldn't be long before she returned permanently. Then she could objectively assess what was going on with Jamie, rather than being led by her… by her what? Heart instead of her head? When had she learned that was such a bad thing?

Jamie approached from the opposite end of the bridge with coffee. She'd very sweetly offered to run back and get one when a jogger had startled Lauren, and she'd thrown her latte in the air. Lauren smiled. Jamie had allowed Lauren to buy her a Boston Red Sox baseball cap, and it looked adorable on her. And in her jeans, snug T-shirt, and boots, she checked off all of Lauren's boxes for sexiness. When she'd picked Jamie up at the ass-crack of dawn to get to the airport, she had been sorely tempted to tell the Uber driver to take them straight to a local motel and order room service instead of heading to Boston. But she'd resisted. And when they got to the hotel, Lauren didn't trust herself to go into the room with Jamie, so they'd left their bags at the reception desk and headed straight out.

"Sorry it took so long. The lines here are crazy. How do you ever get anything done when you have to wait so long for everything?" Jamie handed Lauren her banged up to-go mug.

"I send my assistant out for everything," Lauren said and winked. "That leaves me to get on with the serious stuff."

Jamie held out her arm. Lauren hooked herself on and they walked back toward the hotel.

"Tell me more about the project you're working on right now."

Lauren raised her eyebrows and sighed. She hadn't been working on it much, but she had completed the part she loved the most: the planning and creation of it all. Once a project was up and running, she was happy to let her capable staff tend to the daily grind. It was the crisis work and new initiatives she loved most. Nevertheless, she regaled Jamie with the whole thing, from the kernel of an idea through to its fruition and their hunt for the perfect staff team, which Whit was currently heading up and doing a great job without her. Lauren was proud and disappointed and not for the first time, wondered if she should move on to a new challenge with people who needed her expertise. Maybe she'd done all she needed to do at LitLot. Another NPO, another city, maybe even another country would need her.

"That's impressive. It's no wonder you had to leave Damarron; you've got way too much fire inside for our small town to have ever made you happy."

Lauren didn't miss the hint of sadness in Jamie's voice, but she didn't mention it. The town had been enough for Kayla, but Lauren didn't want to think about that. This weekend was all about the positives and the possibilities. *And* getting to sleep together.

The doorman held open the door for them, and they stepped back inside the hotel.

"Welcome back, ladies. Your luggage is in your room."

The receptionist stopped short of winking, but the gleam in his eye told Lauren how impressed with himself he was for following her simple instructions. "Thank you."

"Enjoy your stay, ladies."

Jamie made a quiet grunt of discontent as she prodded the elevator button. "*Ladies*. Do I look like a lady?" she whispered as they got into the ornately decorated elevator.

Lauren waited until the door had closed before she pushed Jamie against the floor-to-ceiling mirrored wall. "Well, lucky for me you're not a gentleman." She kissed Jamie hard and deep and was satisfied when Jamie softened to her touch.

"I don't have to be one or the other," Jamie said when Lauren pulled away briefly.

Lauren ran her finger from Jamie's lips, down her throat, and to her chest. "What are you then?" She squeezed Jamie's crotch with her other hand and whispered, "I already know you're perfect."

Jamie let out a breathy moan. "I'm yours." She held Lauren's hand and pressed harder.

Lauren traced her tongue over Jamie's lips. "I don't doubt that for a second, but I am intending to claim every inch of you later this evening."

Jamie glanced at the wall clock. "Do we *have* to go to this restaurant? Can't we just order takeout and use each other's bodies as plates?"

Lauren laughed, and the elevator stopped at their floor. She took Jamie's hand and pulled her into the corridor. "Don't you think the wait will make it even more amazing when it actually happens?" Lauren stopped at their door, and Jamie pushed her body against Lauren as she held the keycard to the pad on the wall.

"I've been waiting for over fifteen years," Jamie whispered in her ear. "Don't you think that's long enough?"

Lauren pushed open the door, grabbed a handful of Jamie's T-shirt and dragged her into the room. She closed the door by pressing herself against Jamie, who fell back against it. "That *is* a long time, I agree. But it's only been three weeks for me."

"*Only?*" Jamie put her hands on Lauren's waist and pulled her closer. "How long do you normally make someone wait?"

"I'm not answering that question on the basis that I might incriminate myself." In truth, she wasn't particularly patient when it came to first sex. She had it when it felt right and didn't beat herself up about one-night stands or short-term relationships. She wouldn't be shamed by anyone for being a sexual person.

Jamie wrapped her hand around the back of Lauren's neck. She pulled her into a kiss, and Lauren moaned at Jamie's simple insistence. The kiss deepened, and Lauren pulled away to catch her breath.

"You're not making this easy." Lauren tapped her watch. "We have dinner reservations in an hour, and I want to shower and wash my hair."

Jamie grinned and wiggled her eyebrows. "I'll wash your hair."

Lauren mustered all of her resolve and pressed her hand against Jamie's chest. Against her muscular, hard chest. *Breathe.* "I'll take a raincheck on that, for sure. But when we get back here tonight, there'll be no sleeping. I want you all ways all through the night."

Jamie let out a long, slow breath. "You're killing me."

Lauren laughed gently and ran her fingernail over Jamie's bottom lip. "But what a way to go." She pushed away and did her very best sashay as she walked toward the bathroom. She reached for the door just as Jamie caught her wrist.

Jamie slowly brushed Lauren's hair over her shoulder and exposed her neck. She kissed her and whispered, "Are you sure I can't join you?"

Lauren almost wavered, but she didn't want a quick connection while they were on a schedule. Like Jamie had said, she'd waited years for this, and Lauren wanted it to be worth it. Ten minutes in a wet room didn't fit that bill. She turned to face Jamie, and her resolve faltered a little when she saw the depth of desire in her eyes. "I'm sure. Not because I'm *not* desperate for you, but because I *am* desperate for you. I have a feeling that once we get started, I won't want to stop until my body gives out and runs dry."

Jamie sighed and stepped back. "When you put it like that."

"Just a couple more hours, I promise." Lauren went into the bathroom and locked the door behind her as an extra precaution to keep herself from changing her mind and letting Jamie in. She stripped out of her clothes and turned the shower on extra cold so that it might cool her raging ardor. She didn't hold out much hope.

***

It seemed that Jamie had been saving up all her enthusiasm for the restaurant. Where the city had failed to impress her, the steakhouse blew her away, and she hadn't stopped singing its praises since they'd been seated in a window booth by the exquisitely dressed maître-d'. Lauren imagined that working in a place where they charged three hundred dollars for a steak required an equally expensive work uniform.

Jamie moaned quietly when she took the last mouthful of her medium rare Kobe steak.

"If you don't make noises like that in bed tonight, I'm going to be seriously distressed," Lauren said.

Jamie cocked her head and wrinkled her nose. "After a steak like that, Lauren, I can't promise you a single thing."

"I preferred when you got tongue-tied and nervous." Lauren pouted for effect. "I won't be outdone by a piece of dead animal." She gestured to Jamie's plate but quickly looked away from the pool of blood that was slowly soaking into her fully loaded mashed potatoes.

"That would get your lesbian card revoked for sure, huh?"

Lauren nodded quickly. "Never to be returned. Lifelong exclusion." She pushed away her bowl of strozzapreti pasta, took a sip of the zinfandel their attentive waitress had recommended, and suppressed her own moan of appreciation.

Jamie raised her eyebrow and pointed her fork at Lauren. "I want *that* look all night too."

"Let's get a cocktail at the bar and take a slow walk back to the hotel, and we can give it a damned good shot."

Jamie leaned back in her chair and pressed her hand to her stomach. "The walk sounds like a good idea, but I'm not sure I can fit a cocktail in here. I want to be up all night with you, not with indigestion."

Lauren bit her lip as she glanced at her watch. Morten wasn't due to meet them for another fifteen minutes. She pulled her pasta dish back and picked up her fork. "They've got a great range of whiskey here. I think I spied a bottle of Balvenie on someone's table. A spicy scotch should settle your stomach." She motioned for the attention of the waitress, and she was by their table before Jamie could respond. "Could you bring us two whiskeys, please—whatever you'd recommend."

"Of course. It would be my pleasure."

She quickly went through a variety of questions on background notes and finishes, and after Lauren made it clear she was by no means a connoisseur, the waitress excused herself, saying she had just the right brand in mind.

"Are you trying to get me drunk so you can have your wicked way with me?" Jamie asked when they were alone again. "Because there's really no need. I'm a sure thing." She gestured to her plate. "You didn't even have to buy me this fancy dinner."

Lauren snapped her fingers. "Damn. I wish you'd told me that before we came here. I would've taken you for pizza instead."

Jamie grinned. "Pizza would have been just fine." She sighed and glanced around. "Will you please let me pay the bill?"

Lauren had asked for the menus without prices so that Jamie would choose based on what she wanted and not on the price. Lauren had no doubt that if Jamie *had* seen the cost, she would've insisted on tap water and a baked potato. "I most certainly will not. This was my treat to say thank you for all the support you've given me over the past few weeks. I couldn't have gotten through it without you."

"*That's* what this is about?" Jamie placed her hand over Lauren's. "You definitely don't have to thank me for any of that. Anyone would've done the same."

"But anyone didn't; *you* did." Lauren blinked back the burn of tears and took a moment to breathe. "I'm still crying every day, but I'm crying marginally less, and I think that's got more than a little to do with you." She pulled her hand from beneath Jamie's and interlocked their fingers. "Spending all that time with you, with someone who understood what it's like to lose someone way too soon, has really helped me think about the important things in life and how important it is to live in the moment and enjoy every one of them."

The waitress returned with two glasses of whiskey. "I think this should be perfect, but if it isn't, let me know, and it'll be complimentary."

Lauren thanked her and used her other hand to pick up her drink. "A toast." She waited until Jamie raised her glass. "To second chances and to making the most of the time we have on this cosmic dirtball."

They clinked glasses and sipped. The liquid coursed down her throat and settled like a blanket of fiery comfort on her stomach before its warmth spread through her body. The waitress knew her liquor.

Jamie tilted her head. "I don't know what that is, but it tastes amazing." She locked eyes with Lauren. "*You're* amazing."

The intensity in Jamie's gaze took her breath away. Her eyes revealed so much more than the lust Lauren expected to see. There was a longing, a depth of desire that went beyond physical attraction and hinted at a fire that would burn beyond the initial heat of a new relationship. The look in Jamie's eyes dared Lauren to think that she'd found something and someone special.

A light but insistent tap on the window beside them broke the moment, and Lauren turned her head to see Morten on the sidewalk. He smiled and pointed beyond them as if to say he was coming in, but he had a phone against his ear and motioned that he was wrapping it up. Without knowing it, he'd saved her from delaying the end of their meal any further. She nodded and waved him in.

"Who's that?"

"Morten Thomz. He's an old friend." Lauren tried not to show the excitement that had bubbled up when Morten appeared. It'd been incredibly difficult not to spill the secret and tell Jamie that they were going to meet up with someone who was interested in her art. Lauren couldn't wait to see Jamie's reaction when Morten told her that he wanted to sell her sculptures.

"Big cities aren't as faceless as I expected it to be."

Lauren frowned. "What do you mean?"

Jamie gestured to the spot where Morten had been standing. "You can still run into the people you know even in a huge city like this."

Lauren offered a quick smile and averted her eyes. She hadn't wanted to lie; she'd just wanted this to be a surprise. "I invited him to join us for a drink."

Jamie raised her eyebrows. "What vibe did I give off that made you think I'd be into a threesome with a guy?"

Lauren laughed. "Implying that you'd be into a threesome with a woman?"

"Implying that I was thinking this weekend was all about me and you…connecting."

Jamie looked a little shy, which only made her even more adorable. Lauren squeezed Jamie's hand. "It very much is. And I can't wait to connect back at the hotel room, but I thought we could take an hour to have a meeting about you making the most of your time and talent."

Jamie frowned. "I'm not following."

"Your art, Jamie. It's amazing, and I think you should be sharing it with the world and making a living from it."

Jamie's frown deepened, and she sat up straighter. "What are you talking about? I don't get it."

"Morten is an art dealer. He wants to help you sell your sculptures. I'm so excited for you; it's been killing me not to tell you about this meeting." Lauren smiled widely, but Jamie didn't seem to be sharing her enthusiasm.

"My sculptures aren't for sale. They're just for me."

"They are right now," Lauren said. "But they don't have to be. There are thousands of people out there who'd love to have your kind of art in their homes and gardens. Morten wants to help you make that happen."

Jamie pulled her hand from Lauren's and rubbed the back of her neck. "How does this guy even know about what I do in my barn?"

Lauren tapped her phone. "I sent him photos."

"You did what?" Jamie asked, loud enough that some other diners half-turned to look their way.

Lauren leaned closer to Jamie. "I sent him some photos of your work. I think that hearing a professional opinion will make you see how great your sculptures are. And once you realize that, you can decide where your future lies. You've got so many options, Jamie. You could open your own store; you could have Morten sell your pieces in his outlets; you could be in high-end art stores across the country, even the world. Or all of those things. It's everything you could imagine." Lauren's smile faded as she registered Jamie's jaw clenching and an unfamiliar hardness in her eyes.

"You sneaked into my barn and took photos of my work?"

Lauren shook her head. "Oh god, no. I took them when you first showed me your art."

"I didn't see you taking pictures."

Lauren bit her lip as she began to realize that, for some unfathomable reason, Jamie really didn't want anyone to see her sculptures. "I took them when you went to get Olly for his walk."

Jamie leaned forward and whispered, "So you *knew* that I wouldn't like what you were doing, and you waited until I wasn't there to stop you?"

Lauren shook her head. "It wasn't like that at all. I think you're just lacking self-confidence, Jamie. I think that, deep down, you really want your art in the world. I think you want to be somebody."

Jamie's nostrils flared. She picked up her glass, knocked back the rest of the whiskey, and got out of the booth. She placed her hands on the table and bent down slightly. "I *am* somebody, Lauren, and I'm not like you; I don't need awards, and prizes, and external validation to sleep at night. I'm happy with who I am and where I am." She stood tall and straightened her tie. "Tell your friend I'm sorry I couldn't stay, tell him I'm unwell or whatever you want. You're obviously good at lying." Jamie pulled out her wallet and dropped a small pile of crisp, new twenty-dollar bills onto the table. "I don't need your thanks for helping you out, especially now you've made it so obvious that you're only interested in who you think I should be, not who I actually am."

"No, that's not—" But Jamie had already turned and stalked away. She'd grabbed her jacket and was out of the door before Lauren could even think about trying to follow her.

Their waitress approached, looking cautious. "There's a Morten Thomz waiting in the bar for you."

Lauren nodded, the weariness of the situation weighing heavy on her soul. She collected Jamie's money, slipped it into her purse along with her phone, and got up from the table. "Thank you." She passed the waitress her credit card. "I'll be at the bar."

The waitress smiled. "Of course," she said and hurried away.

Lauren took a deep breath and composed herself to face Morten. She pushed back the swell of tears and disappointment; she'd give them their moment at the hotel later. For now, she had to put on her business face and have the meeting without Jamie. Lauren would make excuses for Jamie in the hope that she might come around, but she didn't hold out much hope. Jamie had shown an assertive side of her that Lauren hadn't expected. She needed some time to process that and to assess her part in completely misreading Jamie and her ambitions, and her own part in making Jamie behave so out of character. Lauren wasn't accustomed to being wrong or misinterpreting people, and she had to wonder if her feelings for Jamie had gotten in the way and muddied her clarity. Whatever the hell had just happened, she had to put it aside, talk to Morten, and convince him Jamie's work was worth waiting for.

And then she'd steel herself to face Jamie again.

CHAPTER TWENTY

Jamie rubbed her eyes with the heels of her hands. She wasn't about to let her emotions turn into tears. Tears didn't solve anything. *That* was bullshit, and she knew it. A good cry released pent-up feelings that would otherwise fester and infect everything good inside. She just wasn't about to let anyone see them, especially the hotel guy who'd called her a lady earlier.

She loosened her tie and opened the top button of her shirt before taking the stairs rather than waiting for the elevator. She took them two at a time, testing the limits of the "stretch-with-you" material of her pants, but the way she felt right now, she didn't care if they tore up like she was the Hulk. She could empathize with his obsession with smashing things, though that desire buzzed inside in an unfamiliar way. She'd held onto her control at the restaurant, but as she stomped back to the hotel, her grip had slipped, and she had a rage inside her that she didn't know what to do with. She hadn't experienced anything like it since she'd lost her dad and become angry at everything and everyone.

She burst through the door onto her floor and headed to their room. She needed to talk to her mom. She was the only one Jamie would be able to listen to, the only one who knew her well enough to decode the explosion of emotions that were bouncing around her brain seeking expression. She opened the door and tossed the keycard onto the sideboard in the entryway. She grabbed the few pieces of toiletries and the other bits she'd unpacked, stuffed them and the clothes she'd worn all day into her overnight bag, and left the room. She checked her watch; in and out in less than five minutes, which was good since she didn't want to run into Lauren again. Jamie hadn't looked back as she'd marched the three blocks back to the hotel, and she had no idea whether Lauren had followed her or stayed to meet her art dealer friend. She took the stairs again, not wanting to take the chance that Lauren might be coming up in the elevator.

She jogged down and pushed the door to the lobby open slowly. She quickly scanned the main area then headed toward the side entrance that wasn't currently staffed. Jamie hurried away but couldn't resist one glance back at the hotel, maybe hoping for a glimpse of Lauren. No, she didn't want to see Lauren. And tonight had proven that Lauren didn't really see her. Jamie bit back the idea that maybe it was the exact opposite, and that Lauren saw *exactly* who Jamie was, or at least, who she wanted to be. That was crazy talk.

When she was a couple of blocks away from the hotel in the opposite direction to the steakhouse, Jamie pulled out her phone and mapped a route to the South station bus terminal so she could get transportation to the airport and hope they would exchange her flight home. She'd had enough of big cities to last her a decade. Her stomach grumbled in disagreement. God, that steak was heavenly, and she'd never tasted a whiskey so smooth.

Shit. The reason Lauren had bought her the whiskey dropped into her mind at completely the wrong time. It had been a delay tactic, nothing more. She'd been so close to finally having sex with Lauren Gray. Part of her wished that Lauren had organized the meeting for tomorrow morning before they were scheduled to go back to Damarron. Then they would've had one night together, one special memory that Jamie could've tucked away into the box in her mind reserved for amazing moments like that, like the last time she'd played catch with her dad in the yard, or when her mom had brought Olly home. She dismissed the notion and chastised herself for thinking about her physical desires when her heart ached with the pain.

Great. Her heart had gotten involved. Jamie had been trying so hard to keep that out of the equation and simply enjoy the time she'd been spending with Lauren. She'd known there was no future in their relationship, deep down in the place that *always* knows best and is *always* right. But she'd also hoped to have that one exceptional night so she could go to her grave without regrets, so that she'd know she'd taken the chance even though Lauren hadn't turned out to be Jamie's happy ever after.

Her GPS indicated she'd arrived at the station, and she made her way to the ticket office. She paid with her credit card since she'd blown the last of her cash for the month at the restaurant. That had been petulant, but she'd done it before she'd really realized that she was completely emptying her wallet.

She made her way to the seat in the ugly, utilitarian lounge farthest away from everyone else and dropped into it. An hour to wallow before her bus departed, and another ninety minutes to stew on the plane back, then another bus back to Damarron. She texted her mom and asked to be picked up from the bus station then checked her phone for messages, but there were none. What was she expecting? An apology? Lauren probably couldn't see that she'd done anything wrong. All she could see was ambition and success. Anyone without those things wasn't worth her time; she'd shown that tonight.

Jamie positioned her bag to use as a pillow, leaned back in her chair, and closed her eyes. All she could do for now was wait and zone out, otherwise she'd bend her mind into a pretzel trying to figure out what was going on and what she should do next.

***

Jamie saw her mom's truck outside the station and let her tears fall before her mom got out and pulled her into her arms. Jamie dropped her bag onto the ground and stayed there, exhausted but safe, and sobbed on her shoulder. She pulled away after a minute or so and half-smiled at the little wet panda face she'd made on her mom's gray marl T-shirt.

"Come on, sweetheart." She opened the passenger door and bundled Jamie into the truck. She picked up Jamie's bag and tossed it in the truck bed.

Jamie fastened her seatbelt, leaned back, and closed her aching eyelids. She just wanted to sleep. Replays of, and thoughts about, what had happened at the restaurant played over and over in her head, denying her rest for the whole journey home. Her mom got in and began the short drive back. She stayed silent, as she knew to do, knowing that Jamie would talk when she was ready.

Olly greeted her at the door, and her mom ushered her in. She hadn't asked if Jamie wanted to go to her house, and Jamie had walked to her mom's door on autopilot. She flopped onto the couch, and her mom lifted her legs so she was horizontal. Olly jumped up and curled into the available space, quietly whining. He lifted his head occasionally and licked at her tears.

Jamie drifted in and out of consciousness, vaguely aware that her mom had taken up guard duty on the opposite sofa. She woke fully when the unmistakable scent of bacon drifted up her nose. Despite the draw of Olly's favorite treat, he remained exactly where he'd snuggled into her hours before. She rubbed his belly. "Come on, boy. Up."

He jumped off the couch but didn't race off to the kitchen. Instead, he waited patiently for Jamie to rise, though his nose twitched like crazy. She swung her feet onto the floor and stood, stretching out until things cracked and clicked into place. She checked the time and shook her head when she saw it was past noon. After tickling Olly's ear, she headed toward the kitchen. "Come on, boy."

"I thought this might raise you from the dead." Her mom turned from the stove top and smiled. "How are you feeling?"

Jamie rolled her shoulders and stretched her neck from side to side. More things creaked. "Like I'm seventy years old."

"People your height aren't meant to sleep on sofas," her mom said and turned back to the frying pan.

"That smells amazing."

"I know. Sit down and drink your juice."

Jamie dutifully sat at the breakfast table and sipped at the fresh OJ. Moments later, her mom slid a plate of bacon and pancakes in front of her and sat opposite with her plate. Jamie broke a piece off and dropped it into Olly's mouth. "Last night didn't go according to plan."

Her mom raised her eyebrows and rubbed a chunk of butter onto her pancakes. "No shit."

"Everything *was* going well until we finished dinner." Jamie retold the events of the day, leaving out the hot make-out session in the hotel room—some things her mom didn't need to know—and ended with her rushing out of the restaurant. She waited for her mom's response, and when it didn't come immediately, she continued to share her breakfast with Olly.

"Tell me why you're angry with her," her mom finally said.

Jamie frowned. "Isn't it obvious? She took photographs of my work and showed it to someone without my permission. She lied to me. She knew I wouldn't be happy about it, and that's why she didn't ask. And she knew I wouldn't meet some fancy art guy, so she organized the meeting at a place she thought I wouldn't just walk out of." She huffed. "But she thought wrong."

"Because you did walk out and leave her alone in the restaurant, and then left the city without a word. Yep, you sure showed her how to behave."

She cut off a piece of pancake and casually popped it into her mouth.

"You're on her side?"

Her mom took a sip of coffee and sighed. "There has to be sides? Aren't you telling me what happened so I can give you my opinion?"

"Of course I am, but I still expect you to see where I'm coming from. You're *my* mom. You're supposed to have my back." Jamie picked up her fork, stabbed a whole pancake, and took a bite.

"No."

Jamie gingerly put the pancake back down and cut a piece off. She shoved it in her mouth, but the gesture was lost on her mom because she'd turned her attention back to her own breakfast.

"I do have your back, honey. I'll always have your back." She patted Jamie's hand. "But I'm not going to tell you what you want to hear unless I think it's justified. So I'm asking again, why are so you angry with Lauren?"

Jamie dropped her fork onto her plate and held up her hands. "I've just told you why. She should've asked, but she didn't because she knew I'd say no. I've told her, and everyone else, that what I do in the barn is *just* for me." Jamie grew more agitated when her mom simply looked at her, as if waiting for more. What the hell did she want Jamie to say? She may as well be talking to Olly for all the support she was getting. Maybe she'd been wrong, and for the first time, her mom didn't know how to help unpick this with her. Maybe she should just call Fran and talk to her. "I don't understand. I'm just tinkering in the barn, that's all. It's not art. It's nothing special. *I'm* nothing special. I'm nothing. And that guy was probably just doing Lauren a favor meeting with her. He was probably just being polite and would've said nice, patronizing things about my small-town provincial *style*, and then he would've gone back to his company and had a good laugh about the hick lesbian welding shit in a stupid shed in the middle of nowhere."

Her mom pointed a fork at Jamie. "*That's* why you're angry, sweetheart." Her mom took a sip of coffee and went back to her bacon.

Jamie waited for her to explain, but she simply continued to munch on her breakfast. "Why are you being so unhelpful, Mom? I need you."

Her mom's face hardened. "Don't you ever say that again."

"What? That I need you?" Jamie shoved her plate away and got up from the table.

"Sit."

Jamie blew out a breath. She was still too tired for this. "I think I'm going to go to bed. I'm exhausted."

"Sit down. Now."

Jamie considered walking out, but she hadn't done that since she was a teenager. Her mom had taught her never to walk out on an argument… so why had she walked out on Lauren? *Damn it*. She retook her seat and shared her final piece of bacon with Olly. He looked up at her with his big brown eyes and whined. At least he felt sorry for her.

"Don't ever say that you're nothing ever again." Her mom put her cutlery down and took Jamie's hands in hers. "You're not nothing, and you *are* special."

Jamie rolled her eyes. "You have to say that; you're my mom."

"I do, and you're right. All children are special to their parents, but you're special in a different way—"

"Sure, as in 'this sidewalk tastes like strawberries when I lick it' kind of special.'"

Her mom laughed and slapped Jamie's hands. "No, not that kind of special. You've got a talent, Jamie, and everyone sees that but you." She shook her head slowly. "I've been waiting for you to come to that realization yourself, but you're over thirty now, and time is a slippery sucker." Sadness flickered across her mom's eyes. "And you never know when yours is done."

The reminder that she'd lost her dad and her mom had lost her soulmate wrapped around her heart like a chain and pulled taut. The darkness of her pain was only ever one thought away. Jamie shook her head. "You're talking about friends and family, Mom. This guy was an art dealer. I don't need someone like that telling me what I already know is true."

Her mom slapped her hands again, and this time, her wedding ring caught a tender spot.

"Ouch, Mom." She pulled her hands back and tucked them under her legs.

"Don't you see that you're just frightened of being rejected? It's why you never asked Lauren out when you were younger. I thought you were coming out of it when you asked her out a couple of weeks ago, but I think you might've used up all the courage you'd been building up."

"Nobody likes being rejected, Mom."

Her mom smiled. "You're right, but that doesn't keep them from putting themselves out there just in case. This isn't just about the art dealer. You could do anything you wanted with the stuff you make in your barn, but you don't. Those school bullies made you think you were worthless, and though you think you've gotten over it, this proves that you haven't gotten over it completely. Sure, you've got a job you like, and you've got a couple of close friends, and you've got me, but all of that is safe. And all of it came relatively easy for you. You stay at the cemetery because it keeps you close to your dad, but he's not there, honey." She leaned farther across the table and placed her hand on Jamie's chest. "He's here, and he'll be with you no matter where you are or what you do."

Jamie's tears fell onto her plate, and her chest heaved as she tried to stop herself from sobbing. She swallowed against the ball of pain that rose in her throat, making it hard to breathe. "I miss him so much."

Her mom got out of her chair and pulled Jamie into a hug. She let herself go and cried into her mom's stomach. She wrapped her arms around her mom's waist and held on tight. It was only when she quieted for a moment that she realized her mom was crying too. Jamie pulled away and looked up.

"I miss him too, but I should've done more for you, Jamie. I should've encouraged you to try new things, and I should've taken you to look at colleges when you graduated."

"Don't say that. You've been an amazing mom." Jamie shook her head. "I never wanted to go to college. I think that was Dad's dream for me, not mine." She let out a deep breath, preparing to say what she'd never really allowed herself to think about, what she'd pushed down every time it had tried to gain its voice. "I love what I do in the barn, Mom. But I've never known what to do about it."

Her mom gave her a final squeeze and sat back down. "And that's—"

"Why I got so mad at Lauren."

"Exactly." Her mom nodded. "She's a tornado, that one, and you got scared when she pulled you up into it. She's done what I should've done years ago." She smiled and tapped the table. "Look at what she's doing for Terri. That girl should have gone to college at eight, she's such a genius. Lauren is one of those people who makes things happen. They see the potential, they see the problem, and they fix it." She shrugged. "Sure, she went about it the wrong way, and she *should* have asked you.

She definitely shouldn't do that again, and you're entitled to be mad at her for that, without question. But she *sees* you, and she knew that you wouldn't let her if she asked your permission. So she went ahead and did it anyway—"

"Because she knew that's what I needed… a kick in the pants."

Her mom chuckled. "Exactly. A good kick in the pants."

Jamie got up again and pulled her mom into a tight embrace. "I love you so much, Mom."

"I love you too, honey."

Olly whined and nuzzled her leg.

"And you, boy. We both love you." Jamie held onto her mom for a little longer. She knew what she'd done wrong now, but that hadn't given her a magic plan on how she should move forward. She thought about Lauren and her returning to the hotel room to find Jamie gone. She probably thought Jamie was a total asshole, and she couldn't blame her.

But Jamie was still angry with her too. Lauren had broken her trust, regardless that she obviously thought she was doing it for the right reasons, and that would take time to rebuild. She hoped her mom was right, and that Lauren saw Jamie for who she was and who she could be. But a niggling doubt scratched at her mind, reminding her they may as well be from two different worlds, and Jamie wasn't good enough to be in Lauren's orbit or anywhere near her tornado, as her mom had called her. Sure, Jamie could think about broadening her horizons a little and maybe see if the folk around town might want to buy the stuff she made, but anything more than that was a fantasy. And she was someone, with or without that forward movement. The question was, would Lauren see that too?

CHAPTER TWENTY-ONE

Her alarm woke Lauren from a fitful sleep, and she reached across the bed, more in hope than in expectation. The bed was empty and cold, just as it had been when she'd gotten back from the restaurant, just as it had been all night, and just like her heart felt. She pulled the comforter up to her neck, stared at the ceiling, and replayed the evening's events in her head. She'd been so sure that Jamie just needed a push in the right direction, and that she wanted to do something more with her art than keep it locked away in a barn where no one else could enjoy it. Morten agreed, otherwise he wouldn't have met with them.

Lauren blew out a long breath, and the pounding in her head registered. After Jamie left, she'd spent an hour with Morten drinking more of the whiskey their waitress had recommended, and then when she'd come back to the hotel to find Jamie had packed up and gone, she'd attacked the mini bar with gusto. She wriggled against something hard beneath her hip and reached beneath the covers. She pulled out an empty vodka miniature. No wonder her head ached. Mixing drinks was never the road to bliss.

She grabbed her phone from the bedside table. No messages from Jamie, but one from Whit confirmed their breakfast meeting in the hotel restaurant. Lauren had hoped to leave Jamie in bed, meet with Whit, and jump back into the sack for more mind-blowing sex. Because it *was* going to be mind-blowing if the kisses were anything to go by. She'd always used the quality of the kiss as a barometer for the standard of sex, and Jamie's kisses had almost defied gravity and lifted Lauren off her feet.

But sex wasn't her priority right now. Where had Jamie gone? Home or to another hotel? Was she still somewhere in the city? And would she come back to the hotel so they could talk things through? Lauren didn't want to entertain the notion that she'd blown it, and that Jamie hated her. She sighed deeply and reluctantly got out of bed for a shower. The hot water would ease her pounding head, but just in case, she grabbed a couple of Advil and washed them down with a mouthful of flat, warm Coke. She showered quickly and decided to let her hair dry naturally. She'd straighten it after she'd had breakfast with Whit. She threw on a simple skirt and blouse, pulled on her heels, and headed downstairs to the restaurant.

Whit was already seated and waved as Lauren was shown to their table. She got up and they hugged, tighter and longer than usual, as if Whit had read her mind or her body language. Between losing Kayla and blowing it with Jamie, life felt like way too much right now.

The waiter poured coffee and retreated quietly.

"I was expecting you to bounce in here looking like you'd won the lottery," Whit said. "But if you'll forgive me for saying so, you look like shit."

Lauren gave a wry laugh and ran her hand through her still-wet hair. "That bad?"

Whit shrugged. "Your hair looks as lustrous as ever, but you look like you haven't slept all night, and not because you were busy having amazing sex."

Lauren looked at the ceiling. "The best laid plans, etcetera. I think I'm losing my touch."

Whit frowned and shook her head. "You had bad sex?" she asked just as the waiter returned for their order.

A barely perceptible twitch of his eyebrow was the only indication he'd registered Whit's too-loud question. He took their order and faded away once again.

Lauren leaned closer and whispered, "I had *no* sex."

Whit smoothed out her napkin and her frown deepened. "You're not making any sense. Spill *everything*."

Lauren took a deep breath then launched into the sorry tale. She furnished the retelling with every detail; there was no point leaving anything out, whether it made her look bad or not, because she needed Whit's honest opinion. When she'd finished, she fixed her coffee and took a long drink. Whit was silent while the waitstaff brought their food and refreshed her coffee.

"You see why I'm thinking I've lost my touch? Being in my hometown has dulled my sixth sense. It looks like I completely misunderstood Jamie. She's happy doing nothing with her talent."

Whit dipped a piece of fresh salmon in the runny yolk of her poached egg and ate it before responding. "You like her a lot, don't you?"

Lauren nodded. "We have a lot of fun together, and it's so…easy. There's no drama or pressure. We feel good together. What's your point?"

"What exactly do you like about her?" Whit asked between forkfuls of food.

"She's smart, *very* sexy, and she's got a wicked sense of humor." Lauren took a moment to think about how good Jamie had looked last night in a suit and tie. It was all Lauren could do not to ravish her before they left for the restaurant. Now she partially wished she had, though this way, she didn't know what she was missing. Lauren pulled off a chunk of bagel, smeared it with honey walnut cream cheese and popped it in her mouth.

"Were you hoping to keep things going when you got back to the city?"

Lauren glanced around the restaurant, hoping she'd see Jamie wander in to join them. "I hadn't really thought that far ahead."

Whit made a harsh buzzing sound. "I call bullshit. You plan everything to the nth degree, and you always know your short, medium, and long-term goals. Try again."

Lauren arched her eyebrow. "You can be disrespectful of our working dynamic sometimes."

"This isn't a business meeting now, *boss*. We're here as friends, and that means I can be as disrespectful as I damn well please—especially when you're being so obtuse." She repeated her original question.

"Yes, I could see it being more than some fun while I was in town."

Whit gave her a searching look.

"Fine. Yes, I wanted it to continue once I got back to the city. So what?"

"Do you think you pushed ahead with Morten Thomz because you wanted Jamie to move away from Damarron and *not* because your spidey sense knew she wanted more for herself and her art?"

Lauren dropped the chunk of bagel she'd just pulled off and leaned back in her chair. "You think I was being selfish?" She hadn't thought of it the way Whit had framed it. She'd considered that her feelings for Jamie had clouded her usually pristine judgment, but not that she'd manipulated the situation for her own gain. And without realizing what she was doing? She *always* knew what she was doing.

Whit shook her fork mid-air. "Not selfish, no. I think you just got a little carried away." She pointed her fork at Lauren when she opened her mouth to respond. "It's understandable. You'd just lost your sister, and you were back in the place you fought so hard to get out of. Jamie was a lifeline, someone familiar but stimulating. But you were always going to come back to Boston, back to your chosen home. I think you didn't want to lose what you'd been experiencing with Jamie, and that morphed into you convincing yourself that she wanted out of the town as bad you did."

Lauren shook her head. "That's a lot of supposition, Whit. I could be wrong, but maybe I'm not, and perhaps she *does* want to do something with her art. What if she's just lacking confidence, and no one's believed in her like I do?"

Whit pressed her lips together before going back to her breakfast. "But you know why she's angry with you, don't you?"

Lauren rolled her eyes. "Sure, but if I hadn't done that, I couldn't have gotten Morten interested." She glanced around the restaurant when Whit gave her a look that said she wasn't impressed. Lauren's dismissive attitude was out of line, and she knew it. "When it works out, the ends justify the means. This didn't work out."

Whit shook her head but smiled widely. "Are you going to apologize?"

Lauren wrinkled her nose and refocused on her suddenly very interesting breakfast. She couldn't get a good bagel in Damarron for love nor money. A tiny part of her thought Jamie was being a smidge ungrateful and more than a little short-sighted, but that was her ego, still sore from the possibility of her instincts being wrong. "Of course I will."

"I hope you'll do it with more grace than that," Whit said and scooped another forkful of egg into her mouth.

Lauren sighed. "I hate to see wasted potential. You know that."

Whit nodded. "I know you do, and even in the relatively short time I've known you, you've helped a lot of people do amazing things with their lives. Heck, I had no idea I could do half of the things I do daily until you took me under your wing and made me your protégé." She waved her hand theatrically.

"There's a but coming, isn't there?" Lauren slathered cream cheese onto the last of her bagel. "I'm not sure the student is quite ready to become the master."

Whit grinned. "I am nowhere *near* that, *but* some people are too scared to put themselves out there, and that fear can be crippling. And it doesn't matter how hugely talented they are, the terror of failure and rejection is far bigger, so they happily stay in their little ponds. And, as hard as it might be for you to believe, other people are simply happy and don't have ambition beyond their daily grind. They like living a life less grand. And it's not for you to say that they're wrong about that."

"'A life less grand,' huh? That sounds like the title of a really uninspiring and deeply depressing memoir." Lauren laughed, but her heart sank. "I can't bear the thought of Jamie's talent being hidden away in a rickety barn for the rest of her life just because she was afraid."

"You're not hearing me, Lauren. She might actually *be* happy. And 'just because she was afraid?' Not everyone's as fearless as you are, and sometimes, maybe you struggle to understand that."

Lauren gritted her teeth briefly. "I don't expect everyone to be like me, Whit. That's not a fair accusation." And she didn't need kicking while she was down either. "I'm going to stay in the city for a few days, do some traveling, and meet the new team. I've nearly finished at Kayla's apartment—Dad could probably do the rest—and I could use the break."

Whit nodded and averted her eyes. Great, now Lauren had upset another important person in her life. This was the problem being friends with colleagues: the lines could blur, and then no one knew where they stood. She sighed. They'd never had that problem before, but then Lauren's judgment had never been so off-kilter before either. "I'm sorry. I shouldn't have snapped at you."

Whit looked up and gave a tight-lipped smile. Her watery eyes added to Lauren's guilt. She reached across the table and took Whit's hand. "I can be an asshole, I'm sorry."

"I guess it proves you are human after all. I've often wondered," Whit said and smiled for real.

"I sometimes wish I wasn't. I'd get so much more done if I didn't have to sleep." Lauren laughed, but Whit's comment got her thinking. Whit made no secret of her heroine-worship of Lauren, and for the most part, it was flattering, but it also meant Whit thought she could do no wrong. And that could be suffocating, or at its worst, believable. Perhaps she'd gotten too swept up in her own reputation and talent-divining abilities. Perhaps the best thing she could do for Jamie was stay away from her and let her live her life exactly the way she wanted. The thought of never seeing her again, especially when Lauren had begun to dream of a future together, settled heavy in her heart. She'd thought they could be something, but last night had proven she might no longer be able to trust her instincts. The sorrow in her soul told her that wouldn't make the letting go any easier.

CHAPTER TWENTY-TWO

I'M SORRY. I SHOULDN'T have taken photos of your work without asking, and I shouldn't have pushed you. I hope you'll forgive me. Take care.

Jamie reread the message as she headed to get her lunch. She'd looked at the words so many times that she'd memorized them, but she still wasn't sure what it meant for her and Lauren. Jamie didn't know what she'd expected to happen, but it hadn't been for Lauren to stay away from Damarron. People fought all the time, then they talked about it and forged a way forward. Was Lauren's response to conflict simply to avoid it? That didn't fit with her CEO personality.

Beth wasn't at the counter, so Jamie couldn't casually ask about Lauren or if she knew when she was coming back. Part of her was relieved. Beth might know that Lauren had no intention of coming back at all, and Jamie wasn't ready to hear that. She'd had four days to process how she felt, and she was still angry. The text had helped with that a little. At least Lauren acknowledged that she'd done wrong, but an apology over text wasn't the same as an apology after they'd had an adult discussion. There were things Jamie wanted to say, but Lauren's text and her absence took that opportunity away from her. And that made her a little angrier. She could've called, of course. Jamie *could've* made the first move, but she was the one who had been wronged, so she shouldn't be the one to extend the olive branch.

Still, finding out what was happening through Rebekah wasn't the same, and the B&B was on her way back to the cemetery. If Rebekah was there, Jamie wouldn't even have to ask about Lauren. As the town's resident grapevine operator, she would volunteer any and all information she had about Lauren. Jamie's plan went out the window when she saw Lauren emerge from a cab and hurry inside Nancy's without looking around. Jamie stopped. Now what? Should she go in there and confront Lauren? Jamie had dared to believe that they had a connection. That was something rare and precious in this world. Were they both prepared to let that go so easily?

No. Jamie wasn't, anyway. She tightened her grip on her bagged lunch and set off toward Nancy's, though she resisted the urge to break into a run.

Rebekah smiled broadly when Jamie entered. "Hi."

"Hey." Jamie offered a quick wave then stuck her hand in her pocket.

"Have you brought lunch for your weary traveler?"

"Huh?"

Rebekah pointed to her lunch. "Lauren just got back. You've got a bag from Beth's. I'm adding up the clues." She frowned. "Are you feeling all right? You look a little pale."

Jamie shook her head and pointed up the stairs. "I'm going up, okay?"

"She's not one of us, you know," Rebekah said.

Jamie turned back as she reached the bottom step. "What do you mean?"

"She'll break your heart and go back to Boston, where she belongs. You'd be better off looking closer to home." Rebekah raised her eyebrow and licked her top lip slowly.

Jamie almost lost her footing. Rebekah had never mentioned she was into women, but their paths didn't cross that often either. Jamie might've been interested before Lauren came back into town and swept her up in a whirlwind of happiness. "I'll be fine," she said and took the stairs two at a time in her rush to get away. She wouldn't be fine, of course. It was way too late for her to put the brakes on the emotions train. That was on a circular track from her mind to her heart, pistons pumping and no sign of letting up. But what were hearts for if you didn't offer them up to be broken or saved?

Jamie knocked on Lauren's door and waited. She smiled, thinking of the last time she'd been up here, with Lauren in her arms, barely conscious and whispering drunken sweet nothings.

Lauren opened the door. "Honestly, I don't—" She sighed and kept the door partially closed. "Hey."

"Can I come in?" It was a minor miracle she'd gotten the question out of her mouth. Seeing Lauren up close again after missing her these past days made her heart skip a beat.

Lauren pressed her lips together and ran her hand through her hair, as if she was contemplating a huge decision.

"Please. We need to talk."

Lauren stepped aside for Jamie to enter. She went in, and Lauren gestured for her to sit on the small sofa in the corner of the room before closing the door quietly and sitting on the edge of her bed six feet away. The gulf between them seemed far greater, and Jamie's tentative optimism began to slide into a deep pit with oiled walls impossible to scale. A number of questions popped into her head, all of them swathed in judgment, and that didn't seem like the best way to begin the conversation. The depth of sadness in Lauren's eyes made Jamie want to forget everything that had happened and just pull her into a long embrace and assure her everything would be fine. But Jamie had no way of knowing where her sadness originated. It was stupid to assume it was because of what had gone down between them. Jamie couldn't forget what had brought Lauren back to Damarron in the first place, and her sister's death must still be raw and destructive.

The silence stretched on, and Jamie fought the instinct to run. But she'd followed Lauren in here. *She* wanted to talk. "I didn't know you were staying in Boston for so long after..." After what? Their ill-fated date/business meeting?

Lauren crossed her legs and fiddled with her nails. "Whit needed me to meet with the new team, and it took longer than I thought it would."

The way Lauren failed to make eye contact told Jamie that might not be entirely true, but she wasn't about to call her a liar. "I got your text."

Lauren raised her eyebrows. "I did wonder, since you didn't respond."

Now it was Jamie's turn to avoid meeting Lauren's questioning gaze. She'd typed and deleted a hundred responses and hadn't hit send on any of them. They'd either been too angry, or too needy, or too accusatory. "I don't think complicated situations can be resolved over text." Way to go. *That* didn't sound harsh at all. "I mean, I'd rather talk to you face-to-face. It's easier. Well, it's not. It's hard, but..." And back she went to not being able to form a coherent sentence.

Lauren leaned forward on the edge of the bed. "I *am* sorry, Jamie. I'm used to doing things that help people achieve their potential, and I'm not used to being wrong." She shrugged and sighed deeply.

Jamie clenched her jaw and tried not to respond immediately to the accusation that she wasn't interested in fulfilling her "potential." It was also incredibly irritating that someone could waltz into her life and see that maybe she *did* need shaking up. Jamie wasn't sure what that meant, or what she was willing to do to make changes in her life. But she'd spent the past few days without Lauren in isolated thought, and she'd recognized that she'd gotten stuck in a comfortable existence, no longer thinking about what life could be. After leaving the high school bullies behind, she'd promised herself never to be scared again, but a silent, stealthy fear had slowly taken over day by day without Jamie ever realizing it.

But she wasn't ready to admit that fully yet, and certainly not out loud. And she was still angry at Lauren, though that feeling was fading fast. With an in-person apology and Lauren's defeated expression, it was increasingly hard to maintain. "I just wished you'd asked me."

Lauren gave a rueful laugh. "And what would you have said?"

"I would've said no, but you knew that. That's why you didn't ask."

Lauren picked at the bedspread. "I'm sorry. I was swept up in the excitement of discovering how amazingly talented you are. I thought you just needed a push. I thought you just needed to hear a professional from the art world tell you how good your work was. I was wrong." She ran her fingers through her hair and sighed. "I'm sorry for pushing you away from where you're clearly happy. It wasn't my place."

That part of the apology sounded a little more judgy. "It's okay to be happy in a small town, Lauren. Kayla loved it here."

Lauren pushed up from the bed and walked to the window. Jamie wanted to pull her words back into her stupid mouth. She got up from the couch and went to stand beside Lauren. She placed her hand on Lauren's shoulder gently, but she shook away Jamie's touch.

"You should leave."

The coldness in Lauren's voice encased Jamie's heart in ice and took her breath away. What did she expect? Bringing Kayla into this conversation was mind-blowingly dumb. "I'm sorry. I have no right to talk about Kayla. I'm just trying to explain that not everyone hates this town as much as you do."

Lauren turned on her quickly. "I don't *hate* this town. I wanted to achieve things that would've been impossible here. I wanted to make a difference to thousands of lives, and I couldn't do that in Damarron." She pushed past Jamie and busied herself unpacking an overnight bag.

Jamie bit her lip and looked out the window. She knew everyone on the street. Simon tidying his floral displays, Beth's parents wandering into the furniture store, and Meryl bent over her walker heading to visit her late husband at the cemetery. What did Jamie *want* to do with the rest of her life? She'd thought she was happy until Lauren showed up, turned her life upside down, and made her think about venturing outside her comfortable reality. She turned back into the room and looked at Lauren. Would she be able to return to that reality if Lauren left? Would the memory of possibilities fade with the setting sun? "That sounded harsh. I didn't mean it like that." Jamie rubbed her forehead. This wasn't going according to plan. She'd gotten the apology she wanted. Weren't they supposed to be able to move past that now? She took a deep breath and ventured over to Lauren. She tentatively reached out but pulled back before making contact. Lauren looked up and shook her head. She'd stopped unpacking though, and she was still looking at Jamie.

"Can we fix this?" Jamie motioned between them. The words had almost stayed lodged in her throat, unwilling to hear the potentially negative response. "I want to move past this. Pick up where we were headed to at the restaurant."

Lauren turned to face Jamie and took a step closer. She took Jamie's hand in hers. "You forgive me?"

"Can you accept me as I am, whatever that might be?"

"I think you're damn near perfect. I really am sorry, and I swear I had good intentions. You know that, right?"

Jamie nodded, unable to form a sentence because all of her focus was on the fiery sensation of Lauren's touch. Lauren leaned in and pressed her lips gently to Jamie's, and everything around her exploded into a million stars. She pulled Lauren into her arms and deepened the kiss. She wouldn't let this moment get away from her, not again. Lauren pulled away and sat on the edge of the bed. She hooked her fingers into Jamie's belt and tugged her closer. Jamie dropped to her knees between Lauren's legs and waited.

Lauren caught the hem of Jamie's T-shirt and pulled it up over her head. Jamie throbbed when Lauren bit her lip, clearly excited by what she saw. She was quick to pull off Jamie's sports bra before taking her in for another world-spinning kiss, leaving Jamie breathless and eager for more, so much more. Lauren broke their connection, but only for the time it took her to shed her own shirt and bra. She pulled Jamie up and fell back, taking Jamie with her. Pressed against Lauren, skin to skin, Jamie's whole body ignited, and desire consumed her every thought.

Everything about Lauren, from the silky softness of her hair to the give of her body beneath Jamie's, felt like it was designed just for her, as if they'd been destined for this since the moment they were created, as if they were drawn together despite the distance that had developed between them over the years. Now, in this moment, the world made sense. All the bad experiences, all the loss, all of it faded away so that Jamie could only concentrate on what was happening in this second. The past and future were distant concepts as she fully inhabited the present and their coming together after years of Jamie dreaming about it. This was really happening.

They shed the rest of their clothes and shoes, and their exploration of each other seemed so soft and unhurried, it was like they'd known each other's bodies for years, had mapped every curve and dip, and knew every inch of skin. "I missed you," Jamie whispered between kisses.

Lauren ran her hand through Jamie's hair and looked deep into her eyes. "I missed you too." She took Jamie's hand and sucked one of her fingertips into her mouth. "Make love to me," she said, guiding Jamie's hand between her legs.

Jamie moaned when her finger slid easily inside Lauren. Her heat coursed up Jamie's hand, while her slick wetness allowed Jamie to drive inside her.

"Hard and slow."

Jamie closed her eyes briefly. Lauren's instruction and the huskiness of her voice tapped into her body and sent a shiver of arousal from her brain right through to her core. She readily complied, her whole being concerned only with Lauren's pleasure and satisfaction. Lauren dug her nails in and dragged them across Jamie's back, leaving trails of golden fire on her skin. She drove in deeper and harder, memorizing every texture and movement beneath her fingertips, mapping a route to Lauren's pleasure and enjoying the slow, scenic route.

Lauren pressed her head into the bed and arched her back, rising to meet Jamie's rhythm and pushing against her. She moaned and her breathing quickened.

"Yes," she whispered. "Yes, that."

Jamie smiled and shook her head slightly, almost disbelieving her eyes. Yes, Lauren was naked beneath her, telling her exactly how she wanted her to move. Yes, Lauren wanted this as much as Jamie ever had. Her hardened nipples jutted out, demanding attention, so Jamie bent to lick one before sucking it into her mouth.

"Oh my god." Lauren grabbed her discarded shirt and bit down on it to muffle her cries.

Jamie closed her eyes for the briefest of seconds; she didn't want to miss a single thing. She wanted every microdetail of the way Lauren moved against her, each one of the sensual sounds she made in response to Jamie's motion, and every emotion that flickered across her expression. All of it, she wanted it emblazoned in her mind. This was a forever memory that would never desert her, one of those times that she'd want to etch into her brain and never let any aspect of it disappear.

Lauren clenched around Jamie's fingers, and she drove her hips upward to meet Jamie's thrusts. She moved faster and harder, moaning and whispering curses into her shirt until she yelled so loudly, Jamie was certain someone would've heard across the street. Lauren collapsed onto the bed, her body shuddering against Jamie's as she rode the shimmering swells of her orgasm.

Unwelcome tears burned at the back of Jamie's eyes, so she pressed her lips to Lauren's neck and began a trail of kisses along her collarbone. She wasn't ready to show her vulnerability. She hadn't been expecting it to show itself that way. Lauren would wonder what the hell was wrong. Who cried after sex? Especially after just giving it. Hell, she'd never felt close to anything like this before… But she'd never made love before. That's what Lauren had asked for, and that's what Jamie had given her, and she'd given it with all her heart. Lauren opened her eyes and looked up at Jamie. She grasped Jamie's wrist to encourage a repeat performance, and Jamie realized she was lost. Lost in Lauren, lost in love. Somewhere along the line, Jamie's heart had thrown itself into the mix, and now she was all in. She didn't know what that meant for her, for them going forward. But she did know that, with Lauren by her side, maybe she could see where her barn-work could go. Maybe she could even begin to call it art.

Those were thoughts for another time. Right now, all she wanted to do was sink into this moment and squeeze every drop of pleasure from it, remember every second, and memorize every move, every sound. She was in bed with Lauren Gray, and in all those years of fantasizing, her imagination had never done this justice. She allowed Lauren to guide her hand and drove deep inside, wanting to give Lauren everything she asked for and everything she desired.

And maybe, *if* she did it right, Lauren would want her to do it over and over again.

CHAPTER TWENTY-THREE

How could it be that the first time simultaneously felt like the last time? Their lovemaking had a power and intensity as if they'd both known they would never touch each other's skin again, as if the world would end the moment they separated. Lauren lay with her head on Jamie's chest, listening to the steady, insistent beat of her lifeblood. She was so strong and yet, so incredibly fragile. Jamie's eyes had blurred with unshed tears. Lauren hadn't missed that even as she came down from the incredible high of her extraordinary orgasm. Was Jamie's sorrow from knowing that the odds were against them, and nothing would probably come of their union? In that moment, Lauren could have easily been swept away with the magnitude of her emotions, overwhelmed by her physical and carnal reaction to their sex. The pleasure hormones swirling around her bloodstream could be interpreted as something deeper, something more meaningful…something like forever.

But Lauren wasn't a character in a romance novel. She was a realist. She was a city girl, and Jamie was a woman content with her small-town existence. Lauren wanted to change the world, and Jamie feared change like the ancient Greeks feared Zeus. There was no meeting in the middle, no compromise that could be had. Jamie's reaction to Boston told her that even before Morten had turned up at the restaurant. And she'd known that before she took Jamie's hand and initiated what had been the most incredible sex of her life. But she hadn't been able to resist the soulful look in Jamie's eyes. Lauren had wanted her so bad in that moment that her awareness of everything else fell away.

And now, in Jamie's strong embrace, breathing in the scent of her sex and fresh sweat, Lauren could allow herself to be carried away on the wings of possibility. But that wouldn't be fair to either of them. She inhaled the moment deeply, wanting to remember every detail of the most perfect feeling she'd ever experienced, and she traced her fingers over Jamie's stomach and hips, too exhausted for more but not yet ready to relinquish the tenderness of their time together.

"What are you thinking?" Jamie whispered.

It was nothing she would want to hear, Lauren was sure of that. "No one's ever made me come that much in a month, let alone a few hours." She chuckled at Jamie's proud grin and batted away her wandering hand. "All right, Romeo, relax. I can't take any more."

Jamie made a whining puppy noise. "Are you sure? Maybe just one more?"

Lauren raised her head and looked at Jamie. She arched her eyebrow and waited.

Jamie held her hands out. "Sorry. No means no."

Lauren shifted and turned so she could rest her head on Jamie's chest and look up at her. "What were *you* thinking?"

Jamie's cheeks colored, and she cleared her throat after glancing away. "I was thinking about how inspirational you are."

Lauren was certain that hadn't been at the forefront of her mind, but she let her get away with it. "Oh, really. How so?"

"You see things most people don't. How do you do it?"

Lauren traced slow circles on Jamie's skin and shrugged. "I'm not sure." She laughed lightly. "Turns out my powers aren't infallible."

Jamie wrinkled her nose. "Maybe they're dead on."

Lauren frowned. "Meaning?"

"Meaning that maybe it takes some people a little more time to come around to what you're saying."

"Go on, I'm listening." She didn't know where Jamie was going with this, but she liked the sound of Jamie's voice, and she wasn't averse to some ego-stroking.

"Some people really are happy with where they're at, and they don't want anything more. But some people are stuck in their lives, pedaling around in their tiny orbit and expecting nothing more."

The way Jamie was struggling to maintain eye contact and how she was lacking specificity began to make sense, but she wasn't about to make another mistake and assume she was right. Jamie had confounded her once already. "*Some* people?"

"Yeah, some people. The ones who have forgotten what it was like to dream because they got so used to struggling to survive. The ones who had their aspirations beaten out of them."

Of course. The incessant bullying Jamie had endured from first grade to high school graduation had left her with mental injuries. She'd seemed so together, so relaxed that Lauren had all but forgotten the timid version of herself that Jamie used to be. Was Jamie really about to roll back on everything she'd said about not wanting to do anything with her art? "Ah, those people… People like you?" She ventured the assumption, unable to help herself.

Jamie nodded. "Do you really think what I do can be called art?"

Lauren pulled herself up to a sitting position so she could observe Jamie more closely. She didn't want to force anything or misinterpret a word. "I do, or I would never have said it. I don't blow smoke, Jamie. That might feel good temporarily, but it never helps anyone in the long run."

Jamie bit her lip and briefly made eye contact. "What if I opened my own store in town? Do you think I could do that? Do you think that people would buy the things I make?"

Lauren didn't attempt to stop her smile, partly from being right all along but mostly from seeing the beginnings of blossoming self-belief. "Is that what you'd like to do?" There was a moment of silence that seemed to stretch on. Lauren wanted it to end, but it was Jamie's question to answer in her own time.

"I think it is—if you think I can do it… If you believe in me, I kind of feel like I might be able to do anything."

Her words rang alarm bells. "You need to believe in yourself, Jamie," Lauren said.

Jamie's phone buzzed. "Oh, shit." She jumped up from the bed and began to pull her shorts on. "I have to get back to work. We've got a grave to fill in. Martin will be wondering where the hell I am." She pulled her phone from her jeans. "Shit. Eight missed calls." She leaned over the bed and kissed Lauren. "I'm so sorry. I've got to go."

"It's okay. I should've realized you were at work. It's my fault. Don't worry."

Jamie quickly dressed and gave Lauren a lingering kiss before she headed for the door. "Can we talk later? About the shop? About the future?"

Lauren smiled. "Of course. I'll be around. We could get dinner?"

"That'd be great. I'll come back at eight, if that's okay?" Jamie returned for another kiss. "Damn, woman, you're hard to let go."

Lauren waved her away. "Go, before you get fired."

Jamie took a deep breath and shook her head before finally leaving. When she'd closed the door, Lauren sank back into the bed and half-wished it would suck her into another world, one far from here, one with less complications and none of these wild emotions flying around. The few days she'd spent back in Boston had been easy, even though she'd met nearly twenty new employees and had intense introductory conversations with them all. Surface level knowledge was a piece of cake; *knowing* someone like she'd been getting to know Jamie, especially the intimate knowledge, was far harder. Deeper. And she felt vulnerable because of it, like an armadillo without its shell.

If that was how she felt, she couldn't imagine what Jamie was going through. She'd just revealed she was prepared to make a huge change in her life and take a chance on her art. Lauren smiled, happy that Jamie had finally recognized her pieces as real art and not merely tinkering around in her barn. But was she only doing it because she thought Lauren might stick around to help her?

Lauren rose from the bed and pulled on sweats, a tank top, and sneakers. She needed to be close to Kayla but couldn't go to the cemetery. She couldn't face Jamie again yet, not while there was so much stuff going on in her head, stuff she'd never had to deal with before. She picked up the keys to Kayla's apartment. Her parents had worked there while Lauren was in Boston and almost everything had been picked up and rehomed, but Kayla's bed remained, and that would have to do.

She got there on autopilot, barely acknowledging Rebekah's attempt at conversation and managing to avoid running into anyone else. Rebekah seemed to have an edge anyway, and Lauren didn't have time for that. She laid on her back in Kayla's apartment and stared at the ceiling, vaguely thinking about all the times Kayla had looked up at the same space. Had she dreamed about their literacy hub while lying in bed?

The sudden realization of the impossibility of creating that hub hit hard. "I can't do our project without you." She didn't want to acknowledge the niggle at the back of her mind that told her it would be the best way to honor Kayla's memory, but equally, the kernel of feelings for Jamie told her to get the hell out of Damarron before she got stuck there and everything that she'd worked so hard for disappeared, before their feelings ruined both of them beyond recovery.

Lauren's life had been on hold since Kayla's death, and the new schools project needed her oversight. She couldn't afford to stay here any longer and expect the trustees to be okay with that. And she couldn't afford to put her career on hold to make Kayla's hub come to life. Whit had said she wasn't ready to step up to the CEO position, and Lauren didn't want to leave the charity in anyone else's hands. Regardless, she wasn't ready to leave the charity. She'd engineered their new expansion, and she wanted to see that through to fruition.

She pounded her fists on the mattress. The only person who could talk her through this was Kayla, and she was gone forever. Lauren thought about calling her mom, but she couldn't bring herself to do it. She wasn't ready to shift confidants so easily. She was nowhere near done missing Kayla, her lifelong sounding board. To talk to someone else—even their mom—seemed like a betrayal, as illogical as that thought was.

She was alone, and this was a crossroads in her life when she had to be solely responsible for her decision. She thought again about Jamie's reaction to their trip. It was a fantasy to believe that Jamie would leave Damarron, her mother, and her job. The possibility of her own gallery in town clearly felt like a massive undertaking; it would be stupid of Lauren to think Jamie would consider moving to Boston to be together.

And Lauren couldn't begin to entertain being back here. She'd built a life in Boston, a life she loved, and she was doing great things. She loved the buzz of the office, the thrill of solving problems when beleaguered colleagues came into her office as if the world would dissolve. Lauren was a fixer, and she couldn't do that here.

She should be happy—she *was* happy—for Jamie. Opening her own shop would be life-changing for her, and it wouldn't have happened if Lauren hadn't pushed her. She recognized, of course, that she'd done it all wrong and should never have photographed Jamie's work without her permission. It was a mistake she wouldn't be in a hurry to repeat. But it *had* achieved the desired result. Jamie had recognized she had talent, and that she should share it outside her scruffy barn, even if just with the residents and tourists of Damarron.

But Lauren's heart ached, and she couldn't get away from that. It was best for them both if she left now. Time apart would heal their hurt and fade the brightness of possibility, and they could both get on with following their life paths. There was no big conflict, no huge argument to be had. They simply had to be adults about their situation and accept that they were worlds apart, that they wanted different things in their lives, and that being together simply wasn't their destiny. They could still be friends, and Lauren would do everything she could to help Jamie set up her new business. But she'd do it from Boston, safely on the other side of a computer screen, and nowhere near Jamie, where she could fall so easily into her eyes and her arms again. And maybe she could run Kayla's project from there one day too.

Lauren sat up and wiped the tears from her face. She'd be strong, like she always was, and she'd focus on her goals, just as she always had. People like her, people driven to help others, didn't have time to pursue their own happiness. And that was okay. It had been until now, and it would be again. She just needed some time to recover and remember who she was when she wasn't in Damarron, when she wasn't around Jamie.

Time. It healed everything…didn't it?

CHAPTER TWENTY-FOUR

Jamie's afternoon went to hell as soon as she got back to work. Martin didn't hide his irritation at her unexplained absence, and her lack of explanation did nothing to help matters. It wasn't like she could tell him that she'd finally fallen into bed with Lauren, even though he knew exactly who she was. Martin was two years older, but he'd also had a crush on Lauren when he was in high school. She didn't want to brag and rub it in his face, and while she was tempted to tell the whole world, or the whole town to start with, that wasn't her style. She'd already texted Fran and Terri, but that was different; they were her best friends, and they'd been rooting for her since she was eight.

One of the webs had broken as they'd lowered the coffin into its grave, the lid had come off, and poor old Mr. Siegel had almost tumbled into the dirt six feet below. It made her a shoo-in for the winning story at tomorrow night's drinking session with her buddies, but at the time, Martin's reaction had made the situation far worse than it had to be. For some reason, she'd always expected him to be the kind of guy who was cool under pressure, but he'd screamed and thrown his hands up in the air, leaving Jamie holding the full weight of the coffin and the corpse. She'd just been glad there were no visitors nearby to witness the performance. If she'd seen it, there'd be no way she'd want her loved ones buried at their cemetery.

But they'd rescued Mr. Siegel and his expensive, top of the line final home, and she had dinner with Lauren to look forward to. Her mom had agreed to take Olly for his evening walk, so all Jamie had to concentrate on was cleaning herself up and getting herself over to pick Lauren up from the B&B, preferably without running into Rebekah. Jamie hadn't thought about Rebekah's vamp act until she was heading home after work, but now that she had, she was in no hurry to see her again. She didn't want to hear anything negative about Lauren, and she definitely didn't want Rebekah fueling her fears about Lauren not wanting to stick around.

They hadn't just had sex. They'd made love. And that meant something, something solid and long-lasting. After four days of non-communication, they were back on track, and Jamie was certain they'd be able to figure out a way for them to be together.

Especially now that Jamie was on board with her new artistic direction and even the possibility of a shop in town. That showed ambition, didn't it? It proved she was ready for change and wanted something bigger and better for herself. That's what Lauren wanted all along, even though she'd approached it all wrong, but it was also what Jamie wanted for herself. And if she really thought about it, she knew it would never have happened without Lauren pushing her off the cliff of her self-doubt.

Jamie got out of the shower, quickly dried herself off, and pulled on the outfit she'd chosen when she'd gotten home. She'd tried to limit overthinking it and gone with a classic button down and jeans combo, something Lauren had repeatedly said she found incredibly attractive. Jamie was hungry and *did* want something to eat, but she was also hoping to work it off by jumping straight back into bed and picking up where they'd left off. And maybe this time she wouldn't cry.

She finished getting ready and headed to Nancy's. As she approached in her truck, she was relieved to see Lauren sitting on a bench a few doors up from the B&B. No awkward run-in with Rebekah then, and there wouldn't be one later if Lauren stayed the night.

She rolled the thought around her head again, and a childish giddiness ran riot in her stomach. She was going to ask Lauren Gray to sleep over, and there was a damn good chance Lauren would say yes. She pulled up, jumped out, and ran around the truck to open the passenger door. Lauren smiled and walked over, looking smoking hot in a cute dress and heels.

She kissed Jamie on the cheek. "Hi."

She looked like she wanted to say something else but had stopped herself. "You look beautiful." Jamie wanted to kiss her properly but didn't want to overstep. *Take it easy.* Lauren blushed adorably.

"Thank you." Lauren got into Jamie's truck. "You're looking very handsome yourself."

Jamie closed the door and rested her hands on the window edge. "I know it's not cool, but I've got to say that I can't believe what we did earlier. I haven't been able to stop thinking about you." That was mostly true. Lauren *hadn't* been on her mind the exact moment Mr. Siegel tried to divebomb into his open grave, but the rest of the time, she—and oh god, the way she'd looked when she'd come—had been front and center.

Lauren glanced away, and her cheek color deepened. "Stop."

Jamie grinned, gently slapped the roof of her truck, and hurried back around to the driver's seat. "Is there anything you're craving to eat?"

Lauren turned in her seat to face Jamie. "Beth delivers," she said. "Your place?"

Oh, mother of monkey nuts. After all this time, they were finally on the same page. Lauren was all Jamie was craving too. She handed Lauren her phone. "Do you want to order while I drive?"

"Sure. Do you want something specific, or should I just get us a selection of dishes?"

"I don't mind, as long as you get some waffle fries." Jamie swung the truck around and headed home. She wasn't about to complain that it was a few hours earlier than she'd anticipated, but her mom would see the truck in the driveway and assume something bad had happened. After Lauren dialed in their order, Jamie took the time at a stop sign to fire off a quick text to her mom, telling her not to disturb them, and everything was all right. Everything was more than all right. Her mom responded immediately with the purple devil face emoji. Jamie rolled her eyes and let out a small laugh.

"What's funny?" Lauren asked.

Jamie tossed her phone onto the dashboard's non-slip mat. "Just my mom being inappropriate. The usual."

On the short drive back to Jamie's, Lauren filled her in on the progress she'd made at Kayla's apartment and that it would be up for sale in the next month. Her voice faltered, and Jamie gently placed her hand on Lauren's thigh. "Are you okay with how fast that's going?"

Lauren nodded slowly. "There's no point delaying it. It's not like my parents or I can afford a second home."

Jamie tried not to visibly react. It was unfair to expect Lauren to be thinking about moving to Damarron, and even if she was, it would probably be too painful to live in her sister's place. It was one thing to hold onto memories but another thing entirely to *live* in those memories. Jamie was moving too fast in the aftermath of her elation at being with Lauren. Tonight was supposed to be about discussing her new plans for the shop and her art. It wasn't about getting caught up in a fairytale ending for her long, drawn-out crush.

She pulled into her drive, and Lauren got out of the car before Jamie could run around to do it. She must've looked disappointed because Lauren smiled.

"I have to open my door occasionally, or I'll get too used to you doing it for me," Lauren said.

Jamie shrugged and headed for her back door. She *wanted* Lauren to get used to it. Her phone pinged after they'd gone into the kitchen, and she checked it. "Our food order is on its way." She pulled out a few plates and put them on the counter. "Do you want something to drink?" Jamie was already at the fridge. She needed a beer to calm her racing heart and quell the sudden onslaught of bouncing balls in her belly. Their first time had been off the charts. How was she supposed to follow that? What if she disappointed Lauren?

"Do you have any vodka?" Lauren asked.

"Sure. With Coke or straight?"

Lauren grinned. "I like my drinks straight but not my women."

Jamie laughed. So Lauren wanted the hard stuff before the night had begun. She was hard to read tonight, and Jamie couldn't tell if wanting liquor already was a good or a bad thing. Surely it didn't signify Lauren was nervous. Jamie thought she had liquid steel running through her blood. She'd never seen anything faze her.

She put some ice in a glass and retrieved a bottle of Absolut from a cabinet. They'd just talked about Kayla so maybe it was to take the edge off that. Jamie poured what she thought was about a double shot and stopped trying to overthink or judge it. Lauren was an adult, and she could drink as much or as little as she wanted for whatever damn reason she wanted.

She got her own beer and clinked her bottle to Lauren's glass. "Cheers. Here's to celebrating new beginnings."

Lauren smiled and sipped her vodka. "You should probably have some paper or a laptop to make notes. When you're just starting out with a new business, the ideas can flow thick and fast, and you don't want to forget anything."

"Oh, okay." Jamie bit her lip and looked around the kitchen. "I don't have a laptop. Should I buy one? I've got a Kindle." Which was of no use at all. What had got her tongue-tied and stuttery again? "I know, I know.

No good. Wait here. I'll grab something from upstairs."

Lauren took a seat at the breakfast bar and raised her glass. "Me and this glass have unfinished business. I'm not going anywhere."

"Good." Jamie rushed out of the kitchen and took the stairs two at a time. She went into her spare room and took a fresh sketchbook from the shelf filled with them. She picked up a fine brush pen from the desk and hurried back downstairs, strangely concerned that Lauren would have finished her drink, changed her mind, and gone home. She stopped at the bottom of the stairs for some self-talk. *Relax.* Lauren was here to stay. She'd suggested they have dinner tonight. It was her idea to eat in. And she'd been the one to kiss Jamie. Lauren wanted this. She *wanted* Jamie.

Jamie danced on the spot as those truths sank in. She pressed her hand to her chest, and her heart thudded beneath her palm. It wasn't the only thing beating to its own rhythm, but she was supposed to be mind-mapping business stuff, not thinking about mapping the planes and contours of Lauren's body with her tongue.

She nearly jumped out of her skin when the doorbell sounded next to her head. She turned and opened the door. A pimply faced high schooler held up a giant bag of food. Lauren must be hungry. It looked like enough food to keep them going all night. Jamie took out her wallet. "How much do I owe you?"

The delivery person shook their head. "Beth says it's on the house. Something about being a special customer, or a special couple. I don't know. I think there's a note in the bag."

"Tell her thank you very much." Jamie offered them five dollars, but they screwed up their face and hesitated. "Come on. The food's free, but your time isn't."

They nodded and took the money. "You're right. Thanks, bruh." They gave Jamie the food and trotted back to their bike.

Jamie laughed. *Bruh?* Did that make her savage? She'd heard that phrase from a teenager at a recent funeral and been surprised when she found out it meant cool. She closed the door and went back into the kitchen. Lauren was finishing off her drink.

"I'm glad I ordered pasta." Lauren held up her glass. "This is stronger than I thought it was. Can I have some water?"

"Sure thing." Jamie placed the bag of food and her pen and pad on the breakfast bar then poured Lauren some filtered water from the fridge dispenser. She sat down and they pulled out all the dishes and laid them out on the countertop.

"I did *not* order all of this," Lauren said.

"They said there was a note in the bag. And they wouldn't take any money."

Lauren hung her head over the giant bag. "Indeed there is." She took out a folded piece of paper and read it to herself. She chuckled but didn't share the contents.

"What did Beth say?" Jamie asked, unable to resist.

"You know how you said your mum was being inappropriate earlier?" Lauren waited and Jamie nodded. "Same with Beth."

"Aw, come on. Spill." Jamie made a grab for the note, but Lauren jerked it away.

She grinned. "Nuh-uh."

Jamie stuck out her bottom lip. "No fair."

Lauren swatted Jamie's nose with the paper. "If you must know—"

"I must."

"If you must know, she was being rude about having enough sustenance to keep us going all night."

Lauren smiled, but there was something else in her expression, a distant sadness, maybe. It was difficult to know where that might be coming from. Jamie's mind had often drifted to thoughts of her dad just after he'd died, and that didn't really ease up for over five years. Even now, a day barely passed without some memory of him finding its way to her consciousness. Her mom had said it was still the same for her, though how she coped with losing the love of her life, Jamie had no idea. She had never experienced a love as all-encompassing as theirs, but her mom's eyes had been raw with tears every morning while Jamie had lived there. For all she knew, she might still wake up that way. Grief didn't fit neatly into anyone's timetable.

"Are you sure you're okay?" Jamie took Lauren's hand gently, and the sorrow seemed to grow darker in her eyes.

Lauren nodded and pulled her hand away. She busied herself opening the food cartons and didn't stop until she found the waffle fries Jamie wanted. After handing them to Jamie, she put a few items on her plate and began to dig in. Jamie did the same but started with the fries. Beth added some secret ingredient to them that Jamie couldn't get enough of. She shoveled a few into her mouth and savored them in silence.

Lauren pointed to the sketchbook Jamie had dropped onto the breakfast bar. "Shall we get started?"

"Sure." She wiped her fingers on a napkin and opened the book. She picked up her pen and hovered over the intimidating blankness of the first page. She was almost too embarrassed to ask, but what was the point of having dinner with the best business brain she knew if she couldn't pick them? Aside from the obvious and very sexy *other* benefit. "What now?"

"Art shops, magazines, websites, artists. You need to do some research. Who are your competitors? Who's doing the same thing you want to do? How are they doing it? Where are they doing it? What's making them successful? What mistakes have they made? And failures—why have they failed? Was it location? Stock choices? Staff issues? Lack of market de—"

"Whoa." Jamie dropped her pen and stretched out her hand. "I can't keep up. Do you mind if I record what you're saying and make notes? Then I can listen to it later and expand on stuff that I missed." She'd started okay, but the legibility of her scribbles rapidly decreased as Lauren's ideas flowed.

"Of course. Sorry. I was going too fast."

Jamie opened the voice recorder on her phone and hit record. "Could you say all of that again?"

Lauren rolled her eyes, but her smile showed she was teasing. She repeated everything, word for word, and Jamie made as many notes as she could. It didn't hurt that she'd get to listen to Lauren's voice whenever she wanted now. It didn't matter that it was just business talk. She had one of those voices Jamie could listen to all day and night, even if she was just reading a dictionary.

For the next two hours, they talked, threw out ideas, ate, drank, and laughed. Jamie had to take a couple of breaks to slow her racing heart and come down from the high of what they were doing. She needed to take a few breaths to keep herself grounded. This was turning out to be one of the best days of her life.

"I can't believe all of this is happening." Jamie put her pen down and got up to get another beer. "And I can't believe I get to do it with you. Do you want more water?"

"I think I'm ready for another vodka."

"You've earned it." Jamie poured the drinks and retook her seat.

Lauren took a hefty swig of her drink. She put her glass down and began to trace her finger along the rim, making it sing. Jamie grinned. *She's making my heart sing.*

"Jamie," Lauren whispered.

Jamie bit her bottom lip. The work was done, now it was time to play. "Yeah," she said, her voice hoarse. She reached out and ran her fingers along Lauren's cheek then over her lips. She leaned in and kissed her softly, tasting the harsh hit of the Absolut.

Lauren pulled back slightly and took Jamie's hand. "I'll help you as much as I can, you know that, don't you?"

Jamie frowned. "You've helped me so much already, but yeah, I thought you would." She wrinkled her nose. "I'm sorry, I shouldn't have just assumed that. I know your time is precious."

"But I won't be *here*, doing it *with* you, as such." Lauren ran her hand over her mouth slowly. "I have to get back to Boston…and my job."

"What?" Jamie pulled her hand from Lauren's. "What about the hub you were planning, the project you and your sister planned? I thought you'd decided to stay and do that."

Lauren shook her head. "I never said that, Jamie. I've never implied that I was staying in Damarron."

Jamie pushed away her sketchbook. "Then what's the point of all this? I thought you were emotionally invested in my art…in me."

"I want you to do this for yourself, not for me. It doesn't matter to me whether you do it or not."

Jamie widened her eyes. Damn, that hurt worse than any bully's gut punch ever had.

Lauren waved her hand and shook her head. "Sorry, that came out all wrong. Of course it matters to me. I'm just trying to say that you should be doing this because it's what you want, not because you think it's what *I* want."

Jamie had no words. She'd misread all of it.

"We'll still see each other," Lauren said. "I'll fly back for your grand opening. And Morten still wants to talk to you about wider distribution, so you can come to the city and see me at the same time."

Weightless. That's what it was. She was falling through the floor and couldn't stop the descent.

"You'll do great things, Jamie. I can feel it. You just need to believe in yourself."

Jamie opened her mouth and let out a noisy breath. "I believed in us." She blinked back the fiery heat of tears behind her eyes. "Why did… This afternoon, didn't that mean anything to you?"

Lauren pressed her lips together and closed her eyes briefly. She sighed deeply. "It meant so much, I can't even tell you—"

"Try." Jamie clenched her jaw. Her stunned heart began to seep an unfamiliar anger into her blood. It was born from pain, she knew that instantly, but she struggled to control it.

"It was precious to share that with you. It really was." She looked away. "I shouldn't have done it, but I couldn't resist. You're so beautiful, and I was so happy that you'd forgiven me. I got carried away with the romanticism of the situation, and I'm sorry that it gave you the impression that I was sticking around. I never meant to deceive or hurt you." She put her hand on Jamie's thigh. "I want to help you with your art. But I can only be your friend. We live such different lives and want different things. I don't see what else I can offer you when I'll be so far away. You deserve someone who puts you at the center of their world."

And that wasn't Lauren. Realization hit her like a steam train. Why had she ever thought she could be? She'd been stupid to think that someone as dynamic as Lauren would ever settle for a small-town hick like her. She couldn't be angry, not really. She should think herself lucky that they'd had this time together at all over the past few weeks. And it made the hours they'd spent in bed earlier more special than it already was. Lauren was offering her friendship, and that was precious. Jamie would take it and hang on to the memories of what could have been—if they were different people. She wasn't about to be the person who'd try to clip the wings of such a magnificent woman, as hard as it would be to let Lauren go. And she couldn't pretend she'd be happy living in the city, closed in by all the buildings and crowded by the hordes of people. She fought the urge to drop to her knees and beg Lauren to reconsider, to think about a long-distance relationship, an open one—whatever Lauren wanted that might make them work. But Jamie wasn't what Lauren wanted, and it wouldn't be enough for Jamie. She wanted to wake with Lauren by her side every morning.

She nodded slowly. Lauren's hand was still on her thigh, and Jamie interlaced their fingers. "I understand. Thank you for what we did share. I'll remember it always." She kissed Lauren gently on the cheek, desperately ignoring the lure of her soft lips. "You've helped me find my way to a self-confidence that would never have been possible without you. I can't thank you enough for that either."

Lauren brought Jamie's hand to her mouth and kissed her knuckles. "You're a special person, Jamie. I'm sorry I can't be *your* special person." She released Jamie and got up from her stool. "I should go. I've got some things to sort out with my parents before I leave."

Jamie didn't want to ask when that would be. She swallowed back the pleas and the tears, and she nodded. "Let me take you back to Nancy's."

Lauren touched Jamie's forearm. "No, that's okay. I can't ask you to do that."

"You're not asking. I'm offering." Jamie offered a weak smile. "It's the least a friend could do when you've helped me so much with all of this." She motioned to the sketchbook, its pages teeming with life and ideas. All Jamie felt was dry and withered inside, her heart an empty nest where once there'd been the burgeoning promise of new life and love.

"Are you sure?"

Jamie nodded. "I'm sure. Let's go."

Lauren gathered her things, and they went out to the truck. Jamie still opened the door for her; friends could do that, and her chivalry hadn't died along with her hopes of a future with Lauren. Jamie closed the passenger door, not just on Lauren, but on their potential life together. It'd been an amazing dream while it had lasted. Now she had to focus that energy on her dreams of a new career. Being with Lauren was a fantasy she'd had since high school. Now all Jamie had to do was place Lauren back in that frame and treasure the friendship that was being offered. She could do no more. But the voice at the back of her mind that screamed, "Bullshit," would take some convincing given how her heart was breaking.

CHAPTER TWENTY-FIVE

LAUREN MOVED UP HER plans to get out of town. She couldn't face running into Jamie again in case her resolve failed her, and she ended up begging Jamie to come to Boston with her. Lauren respected her wishes far too much to do that. The rental company delivered her car to Nancy's at just after eight, and it didn't take long to pack the trunk, especially with Rebekah's overenthusiastic help.

Lauren could've taken a cab but on her way to the airport, she wanted to drive past the spot where Kayla's accident had happened, where Kayla had taken her last breath. It was the only place she hadn't been able to face, and she wanted that closure before she left town for a while. There was no way she was doing that in front of an Uber driver.

She locked the car and wandered across to Beth's to say goodbye.

Beth hugged her, then held her at arm's length. She narrowed her eyes. "I don't understand."

Lauren sighed deeply and motioned toward a booth at the back. "Sit with me?" They sat down, and she laid out what had happened.

"I'm sorry, Lauren. I had no idea you had such strong feelings for Jamie. I thought she was just a distraction from the grief you were feeling."

"I wish it was that." She pressed her hands to her chest. "Then this wouldn't ache so much." She glanced at her watch. Her flight was still six hours away, but she had to see her parents, and she didn't want to rush at Kayla's crash site either. She had no idea how that was going to affect her or how long she'd need there. If she missed her check-in, she'd stay at a motel nearby and get the next flight. Her hurry to get out of town was all about Jamie. "I have to say goodbye to my parents."

They stood and hugged.

"You won't make it so long next time?" Beth asked.

"Definitely not." Lauren wasn't about to dump her resolution to see her parents more often, but after she'd gotten back to reality, it might take a while to reclaim the person she'd been three weeks ago. "Take care."

She hurried out of the restaurant and drove to her parents' house, trying to concentrate on the road instead of the whirr of conflicting thoughts in her mind. When she pulled into the driveway, the familiar sight of her dad working in the front yard was oddly comforting. He wandered over and opened the door when she'd cut the engine.

"Thanks for stopping by before you leave," he said. "We both appreciate it."

"Of course." She was barely out of the driver's seat before he enveloped her in a bone-crushing embrace.

He finally released her and smiled. "Your mom's waiting."

He draped his arm around her shoulder, and they walked awkwardly into the house. Her mom looked up from whatever magazine she was reading, and her eyes were bloodshot. Tears streaked her makeup, but when she smiled, it seemed genuine.

"Hey, Mom."

She got up from the table and hugged her. Lauren couldn't recall this much affection being shown so freely, but she hadn't been around that much either, so what did she really know?

"How are you?"

Lauren almost shared how she truly was. She *almost* told her mom about Jamie, and about how she was fleeing town because everything had gotten way too complicated. "I'm fine. How are you?" She'd try next time she visited, when she'd gotten used to not having Kayla around.

"I'm okay." She pressed her lips together and smiled again, but this time, the sadness was unmistakable.

The weight of grief and loss filled the room and left little space for anything else. They would all have to get used to the hole Kayla had left. Lauren made small talk, and her mom made coffee. They sat around the table for a while, talking about everything and nothing at the same time, and avoiding talking about Kayla at all. It wouldn't be that way forever, would it? Wouldn't they get to a place where they could share their memories of Kayla and all the good times?

"What about your plans for the literacy hub?" her mom asked. "I thought you and your father were going to make that happen."

Lauren had been dreading this topic being raised. "Everything's raw right now, Mom. And there's too much going on with the LitLot expansion. We've employed a whole new team of people." Even as she said them, the words echoed emptily in her heart and mind. She shoved away the intrusive realization. She didn't have to accept it. Once she was home, her passion for the new project would return. It had been her brainchild after all.

Her mom stroked Lauren's arm. "That's someone else's dream, sweetheart. You've made it happen, but it wasn't your dream to begin with."

She glanced across the room, and Lauren followed her gaze to the family photograph they'd posed for over a decade ago. Seeing Kayla looking so vibrant and alive hammered her mom's words home. It was almost verbatim what Kayla had said to her every time they'd gotten together. And Lauren had always responded that they had plenty of time to make their own dream a reality. How wrong she'd been. She'd given nothing but lame excuses, and now it was too late.

Her dad took her hand and pulled her focus back to him. "Whenever you're ready, Lauren. You do whatever's right for you. We'll be here."

Lauren blinked away her tears and fell into another embrace with them both. She thought she knew what was right for her, but maybe she didn't. Without Kayla as her sounding board, and with Whit hundreds of miles away, she had no choice but to make her own decisions. How was that so hard? She was a CEO, and she was thirty-three, not thirteen. Adulting hadn't been this hard before. *Because my heart hasn't been involved before.* Decisions based on logic and strategy were far easier. Emotion clouded judgment and confused the brain. Lauren had protected herself all these years without knowing why, and now that her heart *did* ache, the reason became crystal clear. But what was right for her? That answer was being elusive.

No, she couldn't backtrack. She'd never been one to falter, and she wasn't going to start now. She and Jamie were in two different places, physically and emotionally. It was better this way. "I have to go."

"Don't be a stranger, honey," her dad said.

Was that what she'd become? She and Kayla had often joked about Lauren being adopted, but deep down, she'd treasured the connection to her parents. Trouble was, she'd buried it so deep, she'd somehow managed to lose track of how she really felt about her family. "I promise I won't. I'll be back for Thanksgiving, but I'll try to come home before that."

"There's no pressure. We'd love to see you anytime." Her dad hung his arm over her mom's shoulder and pulled her closer.

"We love you, Lauren." Her mom's bottom lip and chin quivered.

"I love you too." She retreated to her car and reversed down the driveway. She gave one last wave and didn't look back. Moving forward was the only way she knew how to deal with anything. She'd get back to her life and routine, and she was sure everything else would fade away. The desperate agony of losing Kayla would lessen, and the taunting memories of Jamie's touch on her skin would grow faint. Didn't time heal everything?

CHAPTER TWENTY-SIX

JAMIE HAD THROWN HER pre-work morning routine out the window. After making the mistake of hitting play on last night's recorded conversation with Lauren, she'd dropped onto her bed and hadn't moved since. Hearing her voice brought all the pain of her leaving back again. Not that it had gone far; she'd only had respite in a few hours of sleep. The rest of the night, she'd tossed and turned and replayed their conversation, wishing she'd told Lauren that she loved her and that she always had. But it was clear Lauren had made the choice for them. She had a life in Boston, and that didn't include Jamie. How could it? It wasn't like Jamie had made any attempt to compromise on the potential of a long-distance relationship.

She'd spent her teenage years yearning for Lauren, and their one afternoon of passion would have to suffice. She should be realistic and move on. She pressed play again. Torturing herself wouldn't help, but right now, the only thing that would get her through being without Lauren was to listen to her voice and remember how her skin felt beneath Jamie's fingers.

"I'll help you as much as I can, you know that, don't you?"

Jamie grasped onto the sliver of hope Lauren's words offered. Maybe Lauren would come around over time. If they saw each other, even over Zoom or FaceTime, Jamie could try to charm her into coming back, into trying to make a life together in Damarron. She closed her eyes and sighed deeply. What was she thinking? Lauren had big things to achieve still, and she couldn't do that in this town. Jamie couldn't clip Lauren's wings. That would be selfish. She had to let Lauren go.

"Jamie?"

She bolted upright at the sound of her mom's panicked tone. "I'm up here. Are you okay?"

Her mom thudded up the stairs and pushed Jamie's bedroom door open. "Of course I am. It's you I'm worried about. Why haven't you gone to work? Are you sick?"

Lovesick, yeah. Jamie glanced at her watch. She was already an hour late. "No, I'm fine."

Olly thundered into the room and jumped onto her bed. He gave his usual look of sad understanding before flopping his head onto her pillow.

Her mom raised her eyebrow and tilted her head to the side. She cupped Jamie's chin and looked at her through narrowed eyes. "Did something happen last night?"

Jamie stepped back to her bed and stroked Olly, the perfect excuse to break eye contact and stop her mom seeing the agony deep in her soul. "No, nothing happened."

"Ah, now I understand. Sex isn't as important to everyone as it might be to you," her mom said and sat beside Jamie.

"Ew, Mom."

"Do you want to talk about it?"

Jamie shook her head. Hard. "I don't ever want to have another conversation about sex with you. The one we had when I was thirteen was one too many, thanks."

Her mom made a face and shrugged. "Call Fran to talk about it then, but don't mope around the house feeling sorry for yourself. Better yet, talk to Lauren about it. Communication is the key to a successful relationship, honey."

"I'd love to talk to Lauren about anything and everything, but she's leaving." Jamie scrunched Olly's head, but it didn't make her feel better like it was supposed to. *Dog therapy, my ass.* "She came over last night to help me plan my idea for a shop in town and—"

"A shop?" Her mom pressed her hand over her mouth briefly. "Sorry, go on." She tapped Jamie's knee. "But that's so exciting, I want to hear all about it after you've told me about last night."

She should be more excited about that, sure, but it was hard to be passionate about her art when her heart had just been ripped out of her chest. Every dream she'd ever had about being with Lauren was gone. She'd compared every other lover to an ideal of a woman she could never have. It could've stayed a fantasy forever if it hadn't been for the past few weeks. Now, it was all gone. She'd had a shot and blown it. "She's going back to Boston." Jamie lay on her back, and Olly shifted so he could bathe her face in sloppy kisses. She pulled him to her and held tight, putting a stop to the stinky face wash without missing out on his loving cuddle.

"And you just let her go and thanked her for her time? Oh, Jamie, do you really think so little of yourself that you're going to let the love of your life just get on a plane and fly out of your life?"

Her mom's hardline response made her look over the warm mound of fur and love in her arms. "She won't be out of my life. She's going to help me get my shop off the ground. And there are wider distribution options with her contact. And who said she was the love of my life?"

Her mom poked Jamie's thigh. "You did. When you were nine. And again when you were eleven, fourteen, and sixteen. And one more time when you came home drunk at twenty-five." Her mom lay back and shuffled onto her side to face Jamie.

"Kept those loaded in the barrel, didn't you?"

"There are probably other times I don't remember. Menopause hits the memory hard, they say, but I don't remember where I read that."

Jamie laughed gently. "It doesn't matter what I said. She's heading back home. Her life and work are there, and mine's here."

Her mom frowned. "You don't have to stay in Damarron for me. You do know that, don't you?"

"What are you talking about?"

"I mean that I don't want you living your life around me." She waved her hand. "I have plenty of people to keep me company." Her mom shifted and put her head on Olly's back. "Although this pup is the best male company in town."

"I love it here, and I've never liked cities." Jamie shuddered and got up from the bed. She walked over to the window and took in the view. Beyond the wide line of trees, the lake shimmered in the distance. "All those people packed in close proximity makes it difficult to breathe. And that's without the air pollution." She turned back to her mom. "A city would suffocate me."

"And you're sure she wouldn't come back to live here?"

Jamie shrugged. "I didn't ask, but she made it clear she doesn't belong here."

"And did you tell her that you loved her?"

"No." Jamie rubbed her forehead to force away the threat of an ache in her head to match the one in her heart. "I haven't even told myself that I love her yet. Not really."

Her mom joined her at the window and took her hand. "Then you're keeping a big secret from yourself for no reason." Her mom squeezed hard when Jamie rolled her eyes. "Moms are supposed to have all the answers, no matter how old you get."

Jamie smiled. Her mom always had the answers, she couldn't deny that. And really, Jamie was fully aware that she loved Lauren. She always had. She probably always would… "I don't want to complicate her life with extra emotion, Mom. She's struggling with losing Kayla. She doesn't need my shit too."

"Isn't that her decision to make?" her mom asked. Olly whined and made the noise that wasn't quite a bark. "Olly agrees with me. You can't argue with both of us."

Jamie blew out a long breath. "I guess rejection is the worst that could happen, right? Better that than living with the regret of never telling her." Her declaration of love couldn't possibly be enough, but the more she talked about it, the stronger the realization hit that Jamie had to risk it, whatever the outcome. "I'll go to Nancy's. She can't be gone yet."

Her mom kissed Jamie's cheek. "Be brave, honey. Just like your dad."

His loss gripped her heart and squeezed briefly. He'd been strong and faced her mom's parents when they didn't approve of him. He didn't stop fighting for her, and he won out in the end. Maybe history *could* kind of repeat itself.

CHAPTER TWENTY-SEVEN

Lauren gripped the steering wheel tighter as she neared the stretch of road that had taken her sister's life. They'd taken this route together so many times that they could almost drive it with their eyes closed. Tears began to blur Lauren's vision. A blown tire could happen to anyone at any time, but less than two percent ended in fatalities. Why did Kayla have to be a statistic? She hated numbers. Words, she loved. But she'd hated numbers with an unholy passion. Kayla had just been taking a drive to clear her head after a tough day at work; her mom had said she'd gotten a text from her before she took off. Twenty miles outside town, driving with the top down, the wind blowing through her hair, the sun on her face… her last moments would've been filled with peace.

Lauren slowed the car to a stop and pulled into the side of the road. The long run of jet-black rubber marks still marred the light gray surface, their winding path evidence of how she'd braked to swerve away from the young deer. Most everyone in that town would've plowed straight through it, but Kayla had always been a "do no harm" kind of human. And of course, she'd steered her car into the roadside rather than the path of an oncoming car. That would've been fine, had it not been for the giant pothole that had busted her tire and sent the car spiraling out of control into the rockface.

Lauren got out of the car on autopilot and wandered along the gravel. The repair work on the hole was obvious. It should've been attended to before, but it hadn't been. So many what ifs and why nots, but they were useless and would only serve to drive her crazy. There was no time travel to fix the wrongs, no one to answer her questions. There was no grand design she wanted to hear anything about.

Her sister was gone, and she'd left a hole in Lauren's soul that no amount of grief, blame, or rage would heal or fill.

But through losing Kayla, Lauren had found Jamie. And in that precious time they'd spent together, she'd discovered a love she'd never considered pursuing. Fixated on building a solid tomorrow, driven by an all-consuming need to achieve, and bolstered by external validation, Lauren had no concept of living in the moment. The best time is now. She'd heard or read that somewhere. Only recently had she begun to understand what it meant.

She dropped to her knees and pressed her hands against the compacted gravel. Everything was or would be dust and dirt. What was the point of spending her whole life building a future she might not ever get to enjoy? Jamie was in her present. And she wouldn't be around forever. Some other lucky woman would come along, snap her up, and become the focus of her huge capacity for love.

Meanwhile, Lauren worked hard at a charity she hadn't created. *"That's someone else's dream."* Kayla and Lauren's dream had been the literacy hub. What was really stopping her from staying in Damarron to finally realize that dream? She'd built the small town into some kind of villain that sucked away dreams. But it was just a place, nothing more, nothing less. *She* chose what she could and couldn't do, not the town. And what were *her* dreams? Perhaps now was the time to finally think about what would make her happy in an area other than her work life. What did she want? Who did she want? Had she ever known or even stopped to think about that? Being with Jamie had shown her a different life, a different way to be. She had to see where that led before it was too late, because no one got served notice on their life, and no one ever knew when it was too late. So why should she *not* stay to explore her feelings for Jamie?

She huffed. There was nothing to explore. She knew damn well she was in love with Jamie, and that's why she'd run. She'd encouraged Jamie out of her comfort zone to pursue her art, so Lauren should take her own advice and do the same. She should hand in her notice, develop their idea, and be with Jamie.

Lauren gasped for breath as the enormity of it hit her. Her intuition spoke to her. There was no doubt, no fear, no unsteady heart. There was only the certainty that she had to go back and find out if Jamie felt the same. She got to her feet, feeling stronger and more sure of her decision with every step back to the car. She took one last look at the place where her sister had died and smiled. Kayla would always live in her heart and mind, and Lauren would always miss her, but she'd create the hub in her memory so Kayla could live on in the hearts and minds of others.

Lauren got back on the road and turned the car around a little farther along the route. As she left the accident site, she swore she heard Kayla's gentle laugh. "I'll make you proud, sis," Lauren said and drove toward her new dream.

CHAPTER TWENTY-EIGHT

"I DON'T THINK YOU should leave. No. You should stay here. With me. No. I want you to stay. Here. With me." Jamie smacked the steering wheel of her truck. Why did she get so tongue-tied when it was so important that the words come out right? She couldn't tell Lauren that she *should* be doing anything. All she could do was tell Lauren how she felt and leave her to decide what to do. Maybe she should lead with the three words that could be so powerful and so devastating. Lauren's response could lift Jamie higher than the clouds, or it could send her crashing against the rocks, heart smashed into pieces.

Powerful or devastating. Whatever the outcome, Jamie steeled herself as she drove to face it. Rebekah had been particularly unhelpful, but Beth had practically pushed her back out of her restaurant and into her truck to pursue Lauren to the airport. That had to be a good sign. The support of the best friend was like the official seal of approval in every romantic movie Jamie had ever watched. Still, Jamie prepared for rejection and tried hard to channel her dad and stay brave and courageous.

Jamie hit the road that Kayla had died on, and a twist of grief wrapped around her heart. Lauren would have to pass where her sister had come off the highway. The accident was the only thing they hadn't talked about over the past few weeks. In all their conversations, how and where Kayla had died hadn't come up. Jamie had met enough grieving family members, partners, and loved ones to know that the *why* of someone's death was almost always their first thought and the one that stayed in their heads often for months and years afterward. That was especially true when the death had been unexpected or the person too young. When the grave was long grown over, that question remained fresh and eternally unanswered.

In all her years digging and filling in graves, the one lesson Jamie took from it and held close to her heart was that all she ever had was right now. Her dad's death had sown the seed of that belief when she was too young to understand it, but it had flowered with every body she'd returned to the earth.

So she couldn't live with not knowing what might've happened if only she'd offered her heart to Lauren. And even if she was rejected, Jamie could live with the love and loss far better than never having loved at all.

The route was as quiet as it always was, but she slowed to just under the speed limit anyway. After Kayla's death, everyone in town said they did the same. A car came toward her on the other side of the road. As it neared, the lights flashed frantically, and its horn blared.

"What the hell?" Jamie glared into the car as they crossed paths on a corner. "Lauren!" Jamie checked her rearview before slamming on her brakes. She whipped the car around and headed back around the corner only to discover Lauren had done the same, and they sailed past each other again. "Damn it."

Jamie pulled over and cut her engine. She grabbed her phone from the center console and called Lauren. No answer. Should she turn around again? The rental car pulled up behind her, answering her question, and Jamie flung open her door. Her seatbelt halted her progress, and she had a quick fight with it before she jumped out of her truck and ran toward Lauren, who was just closing her door.

Jamie stopped short of picking Lauren up and spinning her around in her arms. She'd turned her car around, that was all. It didn't have to mean anything big. "Hi." She kicked at the gravel and a piece flew up and struck Lauren's shin. "Oh, shit."

"Oww!"

Lauren leaned against the hood of her car, and Jamie dropped to her knees to check the damage.

"Do you have something against my legs?" Lauren asked.

Jamie smacked her forehead with her palm. "Oh god, I'm so sorry."

"You were sorry last time. I'm not sure it means anything if you keep doing the same thing."

Jamie looked up and bit her lip. From every angle, Lauren was beautiful. What the hell was she thinking, kicking the ground? "At least this time I've got a first aid kit." She thumbed toward her truck.

Lauren raised her eyebrow. "No filthy paint rags to dress my war wound? I'm almost disappointed."

Her smile swelled Jamie's heart. She summoned all the courage she had and took a deep, cleansing breath. "I have to tell you something."

Lauren put her hand on Jamie's shoulder. "Can you tell me when you've stopped the bleeding? I'd hate to pass out on you." She wiggled her eyebrows and grinned.

"Fine." Jamie jumped up, raced to her truck, and returned with the emergency kit. Lauren had returned to the driver's seat and sat sideways with her legs out of the car. The bleeding had already stopped, and when Jamie wiped Lauren's leg, she saw it was barely a scratch. "You may need plastic surgery on this. I'm going to have to sell a lot of my pieces to pay for it…unless you'll accept another form of payment?" Jamie looked up into Lauren's eyes, and her heart pounded in her ears. This was it. This was the moment she finally told Lauren how she really felt about her.

"Scars are good reminders of how we've lived. Why would I want to erase where you've maimed me for life?" Lauren laughed.

"That's not overdramatic at all." Jamie continued to hold Lauren's leg even though she'd put the BandAid on. Her soft, warm skin stirred memories of their afternoon together in Lauren's hotel room. God, she wanted repeats of that performance for the rest of her life. "But you don't mind having reminders of me on your body?"

"Where are you going with this, Jamie?"

Jamie wrinkled her nose. She'd put it off long enough. But… "Why were you honking and flashing your lights like a maniac?"

"Now who's being overdramatic?" Lauren shrugged. "I was just saying hi."

Jamie traced light patterns on Lauren's calf. Lauren hadn't pulled her leg away, so Jamie wasn't about to lose contact willingly. "Rebekah said you'd left for the airport. I thought I'd missed saying goodbye."

"Were you going somewhere special?" Lauren ran her fingers along Jamie's tie.

"I wasn't going to a special place, but I was hoping to see a special someone." She was glad she was squatting on the ground. There was no way she'd trust her legs to hold her upright. Every cell and nerve shook with the anticipation of what she was working up to saying.

Lauren straightened and tipped her chin back. "Who do you know out here?"

She almost sounded jealous, but Jamie dismissed that thought as nonsense. "A few people, actually, but I wasn't going to see them. I was doing that dopey romantic thing you see on movies where the jilted lover makes a last-ditch attempt to win the love of her life back with an over-the-top gesture."

Lauren swallowed. Her eyes brightened, and her smile returned, wider than before. "*I'm* your 'someone special.' You were driving to the airport for me?"

Jamie looked down and concentrated on Lauren's leg, still resting on Jamie's thigh. "You sound surprise—"

"*I'm* the love of your life?"

Crap. Lauren's surprise seemed to have turned into disbelief. That phrase put so much pressure on everything. As if just telling Lauren she loved her wouldn't be enough of a shock. "Um, y'know. It's just a saying. That's what they say in the movies. It doesn't mean—"

Lauren pulled Jamie up by her tie and stopped her babbling with a deep kiss. Jamie wrapped her arms around Lauren and held her tight. She hadn't exactly said the words, and she certainly hadn't been as smooth as she'd planned to be, but Lauren's response was perfect.

Lauren grasped the back of Jamie's head and sent all kinds of buzzy signals zinging around Jamie's body. She pulled back slightly and dragged her nail over Jamie's bottom lip. Jamie moaned softly and would've dissolved onto the ground if it wasn't for Lauren's strong grip on her tie.

Lauren broke away, and her smile was almost smug. "Were you chasing me to the airport to tell me you were in love with me?"

Jamie nodded, incapable of speech since all energies were directed elsewhere after *that* kiss. Even breathing properly was a struggle.

Lauren trailed her nails along Jamie's jawbone. "And you were hoping that grand gesture would make me reconsider leaving?"

"Maybe," she whispered hoarsely. "Or maybe just getting you to think about trying to make us work. Somehow. I'll travel. I don't care what I have to do, but I don't want to be without you, Lauren. I can't—"

Lauren put her finger to Jamie's lips. "I'm staying." She pulled Jamie in for another kiss. "I have to create the hub for Kayla, and for me. I can change lives here for now."

Jamie savored Lauren's taste on her lips, but she wasn't convinced. "'For now?' And then you'll go?" She closed her eyes for a moment and mentally whacked herself upside the head. Why spoil the now? Neither of them could know what the future held. The now should be enough.

"And then I'll reassess." She smiled and gently caressed Jamie's cheek.

"If the last few weeks have taught me anything, it's that I can work from anywhere and still make things happen."

Hope rose in Jamie's heart and nearly lifted her off the ground.

Lauren kissed Jamie's nose. "I'll have to fly out for meetings sometimes, but I guess there are worse bases to have than Damarron when there's a super sexy artist in my bed."

Jamie didn't know which part of that sentence she liked best. She'd never been called super sexy or an artist before, and she liked the sound of both. But more mind-blowing than that was Lauren's willingness to live in their hometown and to make her ambitions to change the world work from there too. "I want to meet Morten, if he's still willing. You're right about my art, and I want to do as much as I can with it. Maybe not right away, but eventually, I want to sell it farther from home, maybe even in cities close by." Jamie hadn't said it out loud, but there was only the now, and she wanted to do everything she could in whatever time she had.

"We're doing this?" Lauren asked.

"I love you, Lauren. I've always loved you. I'll do anything to make this work."

Lauren pulled Jamie in for another deep and passionate kiss. Everything was falling into place in ways Jamie had never imagined possible.

Lauren broke away and tugged on Jamie's tie. "And somehow, you've managed to make me fall in love with you so deeply that I'm willing to change my whole life to be with you—just like in the movies."

Jamie clasped her hands over Lauren's. "I don't want you to regret this decision. Are you sure?"

Lauren smiled. "I'm sure about you, and that's all I need. Everything else will follow, and we'll figure it out. But I've had some realizations of my own, and I know this is what I want." She blinked rapidly as her eyes became glassy. "And I think Kayla would be proud of me for growing up a little." She began to undo Jamie's tie. "How about we go to your place and get you out of this restrictive neckwear?" She undid a few of Jamie's shirt buttons and ran her fingers across Jamie's chest. "I feel like rewarding your grand gesture."

Jamie sank a little deeper into her new fantasy reality and let out a husky breath. "I like the sound of that. Let's go." She stood and Lauren shifted, catching the horn and making them both jump, which reminded Jamie of how Lauren had gotten her attention ten minutes ago. "You didn't really answer my question about all the honking and flashing you were doing."

"I did." Lauren fastened her seatbelt and pulled the door closed.

Jamie waited until Lauren lowered the window. "You were just saying hi?"

"Yep."

Jamie bent over and rested her forearms on the door. "The airport's in the other direction."

"Yep." Lauren turned the ignition. "Are we going to your place, or are we playing twenty questions?"

"Were you making a grand gesture of your own?" Jamie grinned, buoyed by the possibility that Lauren had been coming back for her.

Lauren ran her hand through Jamie's hair and dragged her nails across the back of her neck. "I'm pleading the fifth. Get in your truck and lead me home."

Home. She liked the sound of that too. "Sure thing." Jamie kissed Lauren one last time before heading back to her truck. She took a long look back at Lauren before getting in, still not quite ready to believe Lauren would be following her back to her place. Jamie hoped to make it their place as soon as possible. If Lauren was all in, why wait? The best time for everything was right now.

EPILOGUE

Eighteen months later.

Lauren took one last look around. "We're ready."

Jamie tugged the bottom of her vest and messed with her tie. "How do I look? Am *I* ready?"

"You look spectacular." Lauren stepped closer and straightened Jamie's outfit a little. "And there's a part of me that can't wait for this to be over so I can take you back to the hotel and have my way with you."

Jamie tilted her head. "*All* of me can't wait for this to be over, and not just because what you said sounds amazing. Look at this." Jamie held up her phone. "Fran sent me this from outside. Look at all those people."

Lauren nodded. "Impressive. Why are you surprised?"

Jamie wrinkled her nose and glanced at the door. "I know. I shouldn't be. You organized this, so of course lots of people are here for you."

Lauren held Jamie's shoulders and gave her a little shake. "They're here for *you*, and they've have been looking forward to this exhibition and auction for months. Morten's been doing a great job of promoting you, and everyone *loves* a reclusive and reluctant artist."

Darryl, the exhibition's curator, waved from the other side of the room and hurried over. He tapped his watch. "It's time to open the doors, honey. Are you ready for this?"

Jamie didn't respond and looked like she might faint. Lauren stood by her side and gave her arm a light squeeze. "She's ready."

Darryl turned and headed for the entrance.

"Oh my god."

Lauren wrapped her arm around Jamie's shoulders. "Everything's going to be fine." When Jamie still didn't respond, Lauren moved in front of her and held her chin gently. "Thank you for doing this. You've got such a big heart. How did I get to be so lucky?"

Jamie looked up. "You might not think that when nothing sells, and we don't raise a cent for your hub."

"Don't be crazy," Lauren said, finding it hard not to melt at Jamie's adorable show of vulnerability. She had so much to be confident about, and her lack of ego was astonishing. "There are already internet bids on almost everything. You're going to raise enough money to complete the hub and fund the running costs for five years."

Jamie huffed. "No pressure."

Lauren released Jamie's chin and grasped her hands. "I've already done the math. Even if none of that huge crowd out there raise their paddle for any of your lots, the night will still be a huge success."

Jamie gave a small smile. "Really? You're not just trying to make me feel good?"

"I'm always trying to make you feel good, but I promise that's the truth." Lauren lifted Jamie's hands and kissed her fingers. "These are magic."

Jamie wiggled her eyebrows. "It was very different circumstances when you told me that earlier."

Lauren rolled her eyes and released her grip. "You can remind me of those circumstances when we get back to the hotel, but first let's sell out your debut exhibition."

Fran and Terri were the first through the doors with the VIP crowd of family and friends. They embraced, though Lauren thought Jamie's hug with Terri might last the whole night.

"Shouldn't you be studying?" Jamie asked when they finally parted.

"I wouldn't miss this even if I had finals tomorrow—which I don't, so there's no need to worry," Terri said and turned in a circle, taking the space in. "This is incredible."

Fran grabbed an entire tray of champagne from a passing server and handed them around. "Let's toast the great artist."

Lauren raised her glass. "I'll leave the unholy trinity to catch up while I work the room." She kissed Jamie's cheek and squeezed her ass. "See you later, superstar."

Jamie caught hold of Lauren's wrist. "Don't go out of sight, will you? I need to see you to keep me grounded."

Lauren kissed her again. "I promise. Try to enjoy it. This is a huge night for you." She waited until Jamie nodded and took a deep breath. She turned back to Fran and Terri, and Lauren took that as her opportunity to go to Whit, who was coming in at the end of the VIP line.

"I miss you," Whit whispered as they embraced.

"You're too busy to miss me." Lauren offered her glass to Whit, and she took a quick drink before snagging her own.

She clinked her glass to Lauren's. "That's all your fault too."

Lauren smiled. It felt good to be nicely blamed for making something so successful that it was difficult to cope with the work. "How's Charlotte working out as your number one?"

Whit shook her head. "You made mentoring look so easy. If it wasn't for our monthly development sessions, I would've already blown it."

Lauren gave her a light shove. "That's not true. I wouldn't have recommended you as my successor if you weren't ready for the challenge. I'm hearing only good things about your work."

Whit grinned. "I learned from the best." She gestured to the auction stage toward the rear of the room. "Is this where you finally scrape enough money together to buy your Aston Martin?"

"Probably five times over if the starting bids are anything to go by."

Whit's expression turned serious, and she rubbed Lauren's upper arm. "Kayla would've loved this."

Lauren blinked her instant tears away. "Why do you want to ruin my makeup?" She looked over Whit's shoulder and saw her mom and dad coming in. "Saved by the parents."

"I'm sorry," Whit said. "I didn't mean to upset you."

Lauren shook her head. "It's okay. I don't think many of us will get out of here tonight without sobbing. It's a big night." She hugged Whit again. "You're seated up front with us. We'll talk more later."

"Good. If you get ten minutes, I need to pick your brains about the New Jersey education board."

Lauren laughed. "Whatever you need." She turned into her dad's open arms, and his tight squeeze almost took her breath away. She'd already had more hugs tonight than she'd had in the past month. This new family thing was taking some getting used to, but she was happily coping. "I need to breathe, Dad."

He let her go and chuckled. "Sorry, sweetheart."

Her mom took her turn. "Kayla would've been so proud of everything you're doing for your hub, honey."

Lauren let out a long sigh. There was no way waterproof makeup would withstand the next half hour, let alone the rest of the night. She looked over her mom's shoulder and winked at Jamie, who seemed to have relaxed now that her friends were by her side. "I couldn't have done any of it without Jamie."

"And where is our amazing artist?" her dad asked.

Lauren pointed, and they exchanged a wave.

Her mom rubbed her hands together. "I've got a lot to thank her for."

"And she's heard it a hundred times already." Which was probably a massive underestimation of exactly how many times Lauren's mom had vocalized her gratitude to Jamie over the past eighteen months for "bringing my daughter home." Lauren wasn't about to complain. Her new life still fulfilled her ambitions, but it was also making her long-neglected personal life a whole lot more fulfilling too. She stayed busy with the hub development and some consultation work, and the balance she and Jamie had struck at home was something she'd never thought possible. Now she was wondering why she'd waited so long to discover it.

Morten approached with Jamie's mom, Val, hooked into his arm and introduced himself to Lauren's parents. They exchanged pleasantries before he excused himself to attend to some last-minute preparations. Val watched him walk away in much the same way as Lauren always enjoyed watching Jamie walk away.

"Found a new friend?" Lauren asked.

Val answered with a grin. "My lips are sealed—unless you want to get me another glass of this champagne?"

"I'll get you the champagne, but you can keep the details."

Lauren's mom took Val by the forearm and began to lead her away. "She might not want details, but I do." She cast a glance over her shoulder. "I'll be back in a little while, darling."

Her dad laughed and waved her away. "It'd be nice if Val found someone she liked enough to want them to stick around."

Lauren shrugged. Jamie had relayed the story of her parents and their love affair, and it was clear replacing Jamie's father wasn't on her agenda, now or ever. "She had her person, Dad. She doesn't want anything other than some company."

"And what about you? Have you found *your* person?"

Lauren glanced across at Jamie, looking smart and sexy in Lauren's favorite outfit of shirt, tie, and jeans. She couldn't wait to slowly peel those clothes from Jamie's body when this was all over. "Yes. I have."

Her dad smiled broadly, and the overhead spotlights glistened in his eyes. "I'm glad, honey. I wondered if you ever would. You were always so focused on everyone else, I didn't think you'd ever stop to look at what you needed."

Lauren smiled. She'd never stopped to appreciate how in tune her dad was with people, especially his family. Working beside him to design the hub had given her a new sense of how special he really was, and it was time she was grateful for. "Now I get to do what I love and go home to a woman who loves me with all of her heart." She knew she hadn't been ready before, and that no woman she'd slept with would've brought her to this place. No other woman had been as special as Jamie was, and Lauren would never stop being grateful for Jamie putting herself out there the way she had. She shuddered at the thought of how much poorer her life would be without Jamie's love.

As if registering Lauren's thoughts, Jamie came over, grasped her hand, and kissed her lightly.

"Hey, David. Thanks for coming."

"I wouldn't have missed this, Jamie. What you're doing is such a grand gesture."

Lauren and Jamie exchanged a knowing glance. "I'm all for grand gestures. And you know I'll do anything for your daughter."

Her dad nodded. "You're a very special person." He coughed and looked away. "I'm going to find your mother and take a look at the exhibition. See you later."

After he'd left, Jamie pulled Lauren in closer. "I can see where you get your reluctance to show your emotion."

"I resent that." Lauren pouted. "I cultivated my lack of emotion very carefully. It's all my own doing." She ran her fingers over Jamie's tie. "Except elation. You make it exceptionally difficult for me to conceal that."

Jamie grinned. "Oh, yeah? Why's that?"

Lauren extended the fingers of her left hand and admired her engagement ring. "This, for starters. You've promised that this is the happy ever after I never knew I was looking for."

"You were always my happy ever after." Jamie lifted Lauren's hand and kissed each of her fingers. "Everything else has just been chapters along the way while I waited for you to catch up with our story."

"You can be so good with words."

"And I'm exceptional with my hands." Jamie wiggled her eyebrows and gave her a wicked smile.

Lauren deep-sighed. "You are indeed." She tapped her watch. "Let's get this started so we can get back to the hotel, and you can remind me exactly how exceptional you are."

"You got it."

Jamie headed toward Morten on the auction stage, and Lauren unashamedly watched her ass as Jamie swaggered across to him. Her self-doubt had clearly dissipated, and she was practically glowing. Lauren's heart swelled with so many emotions, she couldn't name them. But mostly, it was simple, pure, and unapologetic love. There was an art to that love. Jamie had brought it out in both of them, and Lauren couldn't wait to spend the rest of their lives creating more of it.

What's Your Story?

Global Wordsmiths, CIC, provides an all-encompassing service for all writers, ranging from basic proofreading and cover design to development editing, typesetting, and eBook services. A major part of our work is charity and community focused, delivering writing projects to under-served and under-represented groups across Nottinghamshire, giving voice to the voiceless and visibility to the unseen.

To learn more about what we offer, visit: www.globalwords.co.uk

A selection of books by Global Words Press:
Desire, Love, Identity: with the National Justice Museum
Times Past: with The Workhouse, National Trust
World At War: Farmilo Primary School
Times Past: Young at Heart with AGE UK
In Different Shoes: Stories of Trans Lives

Self-published authors working with Global Wordsmiths:
E.V. Bancroft
Valden Bush
Addison M Conley
Emma Nichols
Dee Griffiths and Ali Holah
Helena Harte
Dani Lovelady Ryan
Karen Klyne
AJ Mason
James Merrick
Robyn Nyx
Simon Smalley
Brey Willows

Other Great Butterworth Books

Let Love Be Enough by Robyn Nyx
When a killer sets her sights on her target, is there any stopping her?
Available on Amazon (ASIN B09YMMZ8XC)

Lyrics of Life by Brey Willows
Sometimes the only way to heal someone's heart is a song from you own.
Coming June 2023 (ISBN 9781915009265)

Scripted Love by Helena Harte
What good is a romance writer who doesn't believe in happy ever after?
Available from Amazon (ASIN B0993QFLNN)

Caribbean Dreams by Karen Klyne
When love sails into your life, do you climb aboard?
Available from Amazon (ASIN B09M41PYM9)

Nero by Valden Bush
Will her destiny reunite her with the love of her life?
Available from Amazon (B09BXN8VTZ)

Warm Pearls and Paper Cranes by E.V. Bancroft
A family torn apart. Love is the only way forward.
Available from Amazon (B09DTBCQ92)

The Helion Band *by AJ Mason*
Rose's only crime was to show kindness to her royal mistress...
Available from Amazon (ASIN B09YM6TYFQ)

That Boy of Yours Wants Looking At by Simon Smalley
A gloriously colourful and heart-rending memoir.
Available from Amazon (ASIN B09HSN9NM8)

Judge Me, Judge Me Not by James Merrick
A memoir of one gay man's battle against the world and himself.
Available from Amazon (ASIN B09CLK91N5)

LesFic Eclectic Volume Three edited by Robyn Nyx
Special edition raising funds for the DEC Ukrainian appeal: available
from Amazon (ASIN B09V39LW2W)